BOOKISH PEOPLE

a novel

SUSAN COLL

ADVANCE PRAISE FOR *BOOKISH PEOPLE*

"As much fun as Coll has with vacuum cleaners—a truly surprising amount—it's literary humor where she slays."

—*KIRKUS REVIEWS*

"*Bookish People* is a delightful, hilarious, and utterly charming novel about a quirky bookstore and its motley crew—ridiculously lovable people who think way too much about words, writing, dead authors, customers' dogs, cats who torment birds, canceled author events, British ovens, readers, vacuum cleaners, and Russian tortoises. The perfect read for bookish people everywhere!"

—ANGIE KIM, INTERNATIONALLY BESTSELLING AUTHOR OF *MIRACLE CREEK*

"A smart, original, laugh-out-loud novel that fans of Tom Perrotta will adore. If you sell, buy, or simply love books, *Bookish People* is for you. I wholeheartedly recommend this quirky gem."

—SARAH PEKKANEN, *NEW YORK TIMES* BESTSELLING CO-AUTHOR OF *THE GOLDEN COUPLE*

"There's not a wittier, zanier, smarter book about books and the people who love them than *Bookish People*. After reading about this single screwball week in the book biz, you'll want to hug your closest bookseller (and maybe apply for a job)."

—LESLIE PIETRZYK, AUTHOR OF *ADMIT THIS TO NO ONE*

"Take a bookstore owner who is sick of books, a pompous poet who has managed to get himself canceled, and a crew of overqualified millennial employees, then add a week of political upheaval and a rare celestial event. The result is *Bookish People*, a sharp yet tender comedy of bookstore manners. Susan Coll has written a love letter to bibliophiles everywhere with too many hilarious parts to list—though the tortoise named Kurt Vonnegut Jr. may be my all-time favorite literary pet."

—LISA ZEIDNER, AUTHOR OF *LOVE BOMB*

BOOKISH PEOPLE

Also by Susan Coll

The Stager
Beach Week
Acceptance
Rockville Pike
Karlmarx.com

BOOKISH PEOPLE

A NOVEL

SUSAN COLL

HARPER MUSE

Published by Harper Muse, an imprint of HarperCollins Focus LLC.

Published in association with the literary agency of HG Literary.

Library of Congress Cataloging-in-Publication Data

Names: Coll, Susan, author.
Title: Bookish people : a novel / Susan Coll.
Description: [Nashville] : Harper Muse, [2022] | Summary: "A perfect storm of comedic proportions erupts in a DC bookstore over the course of one soggy summer week, punctuated by political turmoil, a celestial event, and a perpetually broken vacuum cleaner"-- Provided by publisher.
Identifiers: LCCN 2022003426 (print) | LCCN 2022003427 (ebook) | ISBN 9781400234097 (paperback) | ISBN 9781400234103 (epub) | ISBN 9781400234110
Subjects: LCGFT: Novels.
Classification: LCC PS3553.O474622 B66 2022 (print) | LCC PS3553. O474622 (ebook) | DDC 813/.54--dc23
LC record available at https://lccn.loc.gov/2022003426
LC ebook record available at https://lccn.loc.gov/2022003427

Printed in the United States of America
22 23 24 25 26 LSC 5 4 3 2 1

For Pashka

All these disturbances are very bad for trade. What's the good of a vacuum cleaner if the power's cut off?

GRAHAM GREENE, OUR MAN IN HAVANA

CHAPTER 1

Friday

THE GALLEY

To be clear, Sophie Bernstein did not throw a book at Zhang Li.

By the time the closing shift learned about the incident from the afternoon swing shift, however, the details of this otherwise routine meeting had become so exaggerated that to hear it, you might think Mrs. Bernstein had committed an act of aggravated assault on the young sales representative.

Zhang, who works for one of the country's largest publishing conglomerates, had been in the midst of presenting that spring's offerings when the coffee spilled, or perhaps technically speaking, splattered.

It is true that this was not a completely random event. A galley—an advance copy of a book—was sent aloft, and when it landed on top of the flimsy cardboard cup, on the side of which had been written "Zhang Skim Cap," it resulted in an explosion of the contents. Some drops of coffee, rapidly expelled, splashed onto Zhang's white dress.

They were already twelve minutes into the meeting, so the coffee, which had been procured from the shop on the corner, was mercifully no longer scalding hot.

Mrs. Bernstein later said it was possible that, instead of tossing the galley in the air, she had slammed it on the table. She couldn't say for sure. Whether the galley was tossed or slammed, Mrs. Bernstein's gesture was intended to emphasize her frustration about having to look at yet another book jacket featuring a woman's feet.

She had grabbed a roll of paper towels and blotted the liquid up from Zhang's sleeve—and from the table and the carpet, and also from the wall. She apologized profusely and promised to pay for Zhang's dry cleaning, or if need be, a new dress. There had been handshakes, apologies, and appropriately, no hugs.

Mrs. Bernstein was reasonably sure the meeting ended on a better-than-neutral note, with her promising to follow up with an order of several of the titles that Blowfish, the imprint that employed Zhang, was featuring next spring.

Really, it seemed to end well enough. So Mrs. Bernstein was surprised to see that Zhang appeared to be on the verge of tears as she headed for the door.

CHAPTER 2

Saturday

THE DARKNESS

S ophie does not wish to be at this party, watching her employees get drunk and rowdy. She wants to go to the bookstore, the one that she owns, the one that is causing her deep ambivalence and massive stress.

It is counterintuitive, she knows, that she finds herself longing to be in the very place that is the nexus of her angst, but she has a plan to remedy this contradiction. She is building a refuge inside the store. A room of her own. She has not yet taken up occupancy, but she is slowly preparing to nest. She has even begun to move some essentials—her electric kettle, a small satchel of clothing, a bag stuffed with cash—into the little nook just behind the Fiction room.

It's an architectural fluke, this cozy, tiny space, this little house for a mouse, this parallel universe accessed by depressing a button in the corner of the shelf currently occupied by Graham Greene, although that is not an always reliable landmark since the location of his oeuvre shifts seasonally depending on the alphabetical crapshoot of the latest crop of books. Over the course of many years she has watched various established authors' perches shift radically, like Toni Morrison, who last spring migrated across two entire shelves, and then by the end of the summer season returned to where she began, like the ebb and flow of beachfront sand.

Regardless of which books front the access panel, her private room is there, a constant. No one else knows about it, as far as she knows, apart from Ibrahim, the architect who designed the store and who still helps her out from time to time with small repairs because he is a nice guy. Not much was required to put the room together. The sturdy industrial door had been there for many decades, as was the bookcase that obscured it, but the door was laborious to open. Some six months ago, after the onset of a plague of sleepless nights following the death of her husband, she asked Ibrahim for advice; he offered to bolt the bookcase to the door, grease the hinges, and add a heavy-duty electric gizmo to make it open more easily.

It was $790 well spent. Now the shelter gives her solace and makes her think she has a plan, like the emergency food and water she keeps in the attic at home. She goes up there from time to time, carefully navigating the narrow stairs from the hallway outside her bedroom, just to check, to be sure it's all still there, the five cases of ramen she picked up at Costco, the five gallons of water. She's had these rations since 9/11, however, and she keeps forgetting that it's surely time to refresh.

But right now, this is where she needs to be—here, in this small apartment in Northern Virginia that is crammed full of her employees, most of them young enough to be her kids. Jamal, the store manager, is throwing a party to say goodbye to his colleagues. He is off to study law at the University of Chicago, his first-choice school. Sophie is happy for him. Thrilled. Proud. But she is also bereft; she can't imagine running the store without him.

A vile yellow liquid is being passed around the room, and she watches them drink it on a dare. Apparently it's a Chicago thing, this Malört, and it tastes so horrific that it's been called the most disgusting liquor of all time. Someone has, for better or worse, managed to find a bottle of it in DC.

Sophie watches a young woman with short, spiky, peroxided hair tilt back her head and pour the syrupy yellow liquid into her mouth. She then gasps and chokes and spits it onto the floor. "Blech!" she says. "This is horrible! It tastes like . . . suffering." She grabs at her throat theatrically.

Sophie is having trouble retrieving her name, but she does remember that she fired this young woman a couple of weeks ago, which was a rare and upsetting event. But after a week of hand-wringing and long discussions with Jamal, they agreed that she needed to be let go on account of a belligerent episode with a customer. Sophie wonders why she is even here, at this party.

Ought she be worried that she can't remember her name? Perhaps she is having a deliberate mental block, wishing away the entire bad episode. But who knows; she's owned the bookstore for more than twenty years. Even though she has been grateful to, and frankly even adored, pretty much every one of her employees, and even though she keeps in touch with many of them, by now at least a few of the short-termers have morphed into a pastiche of brainy English majors, most of whom eventually moved on to more lucrative careers.

But this woman, Sophie ought to remember her name. In addition to being rude to customers, she fancied herself some sort of oracle, issuing disturbing and unsolicited prophecies to colleagues and strangers alike.

"Your stars are about to scramble, rearranging your perception of reality forever," she had whispered, unsolicited, in Sophie's ear one day last fall. A week later, Sophie's husband of twenty-five years, Solomon, was dead. It's not as though this young woman was responsible, and yet . . . well, maybe she *was* in some weird, cosmic, woo-woo way. The episode had felt strangely violating, even before the prediction proved true.

Now the former employee—*What is her name?*—grimaces on account of the liquid suffering; she has just taken another deep swig from the bottle. Yellow syrup dribbles down her chin. Sophie fights the urge to reach over and touch the young woman's hair with the palm of her hand just to feel the bristle, to see if it has the same scratchy texture as her late husband's beard.

"Oh, great stuff!" says Noah, taking a sip from the bottle. "Exxon Supreme—high-octane . . . or wait, wait . . ." He takes another sip. "Hmm, I detect a hint of Shell, with a subtle note of isooctane."

Sophie is reassured by her ability to confidently identify this young man. She remembers interviewing Noah when he applied for a job as an entry-level bookseller a year ago, and she has watched with amusement his transformation from a preppy Princeton grad who bragged about his acceptance into one of the eating clubs to, within a week at the store, a skinny, bookish hipster with a fashion style more longshoreman than Ivy Club.

"It tastes like Lady Macbeth's tears," says Clemi, an aspiring novelist whose dramatic red hair spills in ringlets to her waist. Sophie has a soft spot for this kid and has recently given her a promotion.

She hired Clemi straight out of college too. At least half of her employees aspire to become writers, and while most of them will either give up or become worn down by the process, she gets the sense that Clemi might succeed— and not just because her mother is a famous literary agent. She told Sophie she gets up early every morning to write before coming into work, and she has ripped up and begun again multiple drafts. She also seems to revere books—of course, everyone working at a bookstore loves books—but for Clemi, the book love is extreme. It appears to cause her pain when her colleagues disparage a breezy bestseller, or when someone remarks that an author was boring when he spoke in a monotone at an event and should work on improving his act.

"Authors are writers, not trained seals!" Sophie once heard her say.

There is another reason she is partial to Clemi; she reminds Sophie of herself at that age. She, too, was intense and serious and fiercely literary, always talking about and even defending books as if they were kids being bullied on the playground. She took it personally when someone in her seventh-grade classroom raised her hand and delivered a diatribe against *The Catcher in the Rye*, even though Sophie hadn't liked the book much herself.

There is—or was—a physical resemblance too. As a kid Sophie had wild long hair, although it was a darker shade of red than Clemi's. Granted, the rest of the physical resemblance is mostly wishful thinking. She was never quite that thin, or that pretty, or that tall. Only five foot two, Sophie is what you might call stout. She has grown a touch heavier around the hips with each passing year, and she has not been exercising much on account of sometimes excruciating pain in her left shoulder. It seems this is nothing other than an occupational hazard of owning a bookstore and lifting too many boxes. She's only fifty-four, for the love of God. She's too young to have buried a husband or to have a body that is falling apart.

Clemi is now in charge of scheduling and executing all of the store's events, and Sophie has to admit that she does a good job. Possibly even very good. To do a *perfect* job, she'd have to be able to read Sophie's mind, and honestly, Sophie can't even follow her own thoughts these days. She thinks one thing and then second-guesses herself and then a third thought extinguishes its predecessor and she can't remember the original point of the entire thinking episode. There's nothing wrong with her; she is simply addled, and for perfectly good reason. In addition to her personal and professional challenges, which include having recently become widowed, it feels as though the world is in flames.

To wit, she can't believe she has allowed her son, Michael,

to talk her into coming here. It was her fault for mentioning the party when he stopped by the house earlier this morning to pick up some laundry Sophie had agreed to wash. Back when Solomon was alive, there would have been little expectation for her to show up at staff parties. Now that she's alone, she's supposed to stay up late and hoist this Malört stuff and drink craft beer?

Besides, it feels somewhat sacrilegious to be out partying on this particular day, when she's been glued to the television for hours watching the news, horrified and sickened by the bigotry and hatred and rage. "In the name of the commonwealth, you are being commanded to immediately disperse," police officers in riot gear shouted over and over and over in Charlottesville, Virginia.

Things had already become violent last night, when white supremacists gathered on the University of Virginia campus to protest the removal of a Robert E. Lee statue. But then, this morning, it escalated further when a car driven by a white supremacist plowed into a crowd of anti-racist protesters, killing a thirty-two-year-old woman and injuring dozens of others. It was too soon to say how many exactly.

Sophie forced herself to watch, to bear witness, as bystanders stumbled around giving interviews, some of them bloodied and disoriented.

She can still hear the screams. And she can still hear the chants.

"Jews will not replace us."

"Sieg heil." The Nazi salute.

This is a momentously bad day, one she thinks will go down in history like the 1970 shootings of unarmed college students at Kent State. It seems wrong to be out at a party. But as he'd stuffed the contents of the dryer into a duffel bag, Michael had argued, "As horrible as this is, Mom, you're just letting them win if you become a shut-in! You need to set an intention to live."

Who is this once-cynical child who now speaks in platitudes? Could it really be her son, who graduated summa cum laude from college this spring and is currently unemployed? He is building on his liberal arts degree by studying to become a yoga instructor, he says. She would like to go on record as a mother who is supportive, who harbors no particular anti-yogic sentiments, but who nonetheless hopes to see her son earn a living—enough to pay rent in a building with a washer and dryer, or at least within walking distance of a laundromat. She has trouble getting her mind around his latest endeavor. She has never seen him wear sneakers, take a walk, go for a run, or get on a bike, and now he wakes up one morning suddenly transformed into a proselytizing yogi?

She knows Michael has a point, but she has a counterpoint: even on a good day, she doesn't belong at this party. The staff always invite her to their get-togethers, but she knows this is mostly out of politeness and obligation. It's not as if they necessarily expect or want her to come!

Her mistake had been to share with Michael her dismay over the forthcoming loss of Jamal to the legal profession. Jamal is her rock, the one she turns to first when she needs a second opinion. But who can blame him for wanting more professionally? Both of his parents are prominent attorneys, as is his sister, who is a federal judge. He has been contemplating law school for nearly twenty years. Even as the store's highest-paid employee, he lives in a cramped apartment with his husband and five-year-old twins. With shelves of floor-to-ceiling books, the place exudes warmth. On the walls hang poster-size book covers for various contemporary novels that were sent by publishers and are no longer needed at the store, including one for *Unaccustomed Earth* that's been signed with a Sharpie by Jhumpa Lahiri.

"You *have* to go to the party," Michael had continued. "It's important for you to show you care."

"Of course they know I care! I'm their boss. That doesn't mean I have to cross some bridge to godforsaken Virginia and drive on roads named for Jefferson Davis and Robert E. Lee, who started this whole thing! I'm at the store every day. I'm *fully* engaged!"

She knows she was protesting too much and that she was doing so for a classic reason: the opposite is true. She is physically present at the store, but increasingly less absorbed. She is tired. She is burning out. And as yesterday's mortifying incident with Zhang Li possibly indicates, she is even starting to become hostile to the books. Zhang is young and relatively new at her job, and Sophie probably scared her half to death.

Sophie may, herself, prefer fat historical tomes and literary fiction, but she's a book lover as well as a shrewd businesswoman, and she gets that the books with women's perfectly pedicured feet on the covers pay the bills. These and the book products penned by the celebrity chefs and the self-help gurus and the rock stars and the former and would-be presidents and the football players whose devoted fans show up at the crack of dawn and stand in line for hours to get a signed book and a selfie with the author. A bookstore—and its owner!—must embrace all things book, from the intellectually transcendent to bestsellers about how to declutter homes. This is why she opened the store in the first place, so let the trucks haul in all the books, and let the booksellers read them and staff-pick them and hand-sell them, every last one. Just please don't draw any deep meaning from the fact that this bookstore owner is a little bit sick of books.

What really set her off, for the record, had less to do with those stupid airbrushed feet on the galley than a question Zhang had posed:

"Would you like to up your order of *The Girl in Gauzy Blue*?" she'd asked. "I see you've only preordered twenty-four hundred."

The Girl in Gauzy Blue is the literary debut of a twenty-five-year-old Parisian-born Afghani-Irish woman. It's a multigenerational doorstopper of a novel about love and war and identity that has been described as "breathtaking," as "daringly precocious," as "epically transfiguring." Positioned to be a bestseller, it comes out next week. It's the sort of novel that even a year ago Sophie would have lapped up, would have asked for as many more copies as Zhang Li could spare. She might have possibly even written the staff pick herself.

But Sophie is spent. She has trouble understanding how

anyone can really care about this kind of precious literary fiction at this juncture in history.

The Zhang incident was a perfect storm—*The Girl in Gauzy Blue*, the galley with the feet, Jamal's impending move to Chicago—it was an atmospheric disturbance, that's all. Like moist air and cool air converging along with vapors or whatever it is that causes hurricanes to form.

If her son has no interest in taking over—a highly likely scenario, it seems—could it finally be time to give up the bookstore with its endless demands and small-business headaches? The question is not entirely an abstraction. The Pittsburgh-based developer who recently purchased the parking lot behind the store, Ed someone or other, has been trying to reach her for the last couple of weeks to discuss some sort of proposal. She has her suspicions about what that proposal might be, but she's been avoiding his calls.

One thing's for sure: she is not going to tell Michael that there are two other parties she's been invited to. Next Monday, a bunch of her employees are gathering on someone's rooftop to watch the solar eclipse—in the middle of the workday, no less! And the following evening, there's a costume thing: "Come dressed as your favorite superhero," the invitation reads. As if she could or would force herself to dress up as a superhero! The thought makes her want to crawl inside her nook.

It's an accident, her nook. Or really a tangle of escalating confusion and miscommunication from when she and Solomon

13

first purchased the property in 1997. The store was previously a bank. Or, rather, half a bank. The plat was carved into two pieces, and the purchasers of the adjacent property turned their portion into what had, for a time, been an overpriced steak house called, rather uncreatively, the Bank. They turned a cost-cutting measure into an architectural gimmick, keeping most of the industrial bits as well as the furniture, and the entrées were all bank-themed: The Money Market, for instance, was their premier steak dinner—an eleven-ounce fillet, a baked potato, and your choice of fresh vegetable. The Treasury STRIPS was, unsurprisingly, a sixteen-ounce New York prime cut. It was the wrong restaurant at the wrong time in the wrong place; this was a bookstore-and-coffeehouse kind of neighborhood— expensive red-meat joint, not so much. The restaurant collapsed after being panned in a *Washington Post* review. "Don't put your money in this bank," was the kicker and the epitaph. Restaurants are, of course, famously hard to maintain, but this location seemed especially cursed. Over the years it had been a California nouvelle spot serving organic cuisine, a Chinese restaurant, an Indian dhaba, and now, as of two weeks ago, a coffee shop called Verb, from which Zhang had procured the ill-fated skim cappuccino.

Back when the lawyers split the bank in two, the bookstore had been granted a 350-square-foot space with a half bath that jutted awkwardly across the boundaries. It had been the bank manager's office, and the plan had been to use the guts of it for Sophie's office. But then, after the closing, after the construction began, the Bank's lawyers objected and filed a motion claiming the division of the properties had been unfair and based on inadequate information that failed to take into account an easement in the back alley that prohibited the Bank from building an addition. Finalizing of the deed was held up for years, and meantime both properties went ahead with their construction, and the disputed territory was walled off.

In a town full of lawyers, it's hard to believe a legal matter simply evaporated, just went away on its own, but after the Bank was foreclosed on and resold, the matter essentially disappeared. It's now been twenty years; the space next door has changed hands seven times, the lawyers have all moved on to other firms, retired, died, or, in one case, been disbarred.

Sophie's husband, Solomon—a lawyer himself—suffered his fatal heart attack last year. His synagogue book group had drifted off the topic of Thomas L. Friedman's *The Lexus and the Olive Tree* and was instead discussing the constitutionality of requiring immigrants, with the clear goal of targeting Muslims, to sign a registry. Or so she'd been told; Sophie had been at the store that night, hosting an event. This was a topic about which Solomon was particularly incensed. He announced he would register as a Muslim should that dark day come to pass, and he was midsentence, making a point that had to do with Anne Frank's father, Otto, when he clutched at his chest and dropped to the floor. This was not the way he would have wanted to go, because Solomon always completed his points; you could count on that like a cock's crow.

Since his death, Sophie has been haunted by the specter of Anne Frank and has read and reread her diary, wondering what, exactly, Solomon had been trying to say. She's still not sure, but the reminder of Anne's family hiding in an annex behind a wall of books is of course what inspired Sophie to reinvestigate the store's nook. With her husband gone, she and Ibrahim are possibly the only people left in Washington who know this place exists. It's every person's fantasy. A room of one's own, a place only they know how to access, in the most James Bond of ways.

Earlier this year, just before consulting Ibrahim about the door, she had visited the nook for the first time in more than a decade. After the End of Day Report arrived in her inbox—an indication that the doors were about to be locked and the store would be empty—she had driven there at 11:00 p.m. She had been nervous entering alone so late at night. Disarming the alarm system always made her anxious; she entertained visions of setting it off by mistake and then panicking, not being able to remember the code word—was it the name of their first pet bird or their second?—and being hauled off in handcuffs. She knew she should have more confidence: Any idiot could punch in an alarm code, and indeed that evening she managed to enter without incident. She then turned on just enough light to go about her business, which involved finding the small stepladder, climbing to the top shelf in the back of the Fiction room, and removing a face-out stack of *The Quiet American* (Penguin Classics Deluxe Edition), three copies of the mass-market paperback edition (she would have to talk to Antonio, the senior buyer, about that—did they really need to carry two different versions of the same book?), two copies of *The End of the Affair*, one copy of *The Third Man*, and three copies of Greene's collected short stories. Then, using a flashlight, she located the nearly invisible indentation in the corner of the shelf and punched the tiny bull's-eye with the tip of a pen, which caused the latch to release, enabling her to push the shelf open manually, albeit with great difficulty; she had to lean on it with all of her weight. And there it was, still. A tiny, private mecca. A tiny, private, and very, very dusty mecca. One dim overhead light revealed 350 square feet of windowless, dusty solitude. It was even more perfect than she'd remembered, because one thing she had completely forgotten was that she and Solomon had stored a couple of sticks of old furniture in there, including a futon.

The place is much improved now, but it still needs a thorough cleaning and a touch of home—bed linens, some cheery knickknacks, family photographs. Also, a hot plate. Maybe she can even squeeze in a small fridge.

One problem she recently noticed when she tried to plug in her kettle is that the electrical outlets don't work. She will have to figure this out before she can properly begin to inhabit the place, and now, after watching the bodies being carried away on stretchers and seeing those neo-Nazis spewing racist and anti-Semitic dreck, carrying their torches, waving their flags, and chanting, "*Sieg heil*," she will need to accelerate the timeline. She already has flashlights and batteries, and the opening and closing of the door has been much improved by Ibrahim, but now she will need to consult him about making a few additional tweaks.

Is this weird? Probably not. She spent many a Sunday morning as a kid watching grainy filmstrips of Jews being transported to concentration camps, shoved like cattle onto packed trains, and she grew up on a diet of Holocaust literature. It was impossible to grow up Jewish in this world and not have events like those in Charlottesville add to the traumatic inherited memories that already keep you up at night.

Nazis or no Nazis, isn't it some people's ideal to live inside a bookstore? Certainly, it's not unheard of: Shakespeare and Company in Paris famously has an apartment inside the store. And she recently read a sweet novel, *The Storied Life of A. J. Fikry*, in which the owner lived inside the bookstore. Building a cocoon that is in the heart of all these books feels to Sophie the most natural instinct in the world. She has read any number of articles about people scaling down, paring their possessions, moving into tiny spaces, even into tiny houses. It's a trend. Hey, it's even a book!

Does she really see herself moving in here, going into hiding? Maybe yes and maybe no. But it makes her feel better to have a plan, especially given what she watched unfold on television today. Even before today she felt the daily deluge of alarming news related to Russian hackers, nuclear-armed North Koreans, police officers shooting innocent Black children, deranged gunmen popping up like whack-a-moles ambushing schools and holiday parties and church gatherings, people being violently hauled off airplanes, terrorists in Barcelona, melting ice caps, and dying polar bears, and she is on alert, and terrified, about absolutely everything.

Really, if you add it all up, this inclination to nest is an entirely rational response to this moment in time. And she, Sophie Bernstein, is of sound mind and body, as evidenced by the fact that she is here at this party, where around and around the room, a bottle of noxious liquor continues to move.

Live in the moment! Be present! These are things people say nowadays—especially her soon-to-be-a-yoga-teacher son—and she will try, because here she is at a party in a high-rise apartment on Lee Highway, in an indeterminate suburb of Northern Virginia. The bristly-haired young woman is demanding that the bottle make its way back to her, and when it finally does, she holds it over her open mouth and pours the yellow liquid in a steady stream.

"Stop it!" Clemi yells, approaching her and grabbing the bottle. They wrestle for a moment until it falls to the floor, spilling on the rug. The bristly-haired woman dives for it and falls, and a few people gather around to help her stand back up. Sophie sees Clemi take her by the arm and walk with her out the door.

The scene is extremely disturbing to watch. Sophie thinks she should leave before things get even further out of hand. The room is overheated, there is too much alcohol, and it is packed with guests—what Sally Quinn back in the day called a Rat F@#k. (Sophie had been to one of these in the early nineties, when Ben and Sally threw a book party for a mutual friend, and she'd vowed to never return, even if invited.) But this party has only just begun, and there is no way to slip out undetected. She sees Jamal in the back of the room, standing near the door, guardedly watching; his husband, Lewis, is beside him, and on his face is a look of concern. They clearly had not anticipated this mayhem. Sophie wants to talk to them both before she leaves. She decides to give it ten more minutes. She finds her way into the kitchen to get a glass of water and winds up talking to Antonio about his favorite summer reads for longer than expected, until they are both summoned back into the living room.

A shot. A superlative. A grimace. A shot. An even more colorful superlative.

Someone rushing to the bathroom, about to be sick. And suddenly, a chant:

"Mis . . . ses . . . Bern . . . stein. Mis . . . ses . . . Bern . . . stein."

Some thirty pairs of young eyes look in her direction, and in them she thinks she sees a mix of bemusement and affection, as well as a little fear, as if maybe she's about to hurl a book at them.

They continue to chant her name like she's just one of the crowd. Sophie Bernstein—mother, bookstore owner, fifty-four-year-old widow—is being invited to pick up the bottle and throw back a swig.

"Mis . . . ses . . . Bern . . . stein. Mis . . . ses . . . Bern . . . stein. Mis . . . ses . . . Bern . . . stein. Mis . . . ses . . . Bern . . . stein."

Now they are gathered around her. She wishes they would call her Sophie, but she suspects that even her contemporaries retreat to the comfort of calling her Mrs. Bernstein behind her back. This is part of the curse of being Sophie Bernstein; she is more formidable than she wishes to be.

She thinks of the Frank family, right before they went into hiding: "Just enjoy your carefree life while you can," Otto had told his daughter.

"Pass me the bottle!" Sophie says. The room quiets. The bottle makes its way to her. She stares at it a moment, then puts it to her lips and tilts her head back. As the liquid burns the back of her mouth, she envisions a vat of turpentine and rotting yellow grapefruit and, yes, maybe even a hint of petroleum. Her throat ignites, her esophagus is engulfed. It's vile to the nth degree, sure, but it doesn't taste like any form of suffering Sophie has encountered in her life—at least not yet.

"It tastes like . . . napalm."

Someone hoots. She holds tight to the bottle, then takes another swig.

"Oh, great leader, give us your words of wisdom," Noah says, "now that you have drunk from the font."

This is a little much, she thinks, but it's true; she is feeling weirdly visionary.

A new chant begins: "More, more, more." She doesn't know whether they are suggesting she drink more or speak more, so she does a bit of both. Something strange is happening. She is losing her bearings a little, but whether it's because of the vile yellow liquid, the overheated room, the late hour, or all of the above—she has no idea.

"It tastes like dark times," she says, taking one more swig. "Dark times ahead. The darkness will soon descend."

END OF DAY REPORT: Sunday, August 13
OPENING SHIFT: Emma, Jamal, Noah
SWING SHIFT: Carmen, Antonio, Aaron
CLOSING SHIFT: Summer, Yash, Sami
EVENT: Clemi
FLOOR MANAGER COMMENTS: Friends! It's my first EOD report
as store manager! Jamal is still with us in body and (perhaps)
spirit for another week, but I'm taking this over as of today, so
be gentle with me!

- Stop by the information desk and introduce yourself to
  Summer! She comes to us by way of NASA, where she
  worked as a contract specialist for five years, before which
  she had a stint at Barnes & Noble.
- Belinda, from web orders, was not in today. She hasn't
  responded to my texts or calls. If you've been in touch with
  her, please let me know.
- We've had several calls about *The Doodles*, a self-published
  memoir by a dog breeder in Maine who has come up
  with a bunch of weird doodle varieties, including a Micro
  Bernedoodle named Bernie who appeared with the author
  on *Weekend TODAY* this morning and who indeed looks a
  lot like the junior senator from the great state of Vermont.
  We do not carry this book, but Antonio is investigating
  whether we can get some copies on consignment since it
  clearly appeals to our doodle-crazed customers.
- Speaking of animals: We've had a ton of calls about the
  Kuddly Killers event on Saturday. Not sure what that's
  about.
- Ditto for seriously unhappy callers re: Raymond Chaucer,

also appearing this weekend. Sample outtake: "How can you invite that misogynist wife-killing so-called poet to speak at your store?" Direct all relevant questions to Clemi.

And if that isn't exciting enough for you:

- We briefly lost internet midday.
- We ran out of books at the event yesterday evening.
- The vacuum cleaner isn't working properly, but never fear, Noah is on the case! Report from the battlefield: "I'm not sure what's going on. It stopped sucking up dirt. It seems like a little piece of plastic might have gotten stuck in the hose, but I dislodged it with a coat hanger. It's totally under control."

IMPORTANT UPDATE: My Solar Eclipse Party next Monday is shaping up as a must for your social calendar. Stop by and watch from my rooftop. And just a reminder about Sami's Super(S)Hero Party at 9:00 p.m. the following night. Everyone welcome—spouses, significant others, doodles—but you *must* come in costume.

Autumn T

CHAPTER 3

Monday

KURT VONNEGUT JR.

Clemi texts Noah to see whether he has remembered to pick up food for Kurt Vonnegut Jr. on his way in to work. She waits a beat. Then two or three. He does not respond. Perhaps he's still midcommute or stuck on the Metro. She noticed on her newsfeed earlier this morning that a downpour during rush hour has caused massive traffic problems, and also—presumably unrelated—a chunk of the ceiling has fallen in at the Gallery Place station, injuring five people, one critically, and there are now system-wide delays. Or, who knows, maybe Noah's here early, helping a customer somewhere, ignoring his vibrating cell phone.

She leaves her office and walks downstairs to the book floor to see what she can learn. It's 10:24 a.m. on a Monday morning, so the place is relatively quiet but for a couple of regular customers who practically live at the store. There's handsome fortysomething Mr. Zielinski, dapper as always.

He spends at least an hour every morning perusing the travel section, asking questions about the various trips he is perpetually planning, but he never seems to go anywhere. There's Lucy Richards, the octogenarian writer of thrillers who penned a *New York Times* bestseller in 1987 and comes in several times a week to be sure her book remains on the shelf. And there's Cathy—Chatty Cathy, they call her—who lives around the corner and uses the bookstore as a pit stop on her thrice-daily walks with her Shih Tzu, Petunia. She shows up at all of the store's events and is always the first to line up at the microphone with an incomprehensible question that invariably goes on a bit too long. There's also the haggard graduate student who looks like she hasn't slept in a year or, for that matter, taken her hair out of the massive, messy bun inside of which she stores several pens. She has commandeered the table behind the European History section, making a little fortress for herself out of books that the staff has to reshelve every time she leaves. And there's Wayne, who does live here, or rather, just outside, on a bench. He's a former English professor turned bookseller who once worked at a now-defunct chain and has since fallen on hard times. He's refused all offers of help, both from Mrs. Bernstein and from social services.

After patting Petunia on the head, Clemi steps around her and eases herself behind the information desk where Autumn T sits in a swivel chair and taps at the keyboard, the phone pressed to her ear. Her hair hangs in at least a dozen small braids, each ending in a different colored bead, and a pair of chunky tortoiseshell eyeglasses accents her delicate face.

"He's not in yet," she whispers to Clemi, her hand covering the mouthpiece on the phone.

Why the presumption that she's looking for Noah? She is tempted to rebut this, but the thing is, she is.

She takes in the tiny yellow giraffes on Autumn's dress. Or are they birds with long beaks looking skyward? Clemi knows this dress—she almost purchased it on sale at Madewell, but with another week until payday, her bank balance was low.

Autumn T brings up a screen with an inventory card for a book called *Guide to Painless Childbirth, 7th Edition*, then turns to Clemi again.

"He doesn't start today until two, but he's always late," she says nonchalantly, as if always being late is acceptable, which it's not.

Prior to her promotion to store manager, Autumn T was known to be a strict shift supervisor, one who sent out regular emails with harsh edicts warning of repercussions for things like leaving empty coffee cups at the information desk or taking too-long breaks. She has recently sent out an all-staff epistle on how to never say no when talking to a customer—as in, "Do not say, 'We do not have that book,' but rather 'Might I suggest something similar?' or 'We can have it here in two days!'"

Autumn T is better at issuing edicts than at following them herself, however. "Nope! Sorry!" she reports to the customer. She seems almost gleeful to be done with this failed transaction as she plunks down the receiver.

She swivels her chair toward Clemi and glances at the time on her phone. "Plus I just remembered that he said he's running an errand on his way in. Something to do with the vacuum cleaner. I didn't really follow. But he'll be here at some point."

Noah. Charmed Noah. Noah the economics major who before working here had probably never picked up a book that hadn't been assigned. Noah the now self-described voracious reader of small press lit. Everyone is a little bit in love with Noah. Everyone cuts him a ridiculous amount of slack. He can waltz in twenty minutes late in dress code–violating torn jeans, atonal music leaking loudly from his earbuds, and Autumn T just smiles and tells him he's on register three, or that there's a new frontlist shipment she needs him to bring up from the receiving room.

If this little glimpse of what it might be like to be in a relationship with Noah is any indication—he's been avoiding her since Saturday night, when they acquired what she had presumed would be a joint-custody tortoise—the only logical thing for Clemi to do is to run for her life. Which is not to suggest they are in a relationship. Only that there have been months of vague flirtation and, finally, a kiss. More than a kiss, really, since it was not a casual peck on the cheek but rather a full mouth-on-mouth affair that lasted for a couple of explosive minutes, the backdrop for which was aisle seven of the Pets! Pets! Pets! store in Fairfax, Virginia, where they had randomly wound up after Jamal's party. She still can't believe she allowed this to happen.

She had gone back inside after helping fold her increasingly unhinged, and frankly scary, drunk roommate, Florence, into a Lyft, and returned just in time to hear Mrs. Bernstein's weird pronouncement. Noah had looked at her and raised his eyebrows, then pointed to the door. He wanted to step outside to have a smoke. The next thing she knew they were leaning against the building talking and one thing led to another and somehow, weirdly, to the pet store, with its exuberant neon exclamation marks beckoning from across the street. The briefly pleasant memory now feels a bit like a bad dream.

Clemi is certainly not going to stand around the store waiting for Noah to show up. But she doesn't feel like plunging into her work, and when she returns to her windowless office, she just stands there, contemplating the four stacks of bound galleys, piled shoulder high, that lean against her wall. Today was the day she was going to clean this place up. Actually, yesterday was the day, as was the day before that. It's just too depressing to take these books by the armful and carry them out to the bin in the parking lot. She's already tried leaving some in a box in front of the store with a sign that read "Free Books," but at the end of the day only a few of them were gone, so she'd carried them back upstairs.

Hanging on to these copies, saving them from destruction if not, alas, from obscurity, feels like her literary duty. Someone wrote these books, laboring over every word, spending months revising, scrutinizing, and killing off beloved characters at the advice of readers who saw early drafts. After multiple rejections they finally found an agent and then a publisher and gathered some friends to celebrate and popped champagne. Maybe they used the entire advance to buy a used Honda Civic with 87,000 miles on it—such as the one Clemi recently looked at but couldn't afford. And now here it is, an advance copy of their book, meant to generate some prepublication enthusiasm, gathering dust in a dark corner of a bookstore event manager's office.

Only a fraction of these will make it onto the bookstore shelf, even fewer onto bestseller lists. It makes no sense, she knows, but she sometimes imagines that if she does right by these galleys, at least gives them a home and communes with them daily, then maybe the universe will pay it back when her own book is finally written. Clemi also understands that her desire to triage those books that need a little extra TLC runs deep and dark, veering possibly even into Freudian territory. It's part of her rebellion against her mother, a high-profile literary agent. Growing up, Clemi routinely found query letters and partial manuscript pages spilling out of the trash. Sometimes she would pull them out to read, and they were not bad.

Clemi sees the light blinking menacingly from the telephone on her wobbly thrift-store desk. She has no real desire to hear the voice mails that await her, but at least it's a good reason to put off dealing with these galleys for yet another day.

Work is the one thing in her life that is right, except right now it is not. She's been putting in a string of twelve-hour days and it's sucking up all of what she'd hoped would be her time to write. It's always something with this job; in the last week alone she's had two book emergencies. In one case, when a shipment didn't arrive in time for an author event, she had to take the store's van and drive to a bookstore in Maryland to clean them out of *Harvesting Justice:*

Ethical Food in Unethical Times, feeling rather sheepish and frankly unethical as she'd checked out without explaining why, exactly, she needed to purchase every one of their seventy-two copies. And last Friday night, the author of *The Wombats*—a blockbuster work of speculative fiction from Australia just released in the States—went mildly berserk when Clemi brought her the grapefruit juice she'd requested; she had an aversion to plastic and could only drink juice that came in glass containers, a detail that the publicist had failed to convey even though they had exchanged dozens of emails hashing out the author's greenroom needs.

On top of the normal book-related hassles she's grown used to, lately Clemi feels persecuted by Mrs. Bernstein, who is always on her back, texting her at all hours with suggestions and complaints. Part of her initial attraction to the job, apart from the obvious appeal of the books, had been Mrs. Bernstein herself. Clemi had felt a real bond with her in her interview. Their conversation had quickly moved past the requirements of the job to a discussion of Clemi's novel in progress, to their shared love of the movie *Eternal Sunshine of the Spotless Mind*, and then to good Indian restaurants in DC. Mrs. Bernstein had even invited her and a couple of other new booksellers over for dinner at her house just a few weeks after Clemi began. She'd made a delicious lasagna, and they'd all stuck around and talked late into the night. She'd even met the Bernsteins' cute son, Michael. He had just graduated college and was temporarily at home, waiting to move into an apartment in Petworth. But then Mr. Bernstein died, and things were not the same.

And what is up with Autumn T? Did she really need to broadcast that they'd run out of books in the End of Day Report?

Really, divining how many books to order is much trickier than it looks! It's much more art than science. She's tried creating Excel spreadsheets, devising algorithms, consulting with colleagues at other bookstores, but in the end, even when she's pretty sure she's done everything possible, has considered every eventuality, and is semiconfident that she's ordered the right number of books and set up the right number of chairs for people to sit in and listen to the author speak, she still needs to allow for curveballs. Freakish weather, such as the overly soggy summer they are experiencing right now, or the long shot possibility that one of the city's losing sports franchises will miraculously eke out a success resulting in a hastily scheduled hometown playoff game, or a foreign dignitary deciding to pay a visit to the White House, paralyzing traffic in the city for hours with his security detail and ten-car delegation . . . All of these and many other factors go into predicting the turnout and sales at an author event, to the point that getting it right is more of an anomaly than getting it wrong. She can pack a room with a couple hundred people, and only ten of them might buy the book. That's what generally happens with hot-button topics like ISIS, for example. Everyone wants to hear the famous security experts and the talking heads opine, but do they want to plunk down $29.99 for a book about the fact that we are all essentially doomed? The bookstore is the place to hang out. It's a community center, a place to run into friends, to browse new books, to bring your poorly behaved dog in for a treat, to learn something new from the authors Clemi schedules to speak, but that doesn't mean the people sitting in those chairs every night are going to buy any books. The problem is you never know. There are exceptions, like last night, when they bought *every* book.

Standing room only for *Reformed! The Budget and Impoundment Control Act of 1974*. Go figure. Only in Washington DC is that sexy. This isn't much of an excuse for Clemi since she has already made a similar mistake, drastically underordering books for a history of the FDIC—an opus that drew such a large crowd they had to turn people away.

Clemi loves her job. Although maybe what she loves is the *idea* of her job more than its reality. At first, being a bookseller had seemed like a dream for an introverted, book-loving English major just out of college, and it sort of was. But then, after Mr. Bernstein died and Clemi was asked to take on the role of booking events to ease Mrs. Bernstein's daily load, the number of events she was being asked to schedule has more than doubled, and the bookstore is chronically short-staffed.

She's generally a centered person, but work has been unusually stressful these last few weeks—and on top of everything, Florence's struggles are taking a toll on her own well-being. Among other issues, Florence is now obsessed with the forthcoming solar eclipse and has been issuing warnings to Clemi that range from not leaving the laundry outside because it will become contaminated when the sun goes dark, to not making any major changes in her stock portfolio—two pieces of advice that are easy to follow given they have no access to outdoor space at their apartment and Clemi's general lack of funds. Never mind these dire prophecies to do with the eclipse; here on earth there is the horror of Charlottesville to grapple with.

Between all of this and her overflowing inbox, the endless August rain and heat, and Noah being a jerk, she is beginning to feel like she's caught the virus of unrest and imbalance.

When she occasionally slips into a bad loop like this, she tries to center herself with the books to remind herself what it is she loves about working here. Simply walking over to the Fiction room and inhaling the smell of paper and glue is sometimes all it takes to make her okay. She goes back and forth about whether she prefers the smell of new books to the smell of old books, but she leans toward the former: With a new book there is the rush of being the first to turn the pages and discover what's inside, even if the words themselves are age-old. Plus, it's a little embarrassing to admit, but she can't wait to smell her own novel between the pages. She's been practicing her elevator pitch and is prepared to tell whomever that what she's working on is a coming-of-age novel set at an exclusive tiny girls' school in Connecticut, a self-described cross between *Prep* and the magical realism elements of *Swamplandia!* and *One Hundred Years of Solitude*.

Used or new, books give her superpowers. Unless they are damaged or lost or causing her back to spasm from the weight. Long before Sami's party invitation arrived in her inbox, Clemi had already likened herself, privately, to Super Book Girl. Sometimes, when no one is looking, she likes to

33

stand on the top rung of the tall ladder in the Fiction room and put her hands in the air, victorious, like she has just scored a perfect ten on her balance beam routine.

Unfortunately, this centering exercise doesn't always work, especially in the middle of the night, when books become the focus of her anxious dreams. Ordering too many, ordering too few, books that don't arrive, books that can't be found, books they do not have in stock when an author drops by to sign, unannounced.

Last week a shipment arrived just hours before that evening's event with this strange prescription from the printer: "There will be some waviness in the pages when the books are first removed from the carton, but the waviness will subside once the moisture level in the books equalizes with the moisture level in the room." She almost began to weep when she read this note. What was she meant to do with this information? There are so many variables, such an infinite variety of ways in which things can go wrong, that each day feels not like a fresh start so much as a potential minefield of heretofore unimaginable book-related cataclysms.

But all of these concerns pale in comparison to what she knows awaits her today in her teeming inbox and on the store's Facebook, Instagram, and Twitter feeds.

Also, she assumes, on her voice mail.

Forcing herself back to the reality of the day ahead, she picks up the receiver and checks her messages. At least the first few are benign, from customers asking whether she can schedule an event with the author of *The Doodles* or wanting to know if she has his contact information. One caller wonders whether Clemi can help her obtain a Micro Bernedoodle for her son's sixth birthday. A few are calling about the *Kuddly Killers* event on Saturday, which is another creeping concern. Without realizing it, she has scheduled an event that has enraged cat owners; a central thesis of the book, which prepublication reviews have called "balanced," is that free-ranging cats pose a risk to global biodiversity and are responsible for killing as many as four billion birds each year. The book is said to be fair to cats *and* cat owners, and is *not* calling for feline genocide but rather for awareness and solutions, such as putting bells around cats' necks. But as Clemi knows firsthand, nuance is frequently lost in these conversations. It doesn't take much in this current political climate for people to become enraged. Another thing she has learned in her time on this job is that no subject is entirely safe; even an event about flower arranging pegged to Mother's Day this spring brought controversy because the art of putting together bouquets sometimes involves the use of toxic chemicals and plastics, leaves a carbon footprint, etc. Who knew?

The next message consists of one word only: *Kaboom!*

Kaboom. Granted, this is not happening entirely without her agency; Clemi has scheduled the event with a controversial poet—and she has done so for her own controversial reasons. There is no one else to blame. She may have frustrations with her job, but she does have some degree of autonomy. She could have simply said no to Raymond Chaucer's publicist, Fiona. That would have been easy to do, especially since most bookstores have canceled his events in the wake of the shocking *Guardian* profile that appeared about a week ago, which suggested he was responsible for the suicide of his wife, Seema. She died two years ago, but the story has only now begun to make headlines in the wake of the release of his new poetry collection.

Clemi could cancel too. She has done this on rare occasions, plus she doesn't schedule *every* big book that comes along. She's declined to book an event for *The Girl in Gauzy Blue*, for example, even though it was blurbed by pretty much every luminary in the publishing world—including Gary Shteyngart, who wrote: "If you like gauze, girls, and you don't mind blue, this is the book for you!" Plus, the publicist sent her a split of wine and a cookie the size of her head, both sporting the jacket design, as well as a blue branded tote bag. Admittedly she did eat the cookie, but she gave the wine to Autumn T, left the tote bag in the staff room, and doubled down on her position on the grounds that no one shows up for out-of-town authors with debut novels, at least not until a few months later when the book has caught fire, which is in fact mostly true. But that's not really the reason she said no. She is—or *was*—friends with Raina O'Malley, the author. They were in the same dorm when Clemi was a freshman and Raina a junior, and they'd bonded over both wanting to be writers. Then they'd lost touch. Did Clemi not book the event because she is feeling kind of inept and frankly jealous that Raina has managed to sell a novel to a prestigious literary press and is being sent on a cross-country book tour, whereas Clemi is only halfway through her own manuscript and slowly losing confidence in and also terrified of her own, somewhat autobiographical, material? Is she morally required to answer this question?

Okay, so maybe she has made a mistake. Or maybe two or three or ten. It is true that she has invited a reviled poet to speak while declining to book the next mega bestseller. On the upside, she is at least taking a stand for poetry. In general, the store hosts very few poets, something Clemi believes is wrong. Granted, she's not a huge poetry reader, but she wants to be supportive. Also, certain poems have stuck with her over the years, such as Billy Collins's "Her," which she first came across in high school. The lines about the suburbs resonated with her as a kid, perhaps because of her own soulless childhood in affluent Greenwich, where she never felt she belonged. But the line that lodged permanently in her head from that poem is the one that ponders how a bird can get a peep, or a chirp, in edgewise. It's the story of her life. All of her classmates always had so much to say, frequently about nothing at all. It's not that she had all that much to say, but even if she did, everyone around her was clamoring so loudly that it would have been difficult to make herself heard.

An affection for Billy Collins doesn't explain why she's scheduled an event with Raymond Chaucer though. She really does like his poetry, all of which she has read. But that's not the real reason. The real reason is messy and dark and confusing. And it has to do with her mother, the nexus of all things messy and dark and confusing. Her mother is Raymond's literary agent. Her mother and Raymond have always been close. They have, actually, been a little too close. For years. For longer than years. That their relationship transcends the boundaries of the normal agent/client situation is, in fact, widely known in the literary world, and yet it was not publicly acknowledged until the *Guardian* profile. Among other disclosures about the poet's complicated personal life, the reporter included shocking and unflattering quotes from his late wife's friends. Despite the fact that they were obscenely wealthy from his City of London days, he was said to be controlling and cheap and always on Seema's back about their finances. Also, Seema had told her friends that she could no longer abide his infidelities and said the final straw was learning that he had fathered a child outside the marriage some twenty-plus years before.

It's not as if Clemi hasn't occasionally entertained the idea that Raymond might be her biological father. It's just that, until last week, she had no reason to give that thought much credence. Now she can't get it out of her head. She finds herself staring at his picture, looking for any resemblance. There is one, in fact—a dimple in the chin that is just like hers and is difficult to pretend away.

Still, she ought not feel the need to justify the reasons she has booked an event for Raymond Chaucer, even to herself. Raymond Chaucer is the real deal, a prizewinning poet, an internationally known thing. Even though poetry readings typically fail to generate a lot of sales, scheduling an event with Chaucer is still the responsible thing to do. He's a poet rock star. Or maybe, more accurately, a poet criminal. About his most acclaimed collection, *Black Monday*, a *New York Times* critic famously remarked that his sonnets were defined by "the same cold concision that made his name, back when he worked in finance, synonymous with that of Ivan Boesky." He was called by critics, variously, "poetry's own white-collar criminal" and "an insider trader of language."

An open event slot, an acclaimed poet—it seemed wrong to get in the way of the universe. Bad things could happen.

And this was before Clemi even understood that the bad things that might happen were very real. In the wake of the *Guardian* article, he is now being compared to Ted Hughes, considered by many to be responsible for the suicide of his wife, Sylvia Plath. There is even the possibility that Raymond's wife and Sylvia died by similar gas oven means, although Raymond insists that part is untrue. Seema was a poet herself, but unlike Sylvia, she had given up her ambitions to raise the children and had never published any of her work. Making things worse, on the cover of his new collection, a crow carries a stick of dynamite in its beak. The cover design is presumably deliberate, a nod to Ted Hughes's seminal collection, the stick of dynamite suggestive of exploding the narrative, of turning it on its head. The problem is that in real life Raymond Chaucer has not changed the narrative but rather made history repeat—at least, if the rumors and accusations are to be believed.

Clemi feels like sticking her own head in the oven, so to speak. Not really, of course. She's not remotely suicidal, but thinking about meeting Raymond Chaucer—her possible father!—is overwhelming. She doesn't really know what she expects from this encounter. Violins playing while they embrace, as if this is the end of the film version of the story she has been telling herself for years? Or some ugly, or even violent, confrontation? Does she want apologies? A printout of the family tree? Disclosures of ticking genetic bombs in her DNA? Truly, she doesn't know what she is looking for, apart from bringing this story to its conclusion, or at least to some resolution.

Equally unsettling—but completely unrelated—is the Noah kiss, which makes her want to . . . she can't really complete the thought. The thing is, as much as she regrets it, it was also kind of nice. She isn't much of a drinker, but she has learned to keep up, or rather to feign keeping up, by drinking very slowly and nibbling at food to constantly absorb the alcohol, which is what she had been doing the night of Jamal's party. She's not averse to partying, just terrified of turning into her father—by which she means the man who raised her as his daughter, the father who was her father but not her biological father—who was in a fatal car accident after getting behind the wheel, inebriated, at the age of forty-six.

She had been perfectly sober when she and Noah decided, on a whim, to go check out the pet store because . . . because it was open late and across the street from Jamal's apartment, and because they were drunk, or in her case pretending to be drunk. They had wandered up and down each aisle, Noah remarking, sometimes cleverly, sometimes not so much, on various items along the way.

In the dog aisle, they saw a row of toys that stretched the length of a city block. "Perhaps you need a bashful, nerdy-pig latex dog toy?" he had asked.

She'd laughed, probably a beat too long. She felt so self-conscious around Noah, though at the very same time she also thought he was kind of a jerk. An adorable jerk. This was very confusing, her growing attraction to him, and she couldn't quite believe they were there together, alone, but for a couple of Pets! Pets! Pets! employees, including pale, lanky, bespectacled Harold, who had greeted them on the way in. Harold looked like he'd been drained of life, turned reptilian by long hours under fluorescent lights, and soon to be, himself, put in a glass terrarium and sold at 30 percent off, discounted on account of his sickly pallor.

"What do you think Mrs. Bernstein meant by all that stuff about darkness?" she'd asked Noah.

"I don't know; she's getting old. She's just having a little freak-out. Plus, Charlottesville."

"She's only, like, in her fifties, I think."

"That's old, no?"

"I guess," Clemi said, "although my mom is in her fifties and she still goes skiing and hiking. She told me she recently even went to a hookah bar."

"I guess it depends. My mom is fifty and she says she feels pretty old, but maybe that's because my dad just married a twenty-four-year-old."

"Geez. That's like . . . me marrying your dad. Well, in another year."

Noah stared at her for a minute, possibly summing her up as a potential stepmother. "That's too weird. Don't say stuff like that."

"She's also been kind of rude to me lately."

"It's not personal. I don't think she means it. I don't think she likes anyone right now."

"I know. I get it. Her husband died and Jamal's leaving

and everything is just a lot right now. But still, she seems to like *you*."

"Yeah, that's true," Noah said. "Most people do. She probably likes you too. Girls don't have enough confidence."

Clemi was astonished by pretty much every aspect of this remark. He was going to mansplain her lack of confidence to her? What arrogance! And yet, wasn't he right? Why isn't she more self-assured?

"Anyway, what was she doing there at the party? Chugging Malört straight from the bottle? And then saying scary, weird things?" Clemi had asked. "Plus that thing with Zhang! Whatever that was about. I heard Zhang left the store in tears."

"I don't think it's a big deal," Noah said, staring at a pair of bedraggled parakeets. "Any of it. I think everyone is just overreacting. She's just . . . losing it a little. I mean, who isn't? Thelma and Louise."

"Thelma and Louise what?"

"The parakeets. They look like Thelma and Louise."

She stared at them and thought otherwise. Like everything and everyone in this store, they looked to her unwell, more like Cholera and Plague, but again she forced an awkward laugh.

"We have an event on Saturday that has to do with birds. And cats. I haven't read the book, but I think the author says house cats shouldn't be allowed outdoors, or if they are, they should wear bells so birds can hear them coming."

Noah wasn't answering, but he also wasn't *not* answering, so she'd just kept talking: "I was kind of interested in this after reading Jonathan Franzen's *Freedom*. It had a subplot about this—do you remember? That's the book just before *Purity*. I read it a while ago, so I don't remember exactly, but there was this whole thing to do with not letting cats out without bells so birds would have fair warning they were coming." She was making a complete fool of herself. Showing off like she had an encyclopedic knowledge of Franzen novels. Plus, really, who her age reads Franzen? Ought she be embarrassed to admit that *she* does? Jonathan is a friend of her mother's, and he sends her a copy of each new book, signed with warm endearments.

Noah wasn't listening. He was frozen in front of a tank of tropical fish, staring with the intensity of a boy who had drunk too much Malört and then smoked something and ingested who knows what else. Clemi took his arm and pulled him forward until he stopped again in front of a case of tortoises, where she saw three shelled reptiles—motionless, wizened, and the size of tea saucers—in the terrarium.

She and Noah had both stood and stared.

"Are they even alive?" Clemi had asked. By way of reply, one of them, in repose atop a fake rock, extended a front leg and then another and lowered himself off his perch and swiveled his head in their direction.

"Poor guy looks like Kurt Vonnegut Jr.," Noah remarked.

Clemi felt a wave of shame. She hoped no one could hear them being so pretentious with their literary references. She hadn't read any Vonnegut apart from *Slaughterhouse-Five*, which had been assigned in a high school English class. But that had nothing to do with the point of his observation. Noah was sort of right. Inasmuch as a tortoise can resemble a human, he did look a little like Kurt Vonnegut Jr. with his droopy face. She tried to envision what he would look like with a mustache, a cigarette dangling from his tiny tortoise mouth, maybe some eyeglasses.

"He looks depressed," Noah had said. "Maybe we should get him out of here. I mean, he did spend years as a prisoner of war during World War II, and now look at him, stuck in this big-box hell!"

It was true that the tortoise looked depressed.

Clemi stared at the tortoise, locking eyes. Was it her imagination, or was he trying to communicate? Maybe it really was Kurt Vonnegut Jr. in there, or at least his brilliant comic soul packed into a ruddy brown shell.

"Should we take him home?" she had asked, pushing to the back of her mind the fact that the lease on the apartment she shared with Florence and their new roommate, Simon, prohibited pets—an issue the landlord had made a big fuss about, lecturing them to be sure they understood that this included even a tiny caged rodent or a goldfish in a plastic bag.

It was among the most profound moments of her young life thus far, this strange consideration of the turtle, here in aisle seven of Pets! Pets! Pets! in Fairfax, Virginia. It was twelve minutes before closing time, and the lights had begun to flicker. An announcement poured from overhead speakers alerting them to select their final purchases. It was then that Noah—oh so randomly and unexpectedly!— had leaned in for a kiss. His mouth tasted like alcohol and peppermint gum with a hint of cannabis. She made a note of every detail, the way his hand brushed her hair, the way his stubble rubbed against her cheek, the way she wished she could take the stupid hipster wool cap off his head to run her fingers through his hair, the way she felt like devouring him, this unromantic backdrop notwithstanding. Already she was getting ahead of herself, supposing that this tortoise epiphany, accompanied by this kiss, might mark the beginning of something meaningful. Like maybe the tortoise was a gateway pet to be followed up by shared custody of a dog, and then, perhaps . . . who could say?

If so, what happened at the register was inauspicious.

The bill for Kurt Vonnegut Jr., his plastic terrarium, his bedding, a UV light he needed, and a starter supply of food came to $279.85. Noah fumbled around in his wallet unconvincingly before announcing that he seemed to have forgotten to bring his plastic and he didn't have any cash.

"I guess I can put it on my Visa?" Clemi had offered tentatively, hoping he'd intervene. She had a small cushion of savings left over from her mother's graduation present the year before, but big picture–wise, she definitely could not afford this.

"That would be great! I'll reimburse you when we get paid next week." He gave her a kiss on the cheek.

She'd handed the clerk her bank card, even though at this rate she'd barely make it to the next pay period herself.

They had just crossed the Pets! Pets! Pets! threshold when the store went dark, and she heard the sound of the doors being locked behind them. Noah stood triumphant, holding Kurt Vonnegut Jr. in his new traveling case, a bag of what looked like tortoise kale in hand. His cell phone emitted a beep, then another, and he set the acquisitions down on the curb, fished the phone from his pocket, and looked at the screen.

"Hey, Amos and Eli are going to meet up with Brandon and Jimmy . . . I don't think you know them . . . they're friends of Sami's . . . they have a band and a midnight gig tonight at the Wharf . . ."

He'd looked at Clemi and at the Pets! Pets! Pets! bags as if only now realizing the potential glitch in whatever plan he was formulating.

"You're welcome to join," he said. "But . . . you have the tortoise and also you don't really know these guys and I think you would find it kind of boring. And loud."

She hoped he'd propose another solution—like dropping Kurt Vonnegut Jr. off at his apartment and then continuing on to the party together—but instead a dilapidated Toyota Corolla pulled up in front of where he and Clemi stood.

"Actually that's Amos right there. Sorry to leave you here like this. Sure you don't want to come?"

"I'll be fine."

"You're the best," he said, handing her one of the bags. "Bye for now, Kurt," he said to the tortoise. "Sure you can manage?"

She really wasn't so sure. But Noah didn't wait for an answer.

Now, three days into this joint custody arrangement, Clemi can see how deluded she'd been to suppose that beneath the whole hipster façade, including the nearly shredded pair of Toms and the flannel shirt and the guitar he carries around but in truth plays badly, is a responsible boy who would treat her well, who would spontaneously make brunch reservations for them on Sunday mornings, after which they would wander through Room & Board holding hands, fantasizing about one day earning more than eleven dollars an hour and being able to afford to buy a new chair—although at this point she'd settle for a contribution toward the purchase, care, and feeding of a small tortoise.

When Noah finally stops by Clemi's office just before lunch, he's so charming and chill in his usual way that it's impossible for her to get a read on whether he even remembers the kissing part of the pet store episode.

She points to the terrarium that sits atop a bookshelf. "He eats twice a day," she says. "You put a little food right there, and you need to clean the water, and he really likes to come out of the case and wander around on the rug, but keep an eye on him because it's easy to forget he's there and then you might accidentally step on him." She hates every word that comes out of her mouth. She sounds like a mother. Not necessarily her own mother, who she wishes might have worried about someone stepping on *her* when she was growing up, but like her friends' mothers, and ones she's seen on sitcoms and read about in advice columns and in books.

"Also, we're almost out of food."

"How is that possible?" Noah asks. "That bag was huge." An indication, at least, that he remembers something about Saturday night.

"Yeah, there was kind of a problem. My roommate thought

it was from his CSA—he gets produce delivered once a week—and he ate about half the bag last night."

She expects a laugh—it's funny, no? Apparently not.

"I thought you lived with Florence."

"I do. But since she doesn't have any income right now, we took in another roommate."

"She hasn't found another job yet?"

"She has a couple of leads," Clemi lies. "She's having a really rough time right now. I mean, obviously. I've been in touch with her parents. We're all keeping an eye on things for now since she's refusing to move back to Wisconsin and I can't get her to talk to anyone about whatever it is that's going on." She feels protective of Florence, her roommate and former best friend, even though she is not responsible for her spectacular nosedive. She'd been fired for a dozen different reasons, but they all came to a head the day she had a meltdown at the information desk when a customer asked if they had "that book about a bird." Clemi had heard the story related thus:

Customer: "Do you have that book about a bird?"
Florence: "Can you be more specific?"
Customer: "It's on the cover."
Florence: "What's on the cover?"
Customer: "The bird."
Florence: "What kind of stupid bird?"

And it went on from there, with Florence informing the customer that zillions of books about birds exist and that she was fed up with all of these poorly formulated questions, and that people should figure out what they are looking for before walking into a store, until Jamal intervened and stuck a copy of *The Goldfinch* in the customer's hand and took Florence by the arm and led her to the back office for a time-out and, a few meetings later, a letting go.

"Yeah, that's rough. Florence's parents are getting divorced or something, right?"

"Yes, and they're having a lot of other problems. I think her mom just lost her job and they have to move out of their house. And her sister . . . she won't tell me what's going on, exactly, but I heard there is an opioid problem."

"Geez, that's rough," says Noah, who now appears to be done with this conversation. He has just received a text and is, once again, busy with his phone. He taps at it for a minute, then puts it away and picks up the tortoise's case by its handle.

"Thanks, Clem," he says. And then to the tortoise, "We are going to have some good times, my bro."

Clemi watches them walk away and feels a twinge of loss. For Noah, yes, but also, unexpectedly, for Kurt Vonnegut Jr.

END OF DAY REPORT: Monday, August 14
OPENING SHIFT: Carmen, Jamal, Aaron
SWING SHIFT: Luke, Antonio, Noah
CLOSING SHIFT: Summer, Yash, Sami
EVENT: Clemi
FLOOR MANAGER COMMENTS: The rain, the rain, the rain. There are a couple of wet spots to keep an eye on. Jamal has set out buckets and has called the gutter repair people. (What are we going to do without him?)

Speaking of which, Jamal brought donuts! Thank you, Jamal! There are still a few left at the information desk.

A few notes from the day:

- Still no word from Belinda. Web orders are a bit backed up, so just assure customers that everything is on the way. If anyone has heard from Belinda, please let me know.
- People continue to ask about *The Doodles*, which we do not yet have in stock.
- Also they are looking for something called *Antifa Now!*, which is out of print, although the calls continue to pour in like so much rain through the leaky roof of an independent bookstore.
- Ditto for aggrieved calls about all variety of events. We've been transferring calls over to Clemi's voice mail, which—note to Clemi!—is full.
- We briefly lost internet.
- The event for *The Final Act*, winner of last year's PEN/Hemingway Award, was small—"intimate," as we say—and we had to discreetly disappear some chairs. Clemi seemed

to pacify the author; the author seemed to pacify Clemi. No one is quite sure why no one came.

- The police came around and talked to Wayne. They encouraged him to go to a shelter, at least temporarily to get out of the rain. But he said this is home, and he doesn't mind the rain. Sami and I brought him a poncho and some dry clothes, then gave him some money for dinner.
- We conclude this evening's report with a moment of silent prayer and a random joke:

What do you call a whippet crossed with a poodle?
A fasterdoodle!

IMPORTANT VACUUM CLEANER UPDATE: Noah got the thing working again, but you have to kick it a couple of times to loosen up the suction tube before plugging it in.

Autumn T

CHAPTER 4

Tuesday

QUERK III

S ophie finds it hard to be alone inside her house, which is part of why she is here at 5:52 a.m., backing her Subaru up to the rear entrance of the store and retrieving a duffel stuffed with clothes from the passenger seat.

There was a time in her life—not all that long ago—when she longed for a little solitude. What with a young child, the store, all those books to read, the constant invitations to appear on panels at literary festivals, the book parties and fancy dinners with authors and publishers, and a husband who liked to chatter nonstop, loneliness had seemed a foreign concept. She had felt, at times, like she had chickens constantly pecking at her brain. Now the chickens are mostly gone, and it is harder than she could have possibly imagined to be alone.

Which is why it is completely illogical, this fantasy of hers, to hole up—alone!—in the nook. On the other hand, one might argue that it makes complete sense: The store is so busy, so full of life and people and books and book drama, that she has no time to think about herself. Moving into a cozy little spot inside the belly of her store could remedy this. But the thing is, the fantasy—or the nightmare, depending on the circumstances—involves going into hibernation, possibly never coming out. Also there's the fact that she is thinking, or at least allowing herself to entertain the possibility, of selling the store. Okay, so she hasn't entirely thought this through. It's just a fantasy. A thing that gives her peace of mind. No need to fine-tune every little detail, such as: Would she sell the store with herself barricaded inside? What if she died in there? Wouldn't her body decompose? The thing is, she is thinking apocalypse, so who really cares?

It's not like she's the first person in the world to think one thing and then do another. "Do I contradict myself?" Walt Whitman famously wrote. "Very well then I contradict myself, / (I am large, I contain multitudes.)" Adrienne Rich also wrote about life being a contradictory stew. And F. Scott Fitzgerald: The sign of a first-rate intelligence is to be able to hold two opposing ideas at the same time and not have your head explode, he said. Maybe not those words exactly, but something like that.

So maybe Sophie's head is about to explode, or maybe it's not. Whatever. It's complicated. It's 5:52 a.m., so she will give herself a break.

She unlocks the door and successfully disarms the alarm, then drags the duffel up the stairs, across the main book floor, and over to the Fiction room. It's not an especially long walk, but she feels a twinge in her heel and already regrets slipping on her flats made from recycled trees rather than wearing sneakers. This is a not infrequent occurrence, improper footwear; she can't say why she does this to herself over and over and over, although it might have something to do with vanity.

She knows this place so well that she can tell, in a glance, that someone has rearranged the perennial nonfiction display table: *Behind the Beautiful Forevers* has inexplicably swapped spots with *Hillbilly Elegy*. Ditto for the secular saint prayer candles, which have moved from the right of cash register three to the left of cash register four. The supply of James Baldwins has run low, and clearly they have overordered Edgar Allan Poe.

She used to feel such pride entering this store and taking stock of her small literary empire, but lately, sadly, now she mostly feels defeat. She is overwhelmed by all the things that need doing, or even more, need doing right. She tries to delegate, but she's a control freak at heart. Even with Jamal, she respected his opinion yet still couldn't help but weigh in on every little thing.

She hopes she hasn't driven him out by being an overly demanding boss, but then, he's been here for more than twelve years, so she would like to think it couldn't have been that bad. She wants to catch up properly with him before he leaves, to hear about his plans. She hasn't even had a chance to ask about the move—whether he has found a place to live already, whether Lewis has found a new job in Chicago, or how they will manage with the twins so far away from both of their families. When Solomon was alive, they used to have Jamal and Lewis over for dinner every couple of months. Once the twins were born, Solomon would get down on the floor and play with them, pulling out the toys they still had from when Michael was small. He had gone through an intense cow phase, so the collection was bovine-heavy, but Michael had also accumulated enough Legos to build a small metropolis. Solomon especially loved telling the twins jokes; they were too young to understand, but he still managed to crack them up by making ridiculous faces and wiggling his ears and providing various other forms of physical comedy. Sophie makes a mental note to invite Jamal to dinner before he leaves town, then realizes with regret that this thought may have come too late.

She stands before the shelf of Graham Greenes, looking around for the stepladder so she can reach the button to spring open the door. After checking in the usual spots, including in the side closet by the Nature section and leaning against the wall in the employee bathroom, she finally locates it resting on the door to the events closet. Is it her imagination, or is a fishy smell emanating from within? Sophie tries to open the door to inspect, but it is locked and she doesn't know the code. She doesn't like this one bit—being unable to access even this tiny quadrant of her own store. She's going to talk to Clemi about this! But then she remembers an incident to do with theft—an employee's backpack was stolen from inside—and a snippet of a conversation in which putting a keypad on the door might have been her very own idea.

She drags the ladder back to the Fiction room, climbs carefully to the top rung, and removes the Graham Greenes so she can reach the corner of the bookshelf and depress the button. It's a slow process since she is not an octopus and cannot, anatomically, hang on to the ladder, balance an armful of books, and depress the button all at the same time. She needs to dismount to pile the books on the floor. Again she is moving very slowly, being careful with her shoulder, because if she does go into hiding, she will need to be in tip-top shape in order to survive. She thinks about the Frank family, how if one person in the annex became ill, everyone was in danger of infection. Not that this would be a problem since she will be alone, but still, she is one of those people whose colds seem to morph into chest infections, and among the many things she hasn't considered is how she will procure antibiotics should she ever follow this absurd thing through.

After the door releases and glides open easily along its tracks (thank you, Ibrahim!), she repeats the process, mounting and dismounting the ladder until the Greene oeuvre is back in place.

The nook is still there. Each time she sees it she is surprised by the fact of its existence, this beautiful little room of her own. She looks around and tries to imagine a life in here. It's not bad, really. A little claustrophobic, to be sure; a window would be nice, but a person can learn to make do. Michael, who is currently living in a fetid group apartment with an old high school friend and a couple of fellow yogis, has shown her real estate listings for studio apartments in Logan Circle that cost $2,400 a month and are roughly this size. How he expects to pay that kind of rent on a yoga teacher's salary—one he's not yet earning, to boot—she's not sure, and perhaps he is hinting at a loan, but that's not their best subject right now. She would hire him in a heartbeat to work at the store, to see if there is possibly any future here that he can envision, but that's not their best subject either. She asked him recently if he would like to take on a few shifts, either informally or as an actual employee.

"It would mess up our relationship," he'd said.

She refrained from asking him, "*What* relationship?" given that he mostly just pops in and out of the house, dropping off and picking up laundry, perusing the contents of the refrigerator, sometimes borrowing the car. Instead, she explained that he would report to Jamal, and then to Autumn T, and that she would not be his immediate supervisor.

"Sure, I get it, but still, it's best not to mix the personal and professional," he said. "It will just mess up family stuff."

"Okay. Sure. But the thing is, Michael, it's a family business! It is kind of de facto family stuff. If something happens to me, you will inherit a bookstore. You don't even know how to work the register!"

"Geez, Mom, don't be so dark. Nothing is going to happen to you."

She wished she could be so certain of this, but in any case, she hasn't had the fortitude to follow up.

Something catches in her throat and she coughs, then sneezes. It's so dusty in here that she feels her bronchial tubes constrict. This is part of the reason she needs to restore the flow of electricity ASAP—so she can vacuum. She stares at the dead outlet for a few moments and then has a thought: This is precisely the sort of situation for which God created extension cords.

Sophie presses the button on this side of the nook. The thing is supposed to cause the door to glide back open, and for a moment it seems to be stuck. This causes a small wave of panic. Sure, she wants to be in here, and possibly to never emerge, but she also wants to control her own destiny. While it's true that she hasn't thought through some of the finer details of her self-confinement, she does envision occasional visits to the outside world—perhaps not into shopping malls or ice cream parlors or movie theaters or, sadly, to any mountains or to the sea—but at least into the bookstore from time to time, where she can roam the aisles and retrieve new books. That said, it's not as if books are reliably safe spaces; she has never been able to shake the violence of Partition after reading Salman Rushdie's *Midnight's Children*, for example. And ditto for Isabel Allende's *The House of the Spirits*—it's like she lived through military dictatorship in Chile herself, which is indeed the point of great literature. But what she needs right now is good old-fashioned entertainment. A madcap comedy like *Our Man in Havana*, which, now that she thinks about it, is the rare novel that gives a vacuum cleaner a starring role. She read it in college but can't bear to reread; it begins with a horrible racial epithet, and she has been asking herself tough questions about what to do with the books on her shelves that have language, and sometimes values, she cannot abide.

She leans on the door, trying to nudge it along the track,

causing a stab of pain in her shoulder. The door slides open again, but it seems possible that something is funky with the switch on this side. She'll have to see if Ibrahim can look, or help her find someone to look, at this too. Apart from her shoulder situation and her occasionally aching feet, she's in reasonably good shape—but she sometimes feels this store, this thing that once sustained and nourished her, is also doing her in.

Before opening a bookstore, Sophie had not spent any time considering the physicality of books. She imagines that until they are engaged in the nuts and bolts of the business, few people do. Books are words and ideas and stories, but on a more practical level, assembled in carton quantity, they can weigh as much as forty pounds. And that's not factoring in the oversize art or coffee table or cookbooks that with their irregular sizes and pages of glossy photographs can weigh even more. Cookbooks are where her troubles began: Four years earlier there was one in particular by an Israeli chef named Yotam Ottolenghi that was in such demand, no matter how many boxes they brought onto the book floor, they would quickly run out. One night during the Christmas rush Sophie ran downstairs to retrieve a couple of boxes of Ottolenghis—and as she was descending, one of the booksellers yelled to her from the top of the stairs, "Hey, Mrs. Bernstein, while you're down there, can you grab a box of *Vaginas*?" in reference to the new Naomi Wolf book. Sami found a box in the receiving room and added it to the pile in Sophie's arms, which is precisely when she felt the first spasm of pain in her shoulder, thank you very much, Naomi.

Now she is trying to remember whether, during her search for the stepladder, she had come across the extension cord. The vacuum, she assumes, is in the closet in the back of the staff break room. She begins to retrace her steps, preparing to rummage through the various storage spaces scattered discreetly around the store, when she hears a ringing telephone.

A glance at her watch tells her it's now 6:27 a.m. Too early for customers to be calling. Probably a robocall or a wrong number, but for some reason, maybe just habit, she picks up.

"Sophie!" It's a crusty male voice with a British accent, the vocal cords thick with what sounds like decades of nicotine. She knows this voice! She recognizes him before he identifies himself as Charlie Major, an old friend who owns an independent bookstore in North London.

"Charlie! My goodness, how nice to hear from you! I haven't seen you since the London Book Fair in . . . when was I there? At least five years ago. How are you? How's the store doing?"

"We're hanging on, Sophie. It's not the best of times for independents over here. But the lights are still on, and . . . hang on, wait a minute, I was expecting to get your voice mail—I was about to send you an email but figured I'd just give you a ring in case you were there, and there you are. What the heck are you doing at your store so early in the morning?"

"Oh, just catching up on some work," Sophie says, which is not entirely untrue, depending on your definition of work. She is, after all, preparing to vacuum. No need to tell him that she's always up early now that Solomon is gone. Now that she doesn't sleep. Mostly she just lies awake thinking too much, caught in a boring, repetitive anxiety loop: Nazis, loneliness, Michael, meeting payroll, Nazis, Nazis, Nazis. Also possibly squirrels in the attic, chewing through the electrical cords. "To what do I owe the honor of an old-fashioned transcontinental call?"

"I just wanted to give you a heads-up about an event I see you've got scheduled in a few days."

"Which one is that, Charlie?" She's feeling strangely encouraged by this call. In her recent isolation she's forgotten how much she enjoys the camaraderie of this business, and she's always liked Charlie Major—an old-school bookseller, devoted to his store. Sophie has met him several times over the years at conferences and literary festivals, and he has never dropped a hint of any sort of personal life—never mentioned a partner, or even a pet, although he did once mention possibly being a distant cousin of the former prime minister, from a branch of the family that had roots in Senegal. He's a voracious reader, a man of the book.

"All of the stores in the UK have canceled appearances by Raymond Chaucer, Sophie. Most of the stores in the States have too. You are one of the very few that's scheduled him."

Sophie is unaware of this controversy. Although she is hyperaware of the news—she mainlines CNN and reads two newspapers each morning, as much of a habit as brushing her teeth—she has to admit that her eyes glazed over when she saw the headlines about the poet. Given all that is going on in the world, the personal life of a poet seemed more like tabloid fodder than something she needed to absorb.

"We've always been a bit renegade, Charlie." She says this somewhat in jest. She doesn't want to concede that perhaps an error has been made, that she has checked out and left pretty much all of the decision-making to her staff. Still, she's never been a sheep—she's made a name for herself, in part, by taking a stand, by not backing down. Just because other bookstores are canceling his appearances doesn't mean she has to follow suit.

"As a friend, I hope you don't mind my saying that . . . some people might say it's in bad taste to have him, Sophie."

She is taken aback, and her knee-jerk reaction is to become defensive. "I'm not here to pass judgment on the private lives of poets. Did he commit any crimes? Assault? Rape? Murder?"

"Well, no."

"Is he a racist? An anti-Semite?"

"No, not that I'm aware."

"Fraud? Embezzlement? Or . . . wait, did he plagiarize?"

"No, that's not it . . . but he's a bit of a sleaze . . . I mean, there was the awful situation with the wife and the AGA that she used to commit suicide, as I'm sure you've heard."

As Charlie speaks, she does realize, now, that she has absorbed snippets of the news coverage without even trying to. "I heard it wasn't an AGA. I think I read somewhere that it was a very old Bertazzoni oven."

"Whatever, Sophie, that's not the point."

"Yes, obviously. Just saying. But what is the point?"

"The point is that you might want to be prepared. Before we canceled, we had massive protests outside the store. There's a society here of women who still think the name *Hughes* should be removed from Sylvia Plath's headstone—I'm sure you've heard about that, how they are always trying to etch it off the stone—and now they have taken up the Raymond Chaucer cause. They're not fooling around either. Scotland Yard had to come out and defuse a bomb that we found in a bin inside the store."

Okay, now he has her attention. "Good lord! You should have told me that first. *Inside* the store? That's horrible, Charlie. I'm glad no one was hurt!" Freedom of speech versus the possibility of a bomb inside her store—she may have been a firebrand once upon a time, but right now she is all about being safe, or at least choosing her battles. "Thank you, Charlie, I'm going to look into this. I'll call our events coordinator right away, and we'll come up with a plan."

"Hope to see you again sometime soon. Also, my condolences, Sophie. I've been meaning to send a card. I hope you're doing okay. Solomon was a good man. I mean, I didn't know him well, but we threw back a couple of pints last time you were here. He had some good jokes. One that was especially funny—something about a sheep, I think."

"A goat, probably," she says. Solomon had at least three goat jokes in his repertoire, and part of the beauty of their marriage was that she could rarely remember the punch lines, so they made her laugh every time. She does have a specific memory of one of the goat jokes, however.

"Probably the one where the man brings a goat home

and his wife asks him where they'll keep it: 'Under the bed,' he says. And his wife says . . ."

"'But it smells!'"

"Yes, exactly."

"And the husband says"—and here Charlie drifts into a not entirely awful Yiddish accent—"'It's all vright, he'll get used to it.'"

They share a laugh, but then Sophie grows silent. She knows she should say thanks, or no worries, or whatever it is one is supposed to say at such moments, but after nine months, she's run out of steam on this one. It hasn't gotten better, it's only gotten worse—so she simply hangs up.

Sophie inspects the various outlets at the information desk hoping to find what she needs. Three desktop computers here, but no extension cords. But then, wait, the printer seems to be connected to an outlet nearly six feet away, and voilà, there it is. It's a bit frayed, possibly from having chairs rolling over it all day, every day. It's a possible fire hazard, actually, and she makes a mental note to replace it, but right now she just wants to plug the thing in. She's about to bring it back to the nook, but she first pauses and turns on one of the computers to send Clemi an email. She would send her a text, but because Sophie is completely discombobulated, she has forgotten to bring her cell phone. It's still beside her bed, plugged into the wall. It takes an unusually long time for the old desktop to fire up, and she is reminded that Jamal has been telling her for a couple of years now that the store ought to upgrade its computer systems. He may be right. He *is* right. The registers, the inventory system, the point-of-pay system, are all slower than they ought to be, but—his loss—he won't be here to see it when the day finally comes. Instead he'll probably be toiling in some characterless office building with very boring nonglitchy internet where he can check in with his bank account every hour and remember the good old days when he worked in a bookstore and earned approximately 100 percent less.

Once the thing turns on, it takes nearly three long minutes for her to log into her email. She's running out of time: the opening shift will be here in just over an hour, and she still needs to vacuum, so she doesn't mince any words.

Cancel Chaucer event!

Thx,
Sophie

She ought to keep moving, but since she's here, she takes a quick glance through the rest of her inbox. Dozens of authors are asking for one thing or another. Some are people who claim to know her—one message is from the former principal of Michael's middle school, who has written a memoir about . . . being the principal of Michael's middle school. Another is from the niece of a former law partner of Solomon's who has written a dark comedy about war and Hegelian dialectics, narrated by a cat and set in Aleppo.

There's also a query from an old friend of hers from college, a woman who says they lived in the same freshman dorm, but whom she can barely remember. Every one of them has written a book, and they each want Sophie to put it on the shelf, or to have her invite them to speak at the store. Well, *here* are her chickens, pecking at her brain! This can all wait for later. She is preparing to log off when a new message arrives with the subject line: "The Darkness."

She feels a wave of dread. *The darkness will soon descend.* Did she really say this? What had she been thinking? Was she quoting someone, or had she come up with this all by herself—spun it from the darkness in her head, from the soup of terrifying headlines and the events in Charlottesville and passages from *The Diary of Anne Frank* and the prospect of Jamal leaving and all the book galleys with feet on their covers coming to a terrifying boil?

The darkness will soon descend.

As her former employee had told Sophie, her stars are scrambled—which ought to give her carte blanche to say whatever messed-up things she likes.

The disturbing subject line aside, Sophie is intrigued. The email is from Kevin, a relatively new hire who works in the receiving room. If she's remembering correctly, he's got a sweet face, this kid, although it's eclipsed by a long, scraggly beard, and he adorns himself with scary-looking chains that she finds weirdly intriguing.

"I didn't know you were a death metal fan!" the message reads. "I have a few comp tickets for the Darkness at the 9:30 Club a week from Saturday. My brother is the drummer! Let me know if you'd like to come!"

Which is more surprising: that the Darkness is a band, or that this young man thinks death metal is a thing she might enjoy?

She's not even sure what death metal is, but perhaps she ought to embrace this misunderstanding and brush up on her Darkness discography. Being a fifty-four-year-old death metal fan is certainly better than having her staff think she's losing her mind. Obsessing on the possible end-times. On the hard rain that's gonna fall. On the total eclipse of the sun. On the heart of darkness. On the things that make her want to crawl into her nook and never emerge, which is why she's here at the store this morning, now armed with an extension cord and headed downstairs to find the vacuum cleaner.

She enters the staff break room, which she can't help but note could really use a thorough cleaning. She opens the closet and there it is, the vacuum cleaner, just beside the easels and the poster board and the brooms and the various other cleaning supplies. She's not sure she's ever even seen this particular contraption. It's enormous! Aren't appliances supposed to be getting lighter, sleeker, like the Roomba she has at home, or like laptop computers, some of which are now nearly as thin as an ad-deprived magazine? She has heard that these bulky, corded vacuums are a thing of the past—that now they have wireless, dirt-sucking machines that are light, that you can carry in one hand. This one is the size of a small tank.

Now she remembers: It's a Querk III, no ordinary vacuum cleaner. It was imported from Germany and cost just over $1,000. Sophie had initially balked at the price. In her day you could buy a vacuum for about ten times less, and it did basically the same thing; you plugged it in, ran it over the carpet, and sucked up the dirt. What more did you need? But Jamal read aloud to her some of the reviews of the Querk III, and it's true that she has never heard people get quite so worked up over a home appliance. One enthusiast wrote a ten-paragraph review detailing how many times she had already cleaned her carpet before going over it again with the Querk III, posting gruesome pictures of the clumps of hair, dirt, and debris the Querk III had sucked up, including a fist-size spider that was still wriggling. The enthusiast went on another couple of paragraphs about how the Querk III had saved her from inhaling lung-destroying allergens and mites and such. It was a bit over the top. Sophie wasn't that big a fool; she understood that some of these reviews were commissioned, and that she might just as easily be seduced by the virtues of the smooth ride of a new Harley-Davidson. Just because it was the most recognizable motorcycle brand on earth didn't mean she needed to own one.

But Jamal was convincing in a more compelling way; he went through the store's operation ledger and recited to Sophie the number of vacuums purchased over the last twenty or so years, and it was indeed eye-opening, the amount of waste. They had been going through vacuums at a rate of about one every other year. That said, this was a heavy usage situation—hundreds of people passed through the store each day, and someone was assigned to vacuum every night. Nevertheless, this seemed a high rate of turnover. Jamal then highlighted the amount of money spent annually on repairs, as well as on new bags and belts. Also eye-opening. The new Querk III not only came with a seven-year warranty but also was entirely self-contained; it had built-in mechanisms to do all the specialty vacuum stuff, like get into corners or accommodate shag carpeting—no external attachments needed.

It wasn't as if Jamal had any stake in the outcome, yet he was pretty fired up about this particular model. Solomon had passed a month before; she had only been back at work a few days and gave it minimal attention. It's not as though she would have handled it any differently though. She trusted Jamal implicitly and told him to go ahead and buy a vacuum using his best judgment.

The thing has been nothing but trouble, but she doesn't hold it against Jamal. Nor does she hold it against him that, in an effort to secure a better price, he bought the vacuum on eBay for only $850, from what unfortunately turned out to be an unauthorized dealer, and hence the promised seven-year warranty proved nonexistent. It worked for almost seven months before the problems began, which is, granted, longer than the others. When it comes to vacuum cleaners, the store is cursed.

She stares at the Querk III like it's a bull she needs to mount at a rodeo. It's completely intimidating, this machine. For reasons she cannot entirely explain, it makes her think of Arnold Schwarzenegger, if Arnold Schwarzenegger were a vacuum cleaner. She knows she cannot lift the thing, but she will not be defeated. Fortunately it's on spinner wheels that glide surprisingly well, like one of those practically aerodynamic newfangled suitcases, and she manages to get it to the elevator. She presses the button, and while she is waiting for it to arrive—like so much else in the store right now, the lift is slow, makes alarming creaking noises, and needs to be upgraded before something bad occurs—she is seized by a moment of vacuum cleaner déjà vu.

Has she been here before, in this very same hallway, hand on vacuum, waiting for the elevator to arrive? Probably, yes, like a year or two ago, and not necessarily many lifetimes ago when she was perhaps a potbellied pig in Cambodia or a street sweeper in Kolkata.

She has known so many vacuum cleaners over the last five decades that she could write a book! That said, she has no desire to write that book, and of this she's proud. Why does *everyone* think they need to write a book? Why is reading not a sufficient occupation? She thinks of Amos Oz, who, as a boy, wanted to *be* a book. Not an author but a *book*, which to Sophie is the far more noble occupation.

A memoir on vacuum cleaners is not the worst idea. She will not write it, but if she did, each model would head a chapter. She might begin with her Brooklyn childhood, from which she does have a surprisingly clear memory of her mother pushing around a large upright machine that came with a couple of attachments for difficult-to-reach places, like under the couch. It was a big deal, that vacuum. It cost half a month's pay for her father, who had worked in insurance, and she can remember the excitement when he presented it to her mother on her birthday back in an era when a household appliance qualified as an acceptable gift. Then again, maybe they didn't even then—it was the 1960s, after all—but so be it, her father was not the most enlightened man who ever lived. Most memorable to Sophie is the amount of dust stirred up even as the Hoover did its thing, as if it had been designed to ensure its own relevance. And whenever her mother changed the bag, it emitted a brand-new desert storm of dust.

The adult section of the memoir might begin with the first Electrolux, a silver canister contraption that she and Solomon bought when they first married. And here she would reflect, and perhaps even give some unsolicited advice, on marriage. Oh, how she'd loved Solomon! He made her feel loved and supported, even when life was rough. They'd had their struggles over the years of the usual variety—the unfair division of domestic responsibilities, for example, and tensions about money as Solomon worked his way through law school. But that era had eventually given way to one of relative prosperity, which had unfortunately given way to a new problem: Solomon's paralegal, Adele. How painful that had been—the fake business trips, the lipstick on his collar. Really, could he have tried to be less cliché? Sophie still seizes up inside remembering, but she's long gone, Adele, after a rapid, painful death from pancreatic cancer. (Sophie will not say it serves her right and tries to perish such thoughts when they occur, but she is not a perfect human being.) She and Solomon somehow recovered from this, and with the passage of time she was able to let bygones be bygones, to sweep it under—or rather vacuum it into—the rug.

The next model Electrolux, similarly shaped but presumably in one way or another improved, once ingested one of Michael's Power Rangers. She remembers taking Michael with her to the repair shop and hearing her son's squeals of delight when the repairman was able to extract the Morphin Megazord, albeit in multiple and not entirely complete pieces, from the hose. At home, they were able to reattach the limbs, and even though the toy was missing an arm, it was not that much worse from the ordeal. (And here Sophie pauses to reflect on something that tends to get lost in the current climate of fraught, or at least out of sync, interactions with Michael: She was a good mother, and she loved her son with such ferocity that it hurt. At times she wished she'd had a second child so she could spread out her love and make it hurt less, especially should something bad happen to the one. She even contemplated getting pregnant again for this reason only until she read Anne Tyler's *Dinner at the Homesick Restaurant* and learned that having extra children would only endanger her further, as she would then have even more to lose. She cried when Michael cried. And when Michael felt joy, she still cried out of fear the joy might stop.)

Has all of her diligent mothering been negated by the fact that she once hinted clumsily that while she applauds his yogic aspirations, perhaps he could try supplementing his new career with something that puts to use his expensive education? That he might even consider helping his mother out by working in the bookstore? She suspects it's more than that, though. Something between them has changed since Solomon's death. Sure, she sees him frequently—perhaps more now than previously these last few years, since he is back in DC after finishing college—but their interactions are largely transactional. It's not like she wants to sit down at the table and have daily heart-to-hearts, but she feels he is avoiding meaningful conversation.

It had not previously occurred to her that mothering a young adult could be trickier than mothering a young child. It's not as if he needs monitoring; he's not going to swallow a marble or stick his finger in a socket or take a marker and draw all over the walls, and yet those were things she knew how to guard against. Now that he's a young adult, the minefields are harder to see. She can agonize for an hour before speaking, and yet no matter what she says, she'll say the wrong thing.

She urges herself on to more productive memories, recalling the time Solomon's nephew stayed with them for a few weeks while he was looking for an apartment in DC. His poorly behaved pet rabbit destroyed a pair of Sophie's shoes, shredded a brand-new queen-size down duvet, gnawed through a copy of *Ragtime*, and then chewed through the vacuum cleaner cord, cutting it in half.

More recently she has bought herself a robot of sorts, a small disc of an autonomous vacuum. His name is Roomba, and she's a little embarrassed to admit the extent to which she has bonded with the little guy. At night when he is asleep in his docking station, she sometimes locks onto his robot eye and feels as though they are communicating. His blinking light gives her solace. It says he's there, that she is not alone, that she has a companion who is ready to serve. He has little sweeping side brushes that remind her of whiskers, and they appear to wave around as he works. Although his sensors are supposed to prevent him from getting stuck in corners or falling down stairs, she still worries about him like he's a toddler in her charge. It's embarrassing to admit, even to herself, but she kind of loves Roomba. He is an object of comfort in her life, and it occurs to her that once she has been fixed up with electricity, she ought to bring him with her to the nook. She understands that he is a robot vacuum cleaner, that she is a fifty-four-year-old widow, and that this is not really a relationship in the usual sense of the word. And yet it's something.

She is not really going to write a memoir, and the vacuum cleaner romance stops right here. She's not sure she could ever feel such attachment to the hulking metal monster that is Querk III, although she is grateful to him for being so light on his feet. She has no trouble, once the elevator finally arrives, in getting him in and out and to the nook. She then attaches the extension cord to the plug, runs it to an outlet in the Fiction room, and—success! It turns on! But only for a second. Before it can begin to do its sucking thing, she hears a loud popping noise and the lights go out in the entire store.

CHAPTER 5

THE EARLY BIRDS

It offends him deeply, the book tour, the very idea of the book tour. He spends weeks, months, sometimes as long as a year (and sure, sometimes only about ten minutes) working on a poem, and then he is expected to dispense with it, deliver it to the people in an easy-to-consume, bite-size nugget like those breaded slabs of chicken his children used to clamor for, the ones that come with a variety of dipping sauces and a plastic toy.

"The point is to whet their appetites, Ray," Fiona, his publicist, reminds him, her voice breaking up a bit on the phone. They have had this conversation more than once in the days leading up to the transatlantic arm of the tour, such as it is. "Just do your magnificent best, then they will buy the book and spend the rest of their lives reflecting on your brilliance."

"I feel like a walking infomercial for myself. You know, my great friend Jorie once told me—"

"Stop name-dropping. Just do your job and get over

yourself." Fiona is a feisty one, and he likes, and also needs, this. He is ready to let her take charge—navigate his life, be his operating system—even if it's only through the speaker on his phone.

Raymond stares out the window of his sister's apartment in DC, into the strange tableau of the empty ballpark directly across the street. Observed from the fourteenth floor of this glassy modern edifice, it's a view not meant to be, intended neither by God nor any zoning board with a sense of propriety. The place is quiet now, a jarring contrast to the pandemonium of Sunday's doubleheader.

He is not close with his sister. They are what you might call estranged, but in light of his current situation, plus the fact that she is away at a conference in Malaysia, she agreed to let him stay here for a week. The publisher offered to put him up in a hotel, but here he has complete privacy. No need to check in at the front desk, hand over his credit card and passport, and watch the clerk's face register vague confusion and then possibly scorn once he or she realizes why the name Raymond Chaucer rings a bell.

The driver who fetched him from the airport Saturday night told Raymond that even just four years ago, none of this development was here. Now, he said, it's among the trendiest neighborhoods in town. Even so, the driver couldn't locate the building and in frustration finally dropped Raymond on an empty stretch of sidewalk in front of Nationals Park. Raymond had privately wondered if he was being disappeared by his publisher. Maybe he is one of those authors who would sell more books dead.

He stood with his luggage trying to reorient just as a

clap of thunder cracked so loudly he felt the vibration. A light drizzle turned into driving rain as he fumbled with his phone to double-check the address and be sure he was in the right neighborhood, in the right city, on the right planet. As he turned in circles, holding his phone high trying to catch a signal, throngs of very loud, wet, and inebriated people appeared, some of them wearing jerseys and waving gigantic foam fingers in the air. Was this his punishment, his little private hell, to be standing in the middle of a thunderstorm, lost, drenched, and surrounded by a bunch of screaming drunken louts?

There turned out to be a simpler explanation: This was, indeed, where his sister lived, and the baseball game was either over or delayed on account of the rain.

He thinks about Fiona and the last time he saw her, the night before he left for DC. He is a man who likes to infuse his memories with the granular details of his liaisons—what she was wearing or what she was drinking or what shade of lipstick she wore—but in this case he cannot remember much of anything, which is likely because he has moved into a different headspace now, overwhelmed and distracted by the fallout from the *Guardian* article. It's not a good thing, sleeping with his publicist at this particular moment in time. He knows this. But he does his best. He means no harm and he has his needs, and fortunately there is no human resources department to regulate the behavior of poets—at least not insofar as he knows. Not yet.

Wherever they were, whichever of her many sexy wrap dresses she was wearing, whatever variety of leaf she was stabbing with her fork, whatever blend of rare malt he was sipping, he does remember that she reminded him it was quite a coup for her to get him a reading in Washington, that it was a miracle, of sorts, that an event slot had opened up and that the store had not yet canceled his appearance.

"Appreciate me," she'd said.

"I do."

"Do you know what a miracle it was to get you this event? Bookstores don't host many poetry readings," she'd told him, as if this was something he didn't already know. These qualifiers about poetry offend him deeply, although he supposes the problem may simply be that he's become an easily offendable man.

"The event is at seven. The girl at the bookstore asked if you could get there about six. But listen, Ray, I really need to get going. I have a meeting in a few minutes."

"Did you tell her about the pens?" he asked.

"Yes, it's all good."

"You know which kind, right?"

"Yes, it's under control."

"Not just any Sharpies. Ultra-fine point."

"Okay, Ray. Really, I've got it. Forget about the bloody pens. I mean, just remember how lucky you are to be reading there at all!"

But he knows it's not luck; it's fate. He's made a mess of his life, and although he's not entirely sure what set of beliefs he subscribes to when it comes to the governance of such things—whether whatever goes around comes around,

whether each life conforms to an internal narrative structure that demands all the pieces come together in the end,
that what goes up must come down, that all the planes must
land, as much as he resists it—he understands that he must
wind up at that store. He's not sure he deserves forgiveness,
but he'd like to ask for it if he can.

He has four days to kill before his sole US event. Fiona
had to quickly reshuffle his schedule once one store after
another canceled his appearances. He was meant to be in
New York today with two days' worth of readings, then on
to Philadelphia and Baltimore, and on Saturday, the reading
in DC.

This proximity to the ballpark is an unexpected perk,
and he's here during an extremely active week of games. On
Sunday he didn't even leave the apartment—just nursed a
fifth of bourbon and watched baseball out the window the
entire day. He had the game on the television and could see
the field if he stood on the balcony and leaned hard toward
the right. The place went wild when Howie Kendrick hit a
grand slam—the stadium lit up like the Fourth of July.

The Nats are doing well; they will make the playoffs
and will likely play the Cubs in the first round. Bryce
Harper is hurt. Ditto for Jayson Werth. So Raymond was
informed by an exuberant and overly chatty young man he
encountered in the elevator when he'd arrived Saturday
night, exhausted, jet-lagged, disheveled, wrestling his wet
roller bag with its one broken wheel. The man was headed

to the rooftop. He carried in his hands a platter heaped with hunks of raw meat, presumably en route to a place where a grill or a pride of lions waited; Raymond did not inquire. The meat man's drawl was suggestive of a Southern region that Raymond could not confidently identify, plus the man was just a notch too friendly in that American way that, in Raymond's current circumstances, was neither called for nor welcomed.

Still, he was interested in these snippets about the Nats. At one point in his life he counted baseball among his chief pleasures. He travels to this country far less frequently these days, and at the last few games he attended, some five years ago, he found himself abhorring the crowds, not to mention the blaring music, the people sipping beverages from gigantic plastic vats, the orgy of fast food. The nachos he'd eaten, heaped with sour cream and cheese and guacamole, had left him sick for two days. Somewhere along the way he'd stopped feeling the adrenaline surge of a first pitch and had begun looking at the sports pages with detachment, like he was reading a stranger's obituary. One more loss in a long string.

For much of his adult life, the Yankees' schedule had been an organizing principle of his movements, and even of his investments. For a time he and Seema kept a pied-à-terre in New York, and while there were many practical, personal, and professional reasons for this, his consulting arrangements with two New York–based banks among them, the proximity to Yankee Stadium was not an insignificant factor in his desire to own a small piece of real estate in the city. Seema showed no interest in the sport, and he failed to pass his enthusiasm along to any of his children. He couldn't convince Ian, the oldest of his three, to accompany him to a game, even when he threw in the prospect of box seats and first-class air travel.

Eventually he sold the apartment. By then Elena had moved to London anyway, and their not-so-secret ball-park liaisons had been one of the sidebar attractions of the game. There had been other New York women; the philan-thropist's socialite wife, whom he had met at a private MoMA reception for the opening of a Miró retrospective; a young single mother who lived in a one-bedroom flat in Williamsburg, whom he had met at a Starbucks. (And oh, what a mistake that had been! She turned out to be rather unhinged and had pursued him long-distance for a couple of fraught years.)

There had also been an aspiring poet who asked him for advice—Roxana Sánchez was (alas, still *is*) her name—and who lands among his greatest-hits collection of mistakes. Not because their times together were unpleasurable; they were not at all bad. And not because she turned out to be a nutjob; she was among the sane. But because she had hired a lawyer. For what offense, he is not entirely sure, but the threat of whatever she had up her sleeve hovered vaguely, haunting him in his dreams for a few years until, praise the lord, it seemed to disappear.

It's strange, as he ages, the way life falls into such distinct categories that entire phases feel like chapters in a book he once read. If he works hard enough, really puts himself in the zone, he can at least channel the memory of that jolt of pure excitement he'd once felt watching the pitcher roll back his arm, perhaps not unlike a hit of black-tar heroin entering the bloodstream. But by now the memory has become as distant as Sadie, his beloved old dog, a retriever they had when the children were young.

"Watch out. This block, no one walks around here at night after the game crowd clears out," the meat man had warned Raymond, noticing his suitcase. Sunday night he'd stared out the window, fascinated as the game wound down, first a trickle of people and then such large clots that they had trouble squeezing through the gates, everyone rushing to catch the Metro or walking toward their cars or staring at their phones, trying to locate their Ubers. Then the food vendors and the cleaners wearily emerged, the lights went dark, and the only person who remained shouted something about Jesus before slumping against the entrance, which by then had been clamped shut by gates.

So here is Raymond's plan: He's going to hunker down here in this strange industrial apartment building, and he is going to make lemonade from the lemons life has dealt him. He will use this time as a writing retreat—one of those *staycations* people brag about taking, which he has always assumed simply meant they were broke. But it's true, he can already feel the idea for a new poetry cycle beginning to take shape. He can see the arc, the way the baseball narrative will intersect with the coming apart of his marriage, of his family, of his life. The only problem, so far, is that his words are not high-quality stuff.

Here they are, the early birds, moving in
     clusters toward the ballpark:
the couples and the families and the young
     guys in packs
pumped and rowdy and playful.
Some of them wear jerseys,
the occasional foam finger raised high,
     expectant . . .

And here's Fiona again, on the phone, a welcome inter-
ruption to this terrible, juvenile poem.

"Unbelievably good news," she says. "You are not going
to believe this."

"Try me."

"Where to begin? We've got you a spot on Boris this
week. Not sure which day, but before the bookstore. I'm
still sorting it out."

"What's *Onboris*?"

"No, on Boris. The *Boris Lewinsky Show*. NPR, Ray. It's
good. He's a big deal. I'm going to call you back with the
details in a couple of hours. And the *Washington Post* is
also confirmed. They'll send a reporter over for a profile
tomorrow, so you need to pull yourself together. By the way,
can the reporter get into that building? Does she need a
code, or is there a concierge, or will you come down and
let her in?"

"You told her the ground rules, right?"

"Which are?"

"I'm not going to answer any questions about Seema. I
only want to talk about the book."

"We've been over this, Ray. There's really no avoiding it. Just talk about how devastated you are, how she'd been depressed."

"I don't want to get into the thing about the AGA again either."

"Okay, really, just let go of that one. It's not a big deal to anyone but you."

"It *is* a big deal. The *Guardian* said it was an AGA and it wasn't an AGA. That's not who I am."

"Having people judge you for your choice of oven is not your biggest problem right now. If you don't want to get into details like that—which I agree are best avoided—just move yourself away from the questions. Without getting upset, I might add. I think you can manage. But can she get into the building?"

"Who?"

"The reporter."

"Oh, right. Sorry. Just give her my number. I'll sort it out."

"Please do, Ray. This is important. We need to get on top of and change the narrative."

"Yes, Fiona, I've got it. Changing the narrative is what I know how to do."

CHAPTER 6

THE LINCOLNS

Clemi arrives early. So much for working on her novel, which she is having trouble writing. She does not *have* to come into her office two hours before her shift; there is no expectation that she will put in more than an eight-hour day, which means she could technically come in at noon, or even 1:00 p.m., and no one would think she is shirking her duties. Her inbox and voice mail might feel like an ongoing emergency, but truly, everything can hypothetically wait. But then, what excuse would she have for being stuck midway through her latest draft?

Also, she needs to respond to the email from Mrs. Bernstein about canceling the Raymond Chaucer event. This request is fraught on several different levels, and she would like to talk to Mrs. Bernstein before taking any action. No sooner does she have this thought than the phone rings, and Fiona, Chaucer's publicist, is on the line.

"Hey, Clemi, love," she says. "I hate to bother you so early in your day, but I wanted to tell you some great news.

The *Washington Post* is doing a story about Ray. He's in town already; he's meeting up with the reporter this week. Plus, Ray is booked on Boris. Not sure which day yet but definitely before your event. This will be his chance to set the record straight. He feels he's been poorly treated by the press, unfairly maligned."

"Oh, hi! Wow!" Clemi says, absorbing this news, which casts the situation in a slightly different light. "You mean Boris Lewinsky on NPR, right?" She doesn't know what other Boris he might be booked on, but she has learned from experience that it never hurts to ask.

"Yes, yes, they just had a cancellation and are shifting their schedule around—I believe the prime minister of Canada was meant to be talking about his book this week, but there's some plagiarism issue or something."

"Oh, right . . . I think you mean the foreign minister? And isn't it the foreign minister of Norway?"

"Probably. I think you're right. Anyway, his misfortune is our good luck. So that should bring out quite a crowd for the event."

"That's all good news—I'll share with the store's owner. But then again, a crowd isn't always a good thing, especially not an angry crowd. Look, I want to host him . . . obviously, or I wouldn't have booked him . . . but our owner is having some second thoughts. Full disclosure: she wants me to cancel. I'm planning to push back, and I do need to talk to her first—"

"Sure, sure, but you know, he's going to correct the record."

"Sure, but . . . I mean, even the possibly corrected version is still not great. There's the disclosure about the illegitimate child . . ." Clemi winces at her own poor choice of word, *illegitimate*. It is possible, and even quite likely, that she has just described herself. She is not sure what she is doing, what game she is playing, where her allegiance ought to lie. Is she a confused young woman who wants to meet her father? Or is she an events coordinator at an independent bookstore, simply trying to do her job?

"So Ray will be there by 6:00 p.m. A little before."

"Right, if we go forward."

"Also, we need to go over a few ground rules for the event."

"Assuming we go forward, sure."

"First, please do not mention the *Guardian* profile."

"Um, okay, but I can't promise it won't come up during the Q&A."

"It's better if it doesn't."

"Okay . . . I can't entirely control that situation. People are going to have questions."

"I think he can handle most questions—he's no stranger to controversy—but he very much does not want to talk about the AGA."

"I don't even know what an AGA is."

"It's an oven. A fancy British thing. It came up in the *Guardian* interview. Between us—and please don't repeat this—but he seems to be more upset about people thinking that he had an AGA in his kitchen than about the other things that were revealed, like that he had a love child, or that he's been involved inappropriately with his shark of an agent."

Love child has a nice ring to it, but still, Clemi winces.

That's her mother Fiona's talking about. Fortunately Clemi and her mother don't have the same last name, so no one ever connects them.

"What about the AGA is upsetting?"

"I don't know exactly. He's all over the map about it. He insists that it wasn't an AGA. He feels that people will judge him poorly for having an AGA. On the one hand, he's very design conscious, and he thinks an AGA is very middle-class. The stuff of women's fiction. Too bourgeois. That it was the sort of pretentious thing Seema would have wanted. That she was always spending too much. But mostly it seems like he's concerned because that's not really his style. And also because it's simply not true. They did not have an AGA."

"*That's* what sets him off? Not the fact that people think he drove his wife to suicide?"

"Well, Ray is kind of a sensitive soul."

Clemi can't think of any response that won't sound unprofessional. "I'll talk to Mrs. Bernstein," she tells Fiona. "And I promise to get back to you."

"Okay, great . . . hang on, there's one more thing. He needs fine-point Sharpies."

"Got it. I think we already have a bunch."

"Okay. Not regular Sharpies. He needs fine points. He's very fussy about his signature."

"Okay," she says, no longer sure she really wants to have anything to do with this man, her possible father. "I'll get back to you as soon as I connect with our owner."

The chairs are light and flimsy. Cheap and fidget-proof. A mix of Gunde and Nisse styles from IKEA, distinguishable only by the length of the slats on the seat back, they are stored in the events closet in two parallel, tightly packed rows. Clemi typically begins to set up for the daily event at about 5:00 p.m., but she's starting a bit earlier today because it will likely be a big crowd. She used to have help—a rotation of high school students would come in every day and push the heavy fixtures out of the way, set up the chairs, plug in the microphones, and place a bottle of water and a jar of pens on the table for the visiting author—but they have all either left for college or moved on to other things. Her requests to hire new part-time staff have gone unacknowledged by Mrs. Bernstein. She suspects it's just an oversight. The last time she brought it up, Mrs. Bernstein said okay, but first she wanted to make sure they would be in the black that quarter. Things had been unexpectedly slow, given it was a season with no breakthrough bestsellers; they needed Stephen King or Michelle Obama to write another book ASAP. Then she had failed to get back to Clemi, and the last email Clemi had sent on the subject remained unanswered. She knew things sometimes got buried, and lost, in Mrs. Bernstein's inbox, but she didn't have the heart to keep bringing it up.

Florence, skinny but strong, used to help her too. But now Florence is banned from the store. Which is why, as Clemi comes down the stairs from her office and approaches the events closet, the low-grade anxiety she already feels on account of the Raymond Chaucer affair, plus the increasing social media frenzy about the *Kuddly Killers* event, is heightened by the smell, and the sight, of two foreboding things. First—there is a bad sort of swampy odor coming from the back left corner of the store. If pressed, she would have to say it smells suspiciously like eau de tortoise, which can only mean one thing. Second—a customer is camped out on the floor, smack in the middle of where she needs to set up the chairs. Surrounded by a pile of comic books and graphic novels, the person is claiming enough real estate to pitch a tent. Clemi hopes she is only imagining this, but she has a bad feeling that beneath the gray cotton hoodie, which come to think of it looks suspiciously like one she owns, is her problematic friend. She approaches the customer with caution and is not happy to be proven right.

"I'mgettingkindofintoBuffythecomicbookseriesthatis notsomuchtheTVshowin*WolvesattheGate*Buffyhasa onenightstandwithSatsuwhichwasapparentlyacontroversial plottwistsinceBuffypuristsmaintaintheimprobability thatshemighthavesexualfeelingsforawomanIhopeyoudon't mindthatI'mhere."

"What the heck, Florence. Calm down. Are you taking Ritalin or something?"

"I'm. Just. Researching. Superheroes. For. The. Party," she says, sounding like a tape recorder running out of batteries. "Is that slow enough for you?"

"Okay. I'm just urging you to breathe. To calm down."

Clemi racks her brain for some possible silver lining to Florence's recent preoccupation. Well, one of her recent preoccupations, because she has also ramped up her pronouncements about the eclipse. This morning she asked

Clemi if she realized that thousands of years ago, when the sky went dark in the middle of the day, people thought something had eaten the sun.

"Fascinating," Clemi had said, to be polite. Actually, it *is* kind of fascinating, but she's been too busy with the present to think about what is going to happen six days from now.

In addition to Florence's obsession with the eclipse, she has spent the last week researching superheroes in order to decide on a costume to wear to a party to which she is not actually invited. Technically, to which she was once invited but is no longer welcome—a situation that Clemi has perhaps not effectively conveyed. She had discouraged her from coming to Jamal's party, and obviously those efforts had not gone well.

"I've also kind of gotten into Emma Frost and Hellcat and Invisible Woman, and also Jean Grey. Did you know she looks kind of like you?"

"Who does?"

"Jean Grey. At least as she's portrayed in the *X-Men: Apocalypse* movie."

"I have no idea who that is, but it's really interesting. Let's stop talking about this, okay?"

"Okay, one last confession. I think I have a crush."

"That's great, I think. On who?"

"I may have fallen a little bit in love with Kamala Khan."

"Cool!" Clemi says hesitantly. She doesn't know if this is a good thing, like whether this Kamala person is already married or age appropriate or in any way a healthy candidate for a relationship with Florence. It takes her a moment to realize that Kamala is not a real person but a superhero.

She is, evidently, the masked beauty on the cover of *Ms. Marvel: Teenage Wasteland*, volume nine, which is too bad, since it would be helpful to the situation—possibly—if Florence and Kamala could fall in love and live happily ever after. Then, at least, Florence could move out of their apartment, which would potentially solve Clemi's problem of having to share a tiny bedroom with her insolvent roommate—but she'd still have Simon with whom she could split the rent.

"I mean, I totally get that she's not real, that if I go to Jersey City—that's where she lives—and I walk down the street, I'm not going to bump into her, and besides, I also get that she's too young for me. She's still in high school."

"I suppose I ought to be relieved that you aren't seriously contemplating an affair with an underage superhero? Listen, I hate to interrupt, but I've got to set up for the event now. Plus we're both going to get in trouble if Mrs. Bernstein sees you in the store."

"Okay, but you know it's a free country. Sort of a free country. I mean, not so much right now, I guess, but still, I'm a citizen. I have rights! I'm not sure it's even legal to ban me; it's a public place."

"I think she *can* ban you. I mean, I think this is a private place—not like it's federal property or anything. But I'm not a lawyer, so what do I know? But that's not the point. The point is that you've caused a lot of trouble and it's better if you just slip out of here before anyone sees you. If you want, I can borrow a couple of these books and bring them home tonight. Then you can take your time studying, or whatever it is that you're doing."

Florence doesn't budge from this awkward spot on the floor.

"My hoodie looks good on you," Clemi says. "Just borrow it anytime."

"I helped you pick it out. Remember? Thank you. You're welcome."

The Florence situation is bad, and it keeps getting worse.

Now Florence isn't speaking to either of her parents—she is upset about their impending divorce and refuses to discuss the subject. Clemi has been in touch with them, and they understand that Florence needs help and is unemployed, broke, and generally not in a good place. But she won't go home and she doesn't respond to their texts or calls. Clemi is doing the best she can, but it's starting to feel like treading water; whatever Florence needs is out of the realm of anything that she, as a good friend, can provide.

Clemi and Florence have been friends since freshman year of college, when they lived across the hall from each other and bonded over a number of what now seem like superficial similarities. They had the same exact pair of Converse sneakers, they both liked Regina Spektor, and they'd signed up for the same class called "Literature of Desire." They once stayed up all night discussing Maggie Nelson's *Bluets*. Now, here they are five years later, like they're back in college—except, unbelievably, the bedroom in their apartment, on the top floor of a fourth-floor walk-up in Columbia Heights, is even smaller than their cramped dorm room. They live in a funky old building that is architecturally full of charm but in need of repairs, as well as a revamp of the HVAC system. The old steam radiators fail to keep the place warm in winter, and the ancient window unit barely wheezes out enough air to cool the room they now share. Until three months ago they'd had their own rooms, but once Florence lost her job, they decided to double up and take in another roommate to help pay the rent. It had seemed a good idea at the time, but she can't room with Florence much longer. The entire living arrangement is beginning to feel unsustainable. Flo is getting spookier by the day.

Yesterday when Clemi came home, exhausted after working an eleven-hour day, all of the windows in the apartment were open, negating the heroic efforts of the over-taxed air conditioner. The rain was slashing in and the wind was blowing everything around like the twister scene in *The Wizard of* Oz. Florence was perched on the window ledge in a trance, soaking wet.

"Florence? Are you okay? What is happening here?"

"It's cool. I'm just saging our environment," she'd said.

Clemi was, for the first time in all of her troubles with Florence, feeling frightened. "Please come inside. You're all wet and the mosquitoes are getting in and you're doing *what* to our environment?"

"I'm letting all of the negative energy out."

"Great. But what you're really doing is letting all of the rain *in*. The mosquitoes too," she'd said, slapping her arm.

"You'll thank me later, babe. A solar eclipse can usher in a period of utter disarray."

It's not just Florence—it's a huge thing, this solar eclipse. The Great American Eclipse, they are calling it, the first total solar eclipse to span the country since 1918. Clemi has only been paying tangential attention; she will focus more fully when the time comes. Even so, it is impossible not to absorb the hype around her, especially given that Florence has been anticipating this, and talking about it, for weeks. It's basically all anyone is talking about. That and Charlottesville. They are now reporting that more than thirty people were injured when the man drove his car into the crowd, and Virginia remains in a state of emergency. Clemi feels a bit ashamed for living inside her bookstore bubble, and before that, her liberal arts bubble. For her failure to fully grasp that such virulent racism and anti-Semitism are alive and on the rise in America today. She had allowed herself to believe that such extremist views remained on the fringe.

And this frenzy about the eclipse! It's strange to think that a week that began so horribly will be bookended by this rare celestial event. There must be some deeper meaning here—or maybe that's just the would-be novelist in her, looking to connect dots whether or not they ought to join up.

Her brief moment of awestruck reflection was then interrupted by what she saw in the kitchen.

"Oh my God, Florence, speaking of disarray . . . my book!"

Clemi's manuscript was collateral damage, the pages wind-strewn. Part of the latest incarnation of chapter one had settled in the kitchen sink, and several pages straddled the piles of dirty dishes. Clemi remembered all those supposedly terrible submissions her mother regularly tossed in the bin, and the thought made her want to turn on the faucet and feed her own pages down the garbage disposal—not that they have one of those.

As if dealing with Florence isn't enough, their new roommate, Simon, seems to have a little self-contained pocket of psychosis, or maybe just weirdness. Whatever the DSM-5 might have to say about it, Simon's condition is extremely odd; it involves drilling holes in the wall late at night and then plastering them back up.

She doesn't know a lot about Simon, and with hindsight she realizes perhaps she should have done a background check before inviting him to sublet. Yet he is a nice enough guy. She has no idea what in his neurological wiring has caused him to compulsively drill holes, or whether this is a more recent condition or something he's done his whole life—or at least since he became old enough to wield a power tool. Generally speaking, Simon appears to be a likeable, together, amiable, gainfully employed, stable person. He just likes to drill.

Florence is a different matter, at least right now. She's a free spirit, which is part of her appeal, given that Clemi has always felt despairingly conventional. Also, in the context of their friendship, Florence always used to be, or maybe had just seemed to be, the strong, steady one, the one who was entirely self-assured.

The summer after freshman year, for example, she'd decided on a whim to go to Burning Man in Nevada alone. She had just read something about it, or maybe she'd seen something on social media, and she thought it sounded cool, so she got in the car and drove thirty-three hours to the desert and watched, in awe, dancers twirling lassos of fire. "It was mind-blowing," she'd said. She needed to join this beautiful human conflagration. She bought herself a flame-retardant leotard and began to watch videos, teaching herself to twirl flaming Hula-Hoops around her waist. She once performed solo on the quad, and something went wrong: A bit of flame landed on a book that someone had left lying on the grass. It caught fire, and who knows exactly what happened, but somehow that made something else catch fire and campus security had to come with fire extinguishers and long hoses and douse the place. So okay, maybe that wasn't an entirely rational thing to do, and maybe it runs contradictory to being the strong, steady one, but still, Florence at least knew her own mind, and that was impressive to someone like Clemi, who did not.

For as long as Clemi has known her, Florence has been bleaching her dark hair white and wearing it short, and her ears are pierced with raw metal studs that look like salvaged bits from a construction site. She has at least five tattoos, including one of Frida Kahlo on her bicep. Also, intriguingly, she wears a bullet around her neck. The first time Clemi saw it, she thought it was for real and assumed Florence had experienced trauma—maybe a family member had been in a gang, or been killed in Iraq, and this was Florence's way of remembering.

Perhaps she'd been attracted to this idea of who Florence was because of how far removed it was from Clemi's own boring upper-middle-class background. But even after she learned that the bullet necklace had been purchased from a hipster boutique in Milwaukee, and that Florence was the product of an upper-middle-class childhood, Clemi remained intrigued.

She *needs* Florence. Embarrassing as it is to admit, she believes she was awakened, her life changed, by something Florence said to her one night over dinner at a Thai restaurant during sophomore year.

"You are going to be a rock star, Clemi," she'd said as she squeezed lime into her pad Thai and stirred the bean sprouts into the noodles and shrimp.

"A *rock star?*"

"Yeah. A literary rock star. Your novel is going to be huge."

"My novel? I haven't even started writing a novel. I'm just trying to write a short story, but maybe it could become a novel? I hadn't thought about it like that. I mean, I want to be a writer, definitely—I've always wanted to be a writer, but I don't know if I can really *write*. I mean, write anything good." She was so thrown off by this that she found herself babbling defensively. "I can write term papers, and I can write in my journal and stuff, but I don't know if I can write a *book*. Plus, given who my mom is . . . I don't know, it's just too intimidating."

"You can. You will."

It was stupid to lock into this so intensely, she knew. It was no big deal. Florence was always saying stuff like this, sometimes getting weirdly specific. She once told a complete stranger on the Metro that she should consider buying forty-three shares of Hormel stock. Remarkably it did go up, significantly, the next day. And she once told someone in line at the grocery store that she should take her car to be serviced at the Honda dealer on Rockville Pike because she'd heard it was very good. Where Florence had heard this, or why she cared, Clemi had no idea. It turned out the woman *did* drive a Honda but usually took it to be serviced at her local Shell station, and that they were good but not great. Clemi, who witnessed this scene, thought Florence's behavior was intrusive and embarrassing, but the Honda driver seemed invested in what Florence had to say and agreed to give the dealer a call. This then led to an animated conversation about the brand of granola that the woman had just set down on the conveyor belt: How much sugar did it contain, and was there any coconut in the mix? Florence and the woman exchanged contact info before parting ways and agreed to stay in touch, leading Clemi to wonder if she was the one who went about her human interactions all wrong; perhaps she ought to be making more of an effort to make new friends, talking up strangers on the Metro and in the grocery store line.

But not everyone enjoyed being the beneficiary of Florence's unsolicited advice. Sometimes her predictions were dark, like the time Clemi heard her tell someone who was out walking his dog to go back inside because it was an inauspicious day, or when she'd let someone know that his planets were poorly aligned. She was so all over the place that it was hard to say what sort of mystical school she was from. Soothsayer? Fortune-teller? Astrologer? Witch?

Clemi's working theory was that Florence was just being deliberately outrageous, making most of this up on the spot. But every once in a while she got something right. One day shortly after they first met, Florence explained that Mercury was in retrograde and that Clemi ought to be mindful because something was likely to go wrong. Clemi had laughed and said she didn't believe in that sort of thing. But the next day her computer crashed and she lost all of her files, including a term paper she had failed to back up. So maybe there was something to Florence's portents after all.

Even if it had been a Ouija board–level pronouncement made over a mediocre Thai dinner, it was nevertheless the encouragement Clemi had needed—and there are days even now, years later, when she relies on Florence's vision of her as a writer. It's one of those things that's been pushed so far into the recesses of her mind that she can barely admit it even to herself, but she's afraid to sever her friendship with Florence because she worries that if it ends, she'll take her prophecy with her, and then Clemi's creative abilities, such as they are, will freeze. The flip side of this is that supporting Florence right now is time-consuming, expensive, and emotionally draining, contributing to her inability to write.

She tries to remain positive; helping friends through bad times is just a thing friends do. They've switched places for a while, that's all. Clemi wouldn't even be here, in Washington, at this bookstore, were it not for Florence. After graduation, she had followed her here because Florence had a job, whereas Clemi did not. It wasn't just any job; it was a very impressive one. Florence had landed a paid internship at a prestigious nonprofit that provided humanitarian aid to refugees, and she encouraged Clemi to come with her, assuring her she'd have no problem finding a job. DC seemed as good a place as any, even though Clemi was initially concerned about moving to a city she presumed to be wonky and creatively soulless. In her mind DC was full of commuters who wore white tennis shoes and had government ID cards dangling from their necks, which proved to be at least a little true, but that didn't mean they weren't interesting people. It turned out to be a city full of supersmart, friendly, literate types—which was part of what she loved about working at the bookstore.

Still, initially, it proved difficult for a newly minted English major to find work. Clemi applied to anything remotely connected to words—newspapers, magazines, boring-sounding agencies with acronyms she couldn't puzzle out. She was invited to interview for a position writing grant proposals for a global security firm that did a lot of government contracting, but she didn't get the job, which was just as well since the commute to Springfield, Virginia, would have been difficult. Plus she got the sense that she would have been both out of her element and in way over her head. Then, one day while they were browsing in the bookstore, Florence suggested Clemi apply for a job. Florence had even walked over to the information desk to see whether they were hiring. Total Florence-style serendipity ensued: Someone had just quit, and Clemi was ushered right in to meet Mrs. Bernstein, who then summoned Jamal. They offered her a job on the spot.

Clemi had seen this as a temporary gig, something to help pay the rent while she looked for more substantive work. As the days passed, though, she wound up feeling more at home at the bookstore than she'd expected. It was a little bit like being back on a college campus; every day she saw people she had come to know, and they were all people who shared a love of books.

Then, a week after Clemi started at the bookstore, Florence got herself fired from the internship. Clemi suspected there was more to the story, but Florence's version had to do with becoming outraged when her boss asked whether she could possibly wear something other than torn jeans to a forthcoming meeting on Capitol Hill. More details slowly emerged, having to do with Florence issuing a gruesome prophecy involving her boss's cat. Clemi deliberately did not ask any follow-up questions, figuring the less she knew, the better. She felt guilty recommending Florence for a job at the bookstore but thought perhaps the more relaxed environment would suit her. It did not. She spent a brief and rocky tenure behind the information desk before getting fired after three months.

Florence finally stands up and makes a production out of collecting the books around her—moving slowly, scowling, groaning intermittently, as if Clemi has just sent her to Siberia to collect firewood without any gloves. She then begins to reshelve them but is mixing up the graphic novels and the comic books, making little effort to alphabetize. This lack of concern about putting books back where they belong had been just one of many problems she'd caused as a bookstore employee, although it was not what got her fired in the end.

Clemi tries to speed things up. She picks up one of the piles from the floor and is staring at a comic with what appears to be a pregnant Spider-Woman on the cover when a ruckus erupts by the spinner rack of Shinola journals in the alcove near the Fiction room. She turns, books in hand, to see what's happening. There is a situation. Petunia the Shih Tzu. A crying child and an angry, profanity-spewing mother. Clemi sees Autumn T move toward them and attempt to smooth things out. Just another day at the bookstore. She should probably go over there to give Autumn some moral support, but she has her own situation to manage right here.

"Just leave it all be. I'll finish up," Clemi says.

"Okay, but do you want me to help you set up?"

The offer is tempting. Florence may have her problems, but she is very good at setting up for events: She knows the precise spot on the floor where the corner of display-table four lines up with the tape on the carpet that marks the spot where it is meant to return when it is time to push the fixtures back. She knows where the presold books are stored and where they are supposed to be shelved after they are signed. She knows where the inventory is kept for the next day's event and doesn't ever seem to mind retrieving the heavy boxes from downstairs. She knows the combination of numbers that unlocks the keypad entry to the door of the events closet where, at this moment, Clemi is pretty certain a small, smelly tortoise resides.

But right now, what Clemi needs more urgently is for Florence to vacate these premises and get out of the store.

"It's nice of you to offer," Clemi says, "but the event is probably going to be a bore. Just another Lincoln and the whatevers."

Lincoln and the Jews, Lincoln and the Power of the Press, Lincoln and Shakespeare, Lincoln and His Generals . . . These are all real books, many of which have been published in just the time that Clemi has worked at the store.

"*Lincoln and the Root Vegetables,*" Florence replies. "*Lincoln and the Wolf. Lincoln and the Purple Crayon. Lincoln and Cleopatra.*"

This is a little game of theirs, riffing on the absurd number of books that mash up Lincoln with random-seeming subjects.

"*Lincoln and Leopold. Lincoln and Loeb. Lincoln and a Horse That Sings. Lincoln, Paul, and Mary. Lincoln, Marx, Mao, and Marcuse.*"

Florence is on a roll. Clemi wonders if she will stop, ever. She is really not in the mood, but she does think of one and blurts it out:

"*Lincoln and the Doodles.*"

"Doodles?"

"Oh, never mind. It's just a running joke here lately. But no worries about tonight. I've got it under control."

Florence looks wounded. She picks up her backpack and stares at Clemi with disbelief before turning to leave. Clemi hopes she hasn't just had a spell cast on her or isn't about to be the victim of a pin through the spleen of a voodoo doll.

She watches until she sees Florence exit the store, then turns her attention to the next problem. Near the events closet, there is, undeniably, an awful smell. Maybe it has to do with the fact that the electricity was off until about an hour ago—it seems a fuse blew overnight, and it took much of the day to replace. Between the rain, the leaks, and the loss of AC for much of the day, one could suppose the smell might simply be the result of the humid conditions. But the smell is fishy. Perhaps someone left sushi, or a tuna fish sandwich, in the closet overnight. She can think of many possible reasons it might smell bad, and she hopes one of them is not because Kurt Vonnegut Jr., the tortoise, is inside.

Which, alas, he is. Because Noah is an irresponsible jerk.

She turns on the overhead light and walks toward Kurt. He's on the back shelf in his terrarium, surrounded on either side by stacks of *The Lincoln Cookbook*, which is not exactly a Lincoln and the whatevers, but it's close enough to qualify.

He sticks his head up from his perch atop the rock and stares at her. Or so it seems.

Hello!

"Hello?"

Good grief, is the tortoise speaking to her? Is this anxiety virus that's going around causing her to lose her mind?

Please consider me, the tortoise, hungry and thirsty and stuck in a closet!

"Are you talking to me?"

A real shame about the event last night. Sorry no one came, but really, who can blame them? I very much enjoyed hearing that author's lovely lilting voice . . . I mean, I love an Irish accent as much as the next person, but it was a bit too quiet and introspective for my taste. I'm no literary critic, but it seemed like nothing much happened in the book. No real plot. Also, since you asked for feedback . . .

"I'm not sure I asked for feedback."

The question-and-answer session went on a bit too long, and then there was that self-important woman at the end who kept droning on with her long-winded question—why was she asking about NAFTA? Had she stumbled into the wrong event?

"I tried to cut her off, but—"

Also, while I have your attention, are you going to tell Mrs. Bernstein about the people who are threatening to come out to protest the Kuddly Killers *event?*

"No, it will be fine. We have other things to worry about right now, and they're just making a lot of noise. It's really no big deal."

I hear there might be a protest. You might want to keep an eye on the situation.

"It's totally under control."

And are you prepared for tonight's event?

"Yes. I mean, I know enough to introduce the author: Our sixteenth president had a fondness for oysters, bacon, and cheese."

That's all you are going to say?

"No, of course not. I'll give background about the author and stuff. Also that our sixteenth president liked ginger-bread men."

And?

"And, um . . . apples?"

"Hey, Clemi, are you okay in there?"

"Oh yeah, hey, Yash!"

"Who are you talking to?"

"I'm not talking to anyone! Just practicing my intro for tonight."

"Oh, right. I'm just here to tell you that your twenty-four boxes of *Restoration of Sanity* have arrived, and they're blocking the door to the receiving room. Maybe you could move them."

"Sure. Unless . . . I need to set up for the event. Could you give me a hand?"

"With the event setup or with moving the boxes?"

"Either? Both?"

"I wish I could, but you know we're short-staffed and totally backed up downstairs, especially since Belinda hasn't shown up for two days, and the web orders are a mess."

"Okay, sure. Thanks anyway, Yash."

She tries to disguise her annoyance. Yash is a burly former football player, and it would be easy for him to lift the boxes and set them to the side, whereas it's going to take everything she's got to move them herself. Not to mention that it would take him all of ten minutes to help her set up the chairs.

What a jerk! the tortoise says.

"I know, right?"

Yash sticks his head back inside the closet and stares at Clemi for a moment. "You know, don't worry about it," he says. "I'll take care of the boxes. I can see you've got a lot on your hands."

END OF DAY REPORT: Tuesday, August 15
OPENING SHIFT: Carmen, Jamal, Noah
SWING SHIFT: Luke, Antonio, Vashti
CLOSING SHIFT: Summer, Yash, Sami
EVENT: Clemi
FLOOR MANAGER COMMENTS: Today's EOD Report is brought to you by another doodle joke:

> *Outside of a doodle, a book is a man's best friend.*
> *Inside of a doodle, it's too dark to read.*

On that note, it was just your Totally Typical Tuesday in which . . .

- Jamal arrived to find the store dark. He got the electricity back on by midmorning. A fuse in the Fiction room seems to have blown. Probably gremlins.
- It brings me no joy to bring you today's animal update: This afternoon, Petunia grabbed a bagel out of the hand of a kid in a stroller and the mom went nuts, demanded to see her rabies tag, and is now talking about pressing charges and suing everyone. She even called the police, who came around and asked questions.
- Terrifying news about Belinda—as at least a few of you have heard, it turns out she went down to Charlottesville on Friday and was injured when that car plowed into everyone. She is pretty banged up, needed a lot of stitches, and broke her leg, but she's been released from the hospital. I'll keep you updated, but in the meantime, if anyone wants to put in an extra shift or two or ten, we need help on web orders.

- We've had several calls asking whether we'll be scheduling an event for *The Gauzy Blue Whatever*, released today. The author was on *Fresh Air* yesterday and also got rave reviews in the *WP* and the *NYT*. The answer is "no." Direct all questions to Clemi (whose voice mail is still full).
- In case you haven't noticed, it's still raining out there. We have put a bucket between the Nature and Sports sections. Keep an eye on it and please take the bucket out back and do not dump it in the staff bathroom as the sink is clogged.
- Good news: *Antifa Now!* is back in print! Bad news: We sold all twenty-four of our copies. We have more on order. Also, friends, *nota bene*—Antifa is not the same as Antifada. I'm not going to call anyone out by name, but I did overhear someone on the phone yesterday mixing this up.
- Speaking of doodles, people are still looking for *The Doodles*. Antonio has contacted the author and he will be coming in to hand-deliver books this weekend.
- Overflow crowd for *The Lincoln Cookbook*. Too bad we ran out of books again. Also we had a couple of customer complaints about Chatty Cathy monopolizing the Q&A.
- We briefly lost internet, which seems to have been related to the morning power outage, but all is well again.

That's all, friends!

Autumn T

CHAPTER 7

Wednesday

QUERK III, CONT.

*I*t's feeling a little *Groundhog Day,* Sophie muses as she pulls her car perpendicular to the back door of the store and pops open the trunk. By *Groundhog Day,* Sophie is referring not to the February 2 rodent ritual but to the movie where Bill Murray wakes up and is forced to repeat the same day over and over and over until he gets it right.

On the one hand, this repetition is not the worst thing in the world. Sophie is a creature of habit, a woman who thrives best with a routine. For nearly twenty years she has stuck to more or less the same schedule: rising at 6:30 a.m., making coffee, reading the papers, turning on the morning news while showering and dressing, then heading into work about an hour before the store opens at ten. Sure, there have been day-to-day variations—she was usually the one who did the school drop-offs, for example, but not always. Every once in a while, Solomon volunteered. And there were a couple of different pet birds along the way who had unpredictable needs that sometimes threw off her rhythms with their squawking insistence to be let out of the cage. One once flew out the window and perched on the roof, requiring her to climb a ladder and carefully coax him down; although the mission was a success, it threw off her day. And, naturally, meetings and doctors' appointments and household repairs occasionally required changing up her routine. Even when her days were turned upside down, they still made sense because they revolved around the needs of the store.

She had even been hostile to vacations, resenting the idea of mandatory decompression. What an absurd word, *decompression*! She didn't really decompress. On the rare occasions that she indulged in a manicure, for instance, the technician would scold her to relax her hands; she never noticed until those moments that they were scrunched into tight balls. She's not sure she even properly relaxed on the vacations that Solomon insisted they take. He was the one who planned the itineraries, made the reservations, stopped the newspapers, pulled the suitcases out of the attic, and encouraged her to pack. She would protest—she had too much work to take a break! She couldn't possibly leave the store! But once en route, she invariably found herself appreciative of the concentrated family time, as well as the chance to better focus on her never-shrinking pile of to-be-read books.

She had always assumed it was the store that gave her life a daily rhythm, and that all of the little things—the grocery shopping and dinner preparation, the general management of her family and their always just-a-little-bit-too-messy house, the mandatory vacations and pet emergencies and occasional legal functions that Solomon asked her to attend as his spouse—got in the way of her routine. But without these distractions, the entire schema has unraveled. Even her sleep has been thrown off; without Solomon snoring in her ear, something she previously complained about but now realizes was a form of solace, she isn't sleeping well. She is up at strange hours, and even the concept of meals has devolved into eating whatever she can find in the refrigerator when her stomach grumbles, which might mean kung pao chicken out of the cardboard takeout box for breakfast. Also, because she now has all the time in the world to read, she is hardly reading at all.

So it isn't really the Groundhog Day ritual that's the problem but the embarrassing absurdity of her half-baked plan that both makes sense and does not. She tells herself over and over what she is doing; if she repeats it enough, perhaps it will better compute. She is not technically, right this very moment, moving into her nook, but should the time come, she will have a place to go. It's not as though the Frank family spontaneously picked up and moved into their annex. Doing so required months of preparation. Sophie doubts that anyone thought this was crazy behavior on their part; it was clear the darkness was descending, in the same way it is clear to Sophie now. Charlottesville was the warning sign. The possible Kristallnacht, an indication that things are about to get worse.

Besides, even if this move is over the top, she is keeping herself occupied. She could be doing worse things to tamp her anxiety, like gambling or shopping, instead of this constructive little project, this victimless building of a little nest!

So here she is, back at the store before dawn, hauling a few more belongings out of the rear compartment of the Subaru. It's not that big of a deal—she hasn't brought *that* much stuff this time; it's just that as long as she's making the journey, she figures it can't hurt to bring some energy bars and canned foods and eleven pairs of socks.

Also, right now, if she's honest with herself, she is looking to escape something other than her loneliness and fear. She is fleeing the mortifying incident of the dinner party she attended last night, where she met a charming man named Gil.

As soon as she'd arrived at what had been advertised as an impromptu, casual get-together at the house next door, Sophie realized she was being fixed up with her neighbor's uncle, an age-appropriate, white-bearded, soft-spoken man with piercing blue eyes who was visiting from Quebec. They were seated next to one another at dinner. She had been dazzled by his sexy French accent as they talked about opera and books and travel. He told her about his favorite parks in Montreal, and even though dating is not foremost in Sophie's mind, she found herself beginning to think there might be some whole other world out there, another way to live, and she was already skipping ahead to visiting him in Montreal, to walking hand in hand through museums, to meeting his children and grandchildren. Schwartz's smoked meat, Saint Urbain Street, handmade bagels, *The Apprenticeship of Duddy Kravitz*.

The conversation went on and on, quite enjoyably. They discovered a shared passion for Robertson Davies, the Deptford Trilogy in particular. She told him about the time she had been to Toronto, and that she had a couple of friends who had attended McGill. They had so much to talk about that she suggested he come over after dinner for a Cognac.

Live in the moment! she had told herself. *Just enjoy this carefree life while you can!*

But they didn't get very far. As soon as he had walked into the living room and sat on the couch, she began to cry.

What had she been thinking? She and Solomon had lived in this house for nearly twenty-five years. If she was going to date (which she had not been planning to do— this thing had just happened out of the blue!) she ought to at least refresh the house first: paint the walls, buy some new furniture, or perhaps just move some things around to create a new energy.

Also, and this is really stupid, she knows, but she ought to have put Roomba in a different room so she didn't have to see his winking light and wonder if she was being a little bit judged.

Here in the store, engaged in her project, she can push the memory of the evening to the back of her mind.

She returns to the closet in the staff break room, finds Querk III, glides him toward and then into the elevator, and says a little prayer that the lift will safely ascend, which it does, although not without introducing a moment of panic between floors when it stops briefly for no reason before hiccupping back to life, nearly causing Sophie to lose her balance.

She then locates the stepladder, which this time is leaning against the door of the events closet, which still smells oddly aquariumlike, or perhaps more like a fish market. Although she has nothing against sea life—and is intrigued by fish and octopi and even tolerated Michael's hermit crab phase reasonably well—she does not find this to be a pleasant odor.

She removes the Graham Greenes, presses the button, and is about to plug in the vacuum when she remembers the outlet doesn't work and that she needs the extension cord again. Back to the information desk she goes, and then answers the ringing telephone, half hoping it is another early morning call from Charlie Major. She could do with hearing his friendly voice. Alas, it is not.

"Kaboom!" the caller shouts. The voice is so loud that it feels like an aural assault.

She freezes, the receiver still pressed to her ear. "Who is this?" she asks, but the voice is gone, replaced by a dial tone. She imagines a woman unhinged, like Bette Davis in *What Ever Happened to Baby Jane?* Someone in hair curlers and a housecoat, a cigarette dangling from her lips. "We are going to cancel this event, so keep your kabooms to yourself," she would tell this person on the other end of the line, given the chance. Is there a way to capture the number without caller ID? Is *69 still a thing that works? She would like to return this call, but she doesn't know how; she is being done in by technology.

This sort of harassing call is nothing new—there have been lunatics as long as there have been people on this earth—and yet this one unsettles her more than she'd like to admit. It's one thing to hear about these calls, another entirely to have the craziness delivered directly to your ear. She has a meeting scheduled with Clemi to discuss all of this at 9:00 a.m. and now is especially eager to have it resolved. By which she means canceled. Gone. Kaput. *Kaboomed.*

Yes, she feels a little bad about this. As recently as a year ago, she wouldn't have dreamed of canceling an event. Especially when the only issue, as far as she knows, is a private matter. Sure, the poet is known to be a philandering creep, but is that a valid reason to cancel an event? And yes, the suicide of his wife is tragic. Unspeakably so. But again, isn't that, too, a private matter? Not to mention that the world only knows what it knows; extenuating factors might have caused her to wish not to live, factors the public couldn't possibly know.

But now, the world being what it is, who needs to invite more trouble?

If she were more of a diviner, a reader of tea leaves like that troubling young woman she had to fire, she would say this phone call was a sign, or perhaps another sign. On the other hand, maybe she is just looking for signs to justify what she is doing to the nook.

She retrieves the extension cord and plugs it into an outlet in the Fiction room and then connects it to the vacuum cleaner cord and—success! It turns on! The fuse does not blow! Querk III begins to quietly purr.

Maybe this Querk III is not so bad after all. But then, wait: he's running all right, but she can't seem to get him to *move*. She needs the handle to release so she can recline Querk's torso and push him back and forth as one generally does when vacuuming. But how? He stands firm and won't budge. She presses every button she sees, one of which unfortunately ejects the plastic canister that substitutes for the bag. Now the contraption stops working, and a mound of dirt emerges from beneath, swirling in the air before settling into a large heap on the floor.

Oh boy. What has she done? Now the room is even dustier. This entire endeavor is beginning to feel cursed. She unplugs the thing, reattaches the canister, and switches it on again, but still it won't move. She can't believe how much of her time and energy this stupid vacuum cleaner is sucking up, so to speak, yet it won't even pick up dirt! Perhaps she ought to go home and get Roomba, who is blissfully uncomplicated. She just lets him out of the dock and he goes about his business without all of this cajoling.

But she's already here and decides to google her way out of this situation. She goes back out to the information desk and turns on one of the computers, waits five minutes for it to fire up, and then drops into the search engine the words *Querk III Performance*. The first thing to pop up is the Querk.com website, which allows her to peruse new Querk products, or email them with complaints, but if she would like some live customer support, she needs to fill out their form and provide her name and address, the model and serial number of the machine, and the number associated with her warranty—the one she does not have.

She goes back to the search results and is relieved to see a handful of instructional videos on making the Querk III perform.

The first video that pops up appears to be a feature film of sorts. A young woman is pushing the contraption around her living room—it looks like the exact same model as Sophie's obstinate machine!—and it suddenly stops working. The young vacuumist fools with a few buttons, gives the thing a little kick, then pulls her phone out of the pocket of her extremely tight cutoff shorts and makes a call.

Within seconds there is a knock at the door. She opens it, and standing there is a pudgy older gentleman who says, "Did you call for a vacuum cleaner repairman?"

Sophie wishes it were truly that simple.

The would-be vacuumist then replies, "Yes, it is not working!" And the repairman says, "What is the nature of the problem?" And the vacuumist says, "It is not performing!" And he says, "May I show you how to make it properly perform?" And she says, "Yes, please!" And he says, "Before we begin, do you mind if I test the suction power?" And she says, "That sounds a little dirty!" And he says, "That's why we need to fix the vacuum!" And without waiting for her reply, he moves toward her and unbuttons her shirt and Sophie cannot believe she is standing here watching this video, although it is possible that somewhere along the way the answer to her question about how to release and tilt the torso of the vacuum might appear.

She watches for another moment. Things progress, some of it mildly instructive, albeit unfortunately not in a vacuum cleaner–related way. Titillating as this is, she ought not be standing at the information desk at the bookstore watching internet porn.

She forwards to the next video, which is for better or worse a less spicy instructional on how to operate a new Querk III, starring people who remain fully clad. From this she learns about a small indentation in the front of the machine that she is supposed to press with her foot, which releases a mechanism that allows the upper body of the vacuum to recline. She returns to the nook and finds the same indentation on her machine. It is nearly invisible, but it is there. She pushes it with her foot, and the thing begins to move. *Eureka!*

Now that it's fully functioning, Querk III is doing a pretty good job; she can see it effortlessly and quietly devouring the dust. It's like watching a piece of performance art, the way the molecules visibly dance through the transparent outer case. It even manages to gobble up an object with a loud clanking, jangling sound, like a set of keys. She looks more closely; it even looks like a set of keys. Actually, it *is* a set of keys. *Her* keys, now inside the canister and covered in dust—and then the magnificent vacuuming machine sputters and chokes and emits a high-pitched wail. Then Querk III simply dies.

Okay, so this is another setback. It's not the end of the world; she will not let this defeat her. She tries to open the plastic canister again—the very same piece of cheap plastic crap that moments ago fell off—to no avail. She goes back out to the information desk and finds a screwdriver, then uses it to try to pry open the front panel. Still, it will not budge. She kicks it a couple of times in frustration, which unsurprisingly does nothing to help the situation, especially given that she is again wearing a pair of flimsy shoes made, this time, from recycled plastic bottles, as opposed to the other pair made from trees. A wave of pain radiates through her foot. She then goes over to the bank of cash registers, behind which has sat for years, inexplicably—or maybe entirely explicably—a baseball bat, which she uses to take a few swings at Querk III. He stands inert, maintaining a stoic façade as she rages.

Maybe this is a stupid plan on about a dozen different levels, and maybe she deserves this tsoris, but why must every little thing be so difficult? Sophie looks at her watch. It's now after 8:00 a.m.; the opening crew will be here soon, and she needs to piece the store back together before they arrive. Defeated, she closes the nook, puts the stepladder away, drags the stupid idiot vacuum cleaner back to the elevator and down to the ground floor and into the closet in the break room. After her meeting with Clemi, she will retrieve him and take him home and work him over in private until he relinquishes her keys.

She completes all of this just in time. Jamal is arriving, inserting his key in the front door. She watches him from the back of the store, where she tries to make herself look busy, squatting in front of the Sports section and pretending she is rearranging things. He has just a few days left here, and already he is scaling back, letting Autumn T take over most of his managerial responsibilities. She observes how much older he looks these days, which is not hugely surprising since she has known him for over a decade. But when did his hair become tinged with gray? And when did he begin to look so tired? Has this job ground him down? She's feeling sentimental, tearing up thinking about how much she'll miss him.

This is a ridiculous position for her to be in, this crouch. She really ought to get herself into better shape, maybe do some of Michael's yoga. She eases herself upright, accidentally banging her bad shoulder on one of the endcaps and knocking over a stack of Bruce Springsteen's fat memoir, *Born to Run*, which lands with a series of thuds. Jamal looks over in her direction, then comes rushing toward the back of the store.

"You okay, Mrs. Bernstein?"

"I'm great! Totally fine! It's such a beautiful day that I couldn't wait to get up and get to work!"

Jamal seems to be staring at her, thinking. She realizes her response was perhaps overly enthusiastic and that it is not, in fact, a beautiful day; it is cloudy and gray and steaming hot, and it has just begun to rain again.

"I just came in a little early to clear my inbox. I'm crazy behind on everything. But instead, here I am wreaking havoc."

"No problem, let me pick those up for you."

"No, no, my mess! I'm so clumsy. I'll get it, no problem."

They both kneel and begin to pick up the books and place them back in the small plastic bin affixed to the side of the shelf.

The moment feels both awkward and poignant as they stand, books in hand, face-to-face.

"I'm going to miss you so much. I don't know how I will cope without you!"

"You'll be fine, Mrs. Bernstein. Autumn T is great, and you have a terrific staff right now. Things are practically running themselves. Not really, but you know what I mean."

"We do have a great staff right now. I hear Belinda is back in town. Geez. I hope she's doing okay. What a disaster this all is. I'll give her a call later and tell her to take all the time she needs. I hope she has a good lawyer!"

"She does. I put her in touch with a former colleague of my mother's. And yeah, she's doing okay. The whole thing was . . . is . . . pretty scary though. I'm going to drop in on her after work today."

"Thank you, Jamal. Let me know how I can help her. Also, I've been meaning to ask if I could take you and Lewis out to dinner before you leave, or have you over to the house?"

"We'd both love that, Mrs. Bernstein, but honestly we have so much packing to do, and we leave in less than a week. I'll be back soon though. My family is all here, and we'll be in for the holidays. Can I take a rain check for some time around Thanksgiving?"

"Sure. I'm not going anywhere," she says. *Except possibly into hiding about five feet away.* "Also, as I've been telling you for twelve years, you really ought to call me Sophie!"

"Sophie!" he says, laughing. "Sophie!" he tries again, more serious this time. "I'm sorry, Mrs. Bernstein, I don't mean to offend, but you are just always going to be Mrs. Bernstein to me."

"My fault for not scheduling a proper goodbye. I'm sorry. I've just been kind of preoccupied."

"It's been a difficult week. No need to explain. But

listen, thanks for coming to my party. And I'm planning to make it to Autumn T's solar eclipse thing on Monday—if you'll be there, we can raise a glass and say goodbye for real."

"That sounds great," she says. "I'd say until then, but I'll see you here all day."

"And every day until then!"

"I've got to run," she says, looking at her watch. "I've got a meeting in a few minutes."

"Sure thing."

Sophie is not really in any rush, but she is starting to feel emotional again. She's not generally much of a crier, not the sort of person who tears up reading sentimental books or watching couples walk down the aisle. She didn't even cry that much when Solomon died—she grieved terribly, and still does, but tears have never really been her thing. But she unexpectedly opened the floodgate last night with Gil and hasn't managed to plug it back up. And this, too, feels overwhelmingly sad. It's not just that Jamal is leaving but that even after all these years, they haven't quite crossed the barrier to the friendship she wishes they had. At the end of the day he is an employee, and she is his boss, and evidently she will always be Mrs. Bernstein to him too.

She glances over her shoulder as she walks toward her office, and she can see Jamal studying her again, giving her a once-over as if he's performing a quick mental health evaluation. Why everyone is so worried about her lately, she's not sure she understands.

It is only after the store has hummed to life—the registers manned, the phones ringing, the customers streaming through the door, a doodle peeing on the rug—that Sophie remembers her car. Oh boy! She needs to move it! Not only will it be blocking delivery trucks in that tight space, but the new owner of the lot, the guy whose calls she continues to dodge, runs the place like a feudal lord with thirty-two paved spots to his fiefdom—which is to say he's quick to call the tow truck. He is a developer from Pennsylvania who recently purchased the asphalt lot that services the bookstore, as well as Verb and the orthodontist's office on the far end of the block. This man, whoever he is, has for unclear reasons become so obsessed with enforcing his two-hour time limit that he has installed a video camera with which to monitor the goings-on from Pittsburgh. Or so she's heard. She's had many a complaint from customers who have been towed after exceeding the limit by only a few minutes, or who have left the premises to run an errand nearby, but in a store that is not technically serviced by the lot. Sophie pictures him perched in front of a bank of computer screens, passing his days watching cars pull in and out of spaces, his pulse rising each time he catches a scofflaw.

She is definitely not going to give him the satisfaction of having her Subaru hauled away!

She goes to her office, gets her purse, and fishes around for her keys to no avail. She picks up the bag and shakes it, hoping to hear the jangling sound of metal keys but hearing only her tin of breath mints rattling around. The keys do not appear to be anywhere in the office, or in her pockets. Did she leave them at the information desk, or in the nook? Or . . . maybe she left them in her car? She begins retracing her steps and then remembers: They are inside the miserable, stupid, useless, overpriced, underperforming vacuuming appliance. The one that is secured more tightly than Fort Knox.

It's only 9:00 a.m., and already, what a day! Maybe she should postpone the meeting with Clemi and walk home to get her spare keys, then walk back and move the car because, truly, the last thing she needs is to have her car towed. She looks out the window and discovers that it's too late. The rain has turned into a downpour, and the Subaru is gone.

There is a knock at the door, then a voice. "Mrs. Bernstein, is this an okay time?"

"It's not," she says reflexively. "I'm in the middle of a situation."

Sophie turns around to see Clemi standing at the door to her office and remembers their meeting. Her hair is loose and wild, and she is wearing a billowing white top with red embroidery and a short denim skirt and is carrying a huge stack of books. Sophie wishes she could still wear an outfit like that. Not that in reality she ever really could, but it's not a crime to revise these kinds of details about her lost youth, to allow herself to imagine she'd once had the sort of physique that would have made her feel comfortable with a hemline that hit above the knee.

"Um . . . okay?" Clemi says. "I'm around all day if you want to reschedule. No problem."

"No, no, come in," she says, motioning to a chair. "I was

just . . . Something's come up, yes, but it can wait. I'll figure it out. What are these books?"

"They are presold books for the Chaucer event."

"Wow. Since we're canceling, I suppose we can just send them to the customers. Or, for the locals, just tell them they can come in and pick them up."

"I was hoping we could talk about that. I haven't canceled yet. And I have some news from his publicist."

"I don't care what the news is. Just cancel. The sooner the better."

"The *Washington Post* is doing a profile and—"

"Oh great, that's all we need, more bad publicity. People will be out here trying to take off our heads for hosting him."

"It's possible the new profile will cast him in a different light. He is claiming that none of what was reported in the *Guardian* is true. Not none of it, just not all of it. Also, he's going to be on the *Boris Lewinsky Show*. That's a very well-respected show, as you know. I mean, obviously it's up to you—it's your store!—but if you want my opinion, I think we ought to stay the course. He's a prizewinning poet. Plus, it's already on our calendar, it's all over social media, it got picked up by some local press—it's in *Washingtonian*'s 'What to Do in August' listings, plus we've already sold a ton of books! There's even more behind the register that I was hoping I could bring in here.

"I mean, at the very least, we should have him come in and sign if he's going to be in town already for the *Post* and NPR. There's the assumption on the part of the people who bought these that they would be signed."

"Why are they buying them if they hate him?"

"I don't know . . . good question. I guess if they are thinking Ted Hughes, maybe that celebrity trumps notoriety? Maybe they think a signed book will be valuable? I've been doing this job for nearly eight months and I still haven't figured these things out."

"I suppose we could think about it. On the other hand, we could ask the publisher if he can sign nameplates for us to paste in."

"Mrs. Bernstein, I mean, I know it's your call, but is it possible that everyone is overreacting? Isn't what happened a personal matter? Also, he's saying that everyone got it wrong, that his wife's death was an accident. I mean . . . I know he doesn't sound like a very attractive person, but since when are we booking events based on the author's likability?"

This gets Sophie's attention. It's not like Clemi to be particularly assertive, especially not with her. As with Jamal, she realizes that as hard as she tries, she is their boss, *Mrs. Bernstein*, and everyone is a little bit afraid of her. She doesn't know how or why she frightens them and wishes she could soften somehow. She is at least somewhat self-aware, though, and gets that she has never been the most warm and fuzzy person, which is part of the reason she used to have her staff over for dinner on a regular basis, and would also find time to take them, individually, out to lunch. She wanted to demonstrate that even if she is not a hugger and not a big user of emojis, she genuinely cares about, and even loves, each one of them. But maybe those dinners and lunches were dreaded or frightening events.

So while she is glad Clemi feels she has the agency to stand up to her, this seems an odd cause.

Sophie wonders if there is some ulterior motive here but has no idea what it might possibly be. Perhaps it's simply a logistical matter. If the poet doesn't come into the store, Clemi will have to figure out how to distribute all of these books, a pile of which she is still holding.

"Set those books down, for goodness' sake!"

"Yes, sure, thank you. How about . . . right over in the corner? They will be out of the way against the wall over there," she says, pointing to a spot behind Sophie's desk.

"Anywhere!"

"Great. This way, when he's here . . . *if* he's here, I mean . . . they will be ready for him to sign. The closet is overcapacity right now, what with all of the *Kuddly Killers* books. That event is surprisingly generating a lot of buzz. It's a crazy week!"

"It definitely is. Not the best one either."

"Totally, no. I heard that Belinda is doing much better though. She's home now, so that's good." Clemi sets the books down in her designated spot.

"Yes, Jamal told me. Thank goodness. Why don't you sit down for a minute while we talk, Clemi?"

"Sure, thanks," Clemi says. She stops and stares at the wall for a moment. "What's all . . . that?" she asks, pointing to a spot behind Sophie's chair. "And up there, on the ceiling."

Sophie looks up. She hasn't noticed before, but there is more brown splatter—coffee stains from the Zhang Skim Cap debacle that she must have missed when she cleaned up.

"It's just . . . I don't know, it's maybe . . . mold?"

"Mold? We should deal with it if it's mold, you know. It could be toxic."

"No, it's not mold! It's just . . . the rain. I mean, there's a leak in the ceiling. I keep meaning to get it patched," she says. "I'll get someone to take a look . . . So listen, the thing is, I had a call from a friend who owns a bookstore in London, and he said all the stores in the UK have canceled, and he seems to think we are pretty much the only store in the country that's hosting him."

Clemi looks at Sophie hesitantly, glances down at a notebook that rests in her lap, and begins to speak.

"I know this is . . . I thought, based on our previous conversations . . . especially when I first took this job, and you were giving me some pointers . . . that we basically are here to promote freedom of expression, and that . . ."

Sophie realizes that Clemi is not going to give up. She has even prepared talking points. Clemi is, indeed, prepared to do battle over this event. It would seem to Sophie that most young women—most women of any age—would agree that this poet is a narcissistic, misogynist jerk.

"What exactly are you trying to say? I'm all for freedom of speech, but what if it crosses the line to hate speech?"

Sophie realizes that she is derailing the conversation. They are not talking about hate speech. Plus this probably sounds harsher than intended. But she is overwhelmed with this car situation and needs to get out of here to figure out next steps. She agrees with Clemi but is also gripped by fear. She just wants this conversation to end and for the poet to not appear.

"Yes, I agree. I'm just trying to say that . . . as I just

said, maybe we shouldn't be so quick to cave in to popular opinion when we don't even know all of the circumstances. On top of which . . . I don't know what I'm trying to say exactly except that I don't think we should be so quick to cancel."

"Sure. I hear you. But this poet, he . . ." Now Sophie is the one who can't finish her sentence because she is aware that what she is going to say does not fully compute, and that she is trying to talk herself into a position she cannot defend. This poet hasn't committed any crimes, at least not insofar as she knows. So maybe he's a creep. Maybe his behavior led to his wife's suicide. Maybe it did not. Maybe she suffered from depression. Maybe she had other things going on in her life. Sophie has read enough novels, watched enough films, to know there might be a twist. Maybe she, personally, wouldn't have invited him to speak at the store, but Clemi has booked this event, and Sophie understands that she ought to get out of the way and let Clemi do her job. Just because everyone else has canceled doesn't mean that she has to. Again, she reminds herself, she has never been a sheep!

Then again, she thinks of Charlottesville. Of Belinda. Of all the ugliness that has been unleashed, just a little over a hundred miles down the road. If a person were ever to go ovine, this might be the logical time.

"Mrs. Bernstein, are you okay?"

"No. Yes. I'm totally fine. I was just going to say, why don't we—"

They are interrupted by Noah, who is standing at the open door, his hand resting on the handle of Querk III.

"Hey, you guys," Noah says. "Sorry to interrupt, but this seems like a possible emergency. I don't really know what's going on here, but I just opened the storage closet to get more paper towels and noticed the vacuum cleaner is . . . I don't know how to put this, but it looks like it's been attacked. The plastic in front is all bashed in. It's suffered multiple blows. I've never seen anything like it."

"Holy cow. Who would do that? Should we call the police?" Clemi asks.

"Does DC's finest have a cleaning-devices protection unit?" Noah asks. "You know, they probably do," he says. "Probably also a shelter for abused appliances, like a place they offer support to battered printers, or old desktops people throw out the window when they won't reboot."

Sophie is not finding this amusing. Is it her imagination, or does Clemi seem to brighten whenever Noah enters the room? She even appears to be laughing at Noah's stupid joke. She sees Clemi brush her hair over her shoulder and sit up straight. Sophie doesn't like this one bit. Although the employee handbook, such as it is—a stapled-together and relatively fluid set of rules—does not prohibit colleagues from dating one another, she sometimes wonders whether it should. Her employees frequently couple up, and it tends to spill over to disruptive workplace drama. She had one former couple who refused to work the same shift, and another love triangle turned into a similarly disruptive scheduling problem. Plus, the mother in her doesn't see this as a good fit.

"Poor thing! Does it still work?" Clemi asks.

"Good question. Let's plug it in."

"No, let's not," Sophie shrieks, jumping out of her chair.

She rushes over and grabs the neck of the vacuum from Noah and drags it to the corner. "Just leave it here," she says. "I'll take care of it."

"Are you sure, Mrs. Bernstein? I'm happy to deal with it. I've become the unofficial vacuum cleaner repairman."

"I've got it. It's completely under control. You can go now." She suspects she did not succeed in striking the intended carefree tone here, the one meant to convey that this is no big deal, that she is not at all obsessed with the vacuum cleaner, not at all determined to keep this greedy, key-snorting vacuum cleaner close by. Never mind trying to convey that she is a loving, soft-spoken boss.

"I have a vacuum at home I can bring in later. It's one of those small robot things, a Roomba. Not really heavy-duty enough for the store, but it will do until I get this one sorted out."

"Cool," he says, saluting theatrically before leaving the room. But just as quickly, he is back.

"Oh, I forgot, one more thing: Clemi, your mother called. She said to call her back. She said it's urgent."

"My mother called *you*?"

"Of course not. She called the store. Autumn T took the message. She told me to tell you."

"Got it," says Clemi.

Sophie stares at Noah until he backs out of the room.

"Do you want to go call her?" Sophie asks.

"Call who?"

"Your mother. He said it was urgent."

"No, it's fine. It can wait. So where are we on the event situation?"

"We are canceling." Sophie decides this on the spot, even though a moment earlier she had been about to take a bold stance. "Just tell people we are . . . sick. Tell them we are sick and our vacuum cleaner is broken and also we are closing for repairs."

Clemi looks at her like she's gone mad. Now someone else is tapping at the door. It's that new employee, Summer. She is so blond, her teeth so white, her skin so tanned, that she looks like she should wear a sash that reads "Miss June 22."

"Mrs., B, there's a call for you on line three, plus some guy at the information desk looking for you."

"And?"

"He says it's important."

"Which one is important?"

"What do you mean?"

"Is the call on line three important or the guy at the information desk?"

"Honestly, I don't know."

"Perhaps you can get more information?"

"Um, sure. I'll try."

Summer turns to leave.

This pileup of problems today, this week, this year—her life is beginning to feel like an overstuffed screwball comedy, apart from the several pieces that are not in the least bit funny.

"So, wait, you want me to tell people that we are going to shut down the entire store?" Clemi asks. She looks completely addled, puzzled, farklempt.

"No, that's not what I meant. Tell them . . . the poet is sick."

"What do we tell the poet?"

"You're smart, you'll think of something."

"But, Mrs. Bernstein . . ."

Now Summer is back. "The man on the phone says his name is Ed. He is coming to town on Friday. He would like to schedule a time to meet with you to discuss something to do with the store, or the parking lot, or maybe both. Also, I have something for you from Zhang," she says, handing her an envelope.

"For goodness' sake, I'm in a meeting," Sophie barks. "Tell the guy on the phone that I'm busy!" She looks at Summer, at Clemi, at the vacuum cleaner, out the window at the parking lot from which her car has disappeared, then puts her head in her hands on the desk.

Now yet another person is at the door, and he is calling her *Mom*.

"Oh, hey, sorry, I didn't realize you were busy," he says. "Hi, Clemi . . . and . . . ," he says, turning to Summer. "I'm not sure we've met. I'm Michael, Sophie's son."

"Hi, Michael, I'm Summer. Like the season," Summer says, leaning in to shake his hand.

He is wearing yoga shorts and a T-shirt that has a drawing of an animal sporting sunglasses, and it is emblazoned with the words "No Drama Llama." His hair is shaggy and he has the beginnings of a beard. Sophie thinks he could do with a shave and a cut, but she will keep this thought to herself.

"Haven't seen you around much," Clemi says.

"Yeah, I've been super busy. Yoga teacher training and looking for a new apartment and just general stuff." He hesitates for a minute, like he's thinking. "Also catching up on my reading."

"What are you reading?" Clemi asks.

"Um . . . I've got a big fat pile, but it's been hard to find the time."

"Yeah, I get it."

"What *should* I read?" he asks.

Sophie is somewhat astonished. She gives Michael about five book recommendations per week, and he just tunes her out as if she's telling him to eat his vegetables. He does eat vegetables now, religiously and even somewhat pompously, touting his healthy eating habits whenever Sophie suggests they go out for burgers or a pizza. When he was a kid she struggled to get him to eat so much as a pea.

"Oh my gosh, there is so much good fiction coming out this fall, it's hard to know where to begin, but you might like the debut novel by this guy who lives in the Hudson Valley and is a yoga instructor. It has to do with raising organic chickens, but also there is a lot of yoga in the mix. Plus there's a backstory to do with his parents coming over from Ireland, and his sister has this horrible disease, and even though it doesn't sound like it, there's a thriller element. But I'll stop talking—don't want to ruin it for you. Would you like a galley?"

"Sure! That sounds amazing!"

Sophie clears her throat to get his attention. She is very happy to hear Michael talking to Clemi about books but is also pretty sure he is just bluffing, feigning interest in this poultry yoga novel, and she would really like to end this meeting and clear everyone out.

"Oh, sorry, Mom," he says. "I didn't mean to interrupt, but I left some stuff in the back of your car. And as long as I'm here I was also wondering if I could . . . maybe . . . well, I walked over here and it's kind of a lot to walk back in the rain, plus I have a few things I need to do later today, so maybe . . . could I borrow the car?"

"Oh, sure," she says, relieved to have a reason to definitively end these various unsettling conversational threads. "I just need you to give me a ride so we can pick it up."

"Um, that's confusing, but sure. Whatever. Can I get the galley from Clemi first?"

"Hang on, I'll just run upstairs and grab it. I'll be right back down."

"Seriously, Mom? You've lost your car *and* your keys?"

Perhaps there is some positive way to spin the fact that Michael feels free to talk to her in this sarcastic tone? Maybe it's just a sign that they are close, that they can dispose of the niceties? She thinks not though. It's more likely indicative of the opposite. If anything, since Solomon died, they have drifted apart. He returned from college and they got through the funeral and the mourning period, and then he went back to school, and then it was winter break and he decided that, instead of going home, he would go to Bali with some friends, and that's where he started doing yoga. Sophie can see the myriad ways that this has been a good thing for him, a way to channel grief and take some time to figure out next steps. She does not want to be one of those mothers who measures success with a paycheck or a diploma or a fancy title, and really, she's not. Or maybe she is, but she'd like to think she's not. What troubles her is that Michael is, or at least seems to be, adrift, bouncing from idea to idea. He was planning on graduate school in international relations, and then he was going to go to law school, and then he was talking about getting his MFA in studio arts, even though he has no artistic bent, at least none that Sophie has ever been aware of. He has talked about going to teach in South Korea, joining the Peace Corps, applying to Teach for America, and moving to Los Angeles to write screenplays. He has said all of these things in the span of four months and not followed up on a single one. Working at the store, even just as a temporary measure, is not among the things he contemplates, even in passing, although he has talked about possibly applying for a job as a barista at Verb next door.

The traffic isn't helping. They have been idling for thirty minutes now, en route to the impoundment lot in Germantown. According to the GPS on Michael's phone, they are only fifteen miles from their destination, but in current traffic conditions, that's still a good forty minutes away. Whatever accident or incident has them stopped must be epic. It's a well-known fact that Washington-area drivers are completely inept in the rain.

"I haven't *lost* anything! I haven't *lost* my car. It's just been towed!" Sophie protests. "And I know exactly where my keys are. I just can't access them right now, and if it's okay with you, I'd rather not get into it. Anyway, it's serendipitous that you showed up when you did because I was going to have to call you to get a key to the house. Plus I needed this ride."

"Yeah, but you didn't tell me it was going to take so long. I thought I was just dropping you off at, like, the car dealer or something. I mean, why would anyone tow a car from DC all the way out here? I have a meeting at eleven thirty."

"I have no idea. He must have an arrangement with the tow company to bring it to this lot. Probably it's owned by the same person, and he got a good deal? Don't ask me. It's clearly not my area of expertise!"

Sophie wonders what kind of meeting Michael has at eleven thirty, but she doesn't want to pry. He takes his eyes off the road to look at his phone, swerving slightly and causing Sophie to grip the armrest of the store van, which they have borrowed for this trip. "It's already ten thirty. Will you at least let me have a smoke? I'll open the window."

"No!" she shrieks. "Not in the store van! When did you start smoking? I don't understand."

"I don't need a lecture, okay? I'm doing you a favor as it is!"

"Okay. Fine. Don't do me any favors. Why don't you drop me off right here," she says, waving toward the shoulder of the interstate. "I'll just take an Uber."

Michael looks toward the shoulder like he's seriously considering this option.

"I don't know . . . I wouldn't feel right leaving you there. It might be tricky to get an Uber on the highway. I don't know if they are legally allowed to stop on the shoulder, plus it's probably not safe for you. I don't think we even have an umbrella. Unless maybe there's one in the back somewhere?"

She's glad he can at least muster this level of concern, especially since she doesn't have the Uber app.

She looks out at the five lanes of traffic crawling north and sees a UPS truck, four nearly identical silver Toyota Corollas, a Subaru not unlike her own, a blue Acura MDX, a motorcycle, a school bus, a couple of trucks, a black Mercedes sporting dealer plates, and a flatbed hauling chickens in wire cages. Poor dumb happy nattering things, likely on their way to slaughter, and then to someplace like Popeyes where they will be coated in batter and plunged into a vat of boiling oil.

"Just enjoy your carefree life while you can!"

"What?"

"*What*, what?"

"What did you just say, about your carefree life?"

"I was talking to the chickens."

"Great sign, Mom, talking to the chickens."

"Sorry, I'm just thinking out loud. It's just something from a book I'm reading."

"Oh, the same one Clemi was talking about, about the organic chicken farmer–yoga instructor?"

"No, a different book." Sophie hesitates before continuing. She doesn't especially want to hear what Michael will have to say about her current preoccupation. And yet he's opening the door to the rare opportunity for an almost intimate mother-son conversation, so why not? Who knows what wisdom he might have locked inside that expensively educated brain?

"I'm reading . . . rereading, really, *The Diary of Anne Frank*."

"Seriously? With that store full of amazing books, *that's* what you're reading? Why?"

"I don't know, Michael. Maybe *Charlottesville*?" This is not a truthful answer. She had been dipping in and out of this book since Solomon died while quoting Otto Frank. But events in Charlottesville certainly lend it more urgency.

"Instead of reading about a family that went into hiding, Mom, you should read a book about picking up a baseball bat and crushing these racist, ignorant a-holes."

Sophie has never heard him speak like this. She didn't know he had an activist bone in his body, never mind a violent streak.

"That's not a very yogic thing to say."

"I'm bifurcating. My practice and my politics are two separate things."

Sophie thinks about this. She doesn't entirely disagree. A part of her would like to show up at the next Charlottesville—whatever that event may be—with a baseball bat. Alas, she won't. That's not who she is. Her choice of weapon is words. As if, maybe, she could hand them all a copy of Martin Luther King Jr.'s "I Have a Dream" speech and they would drop their weapons and give each other hugs.

The word *bifurcating* makes her think, weirdly, of the superhero party she's been invited to.

"Is that your special power? Bifurcating?" she asks. "Staring into the chasm between your cognitive dissonance and your spiritual wholeness?"

"What do you mean?"

"Your bifurcation. Your violence and nonviolence co-existing. That sounds like a superpower."

"If I had a superpower, I would fly around the world making sure people practicing yoga don't hyperextend."

"Ha! Believe it or not, I might borrow that somehow. Your old mom is invited to a superhero party next week. Two parties! Monday there's a solar eclipse party. Tuesday is the superhero thing. Don't ask. I need to come in costume. Maybe I'll go as a yoga instructor and help people hyperextend."

"No, you want them to *not* hyperextend."

"Oh. Got it. *Not* hyperextend. You can come to the party if you want. It will be fun!"

Michael laughs. At first just politely, but then, as the thought settles in, he seems to find it hilarious. He is laughing so hard she worries he might veer out of his lane. She's not sure which part is funny.

"You've got quite the social life, Mom."

"Maybe I do," she says, insulted. "I went to a dinner party last night. I met a nice man!"

"You did? Wow! Tell me more!"

"That's all I've got. His name was Gil. From Montreal."

"That's great. Will you see him again?"

"Probably not. I invited him over for a drink, but the minute he walked in the door I started to cry."

"Oh, Mom. That's awful. You really ought to talk to someone. I know it's been tough."

"I don't want to talk about it."

They drive in silence for a while. She considers taking

this opportunity, where the door has cracked open ever so slightly, to talk more intimately. Maybe she *does* want to talk about it. Maybe they should. She ought to ask him how *he's* doing, really. To share her own struggles since Solomon passed, to urge Michael to share his.

Perhaps she would even tell Michael about her nook, about her creeping terror and inability to cope. She knows she ought to tell him that she has been dodging the calls of the Pittsburgh-based parking and towing cretin who is possibly angling to purchase her store, and that the thought is not entirely unappealing.

Perhaps Michael might have some advice, if not practical, then at least theoretical. He was a philosophy major, after all, with a minor in political theory, so maybe he could share some wisdom about this particular awful moment in time, about the cyclical nature of history, about how these bad loops are not always definitive. Maybe he'd say something encouraging and even transformative about the resilience of people—how they just need to keep up the good fight. How the last thing they should do is cancel a controversial event or go into hiding in bookstore nooks. How the events in Charlottesville were anomalous and not necessarily pre-dictors of dark times to come.

But she doesn't say a word.

At long last, they exit the highway. The voice on the navigation system guides them through some narrow, windy streets to a dead-end row of warehouses in a neighborhood in Germantown that is beginning to feel like both the end of suburbia and the end of the world. It is not quite the end, however. There is still cell service, and Michael's phone rings.

"Yeah, sorry, man. I'm not gonna make it. My mom's having some issues."

Sophie can hear a voice coming from the phone but can't make out what it says, just a series of blurts that sound like Charlie Brown's incomprehensible cartoon teacher.

Having some issues. This is insulting, but not untrue.

They arrive at last, passing through a chain-link fence, beyond which stands a small ramshackle structure that looks like a roadside soft-serve ice cream and burger shack.

She approaches the attendant, a skinny kid with a bad case of weeping acne, and introduces herself, describing her impounded vehicle. Paperwork is produced, a credit card is extracted from her wallet, and the fee is paid. The boy tells her to have a nice day, pointing toward her car, which sits forlornly between a neon yellow Kia SUV and a silver Mercedes sedan. The impoundment lot, a great equalizer of sorts.

Michael remains behind the wheel in the van, where he continues to work his phone. Sophie is about to tell him to leave, but mercifully does not, because when she approaches the Subaru and tries to open it, she realizes that she doesn't have the key.

She has the key, just to the wrong car.

She failed to realize that she grabbed the spare key not to *her* car, but to Solomon's Outback, which she no longer owns. A car key is a car key is a car key. It was an understandable, honest mistake, not one necessarily sugges-tive of her losing her mind. Michael himself might have made the same mistake!

Nevertheless, here they are, twenty-two miles plus traffic

from home, the detritus of Michael's busy yogic life piling up on his beeping and vibrating phone.

"How about I hot-wire it?" says the kid.

"You can't hot-wire a new Subaru," says a tall, thin, balding man wearing a cap that says "Yeshevsky Boot and Tow." He looks just like the boy, but instead of pimples he's sprouting a few days' growth of facial hair. He has just pulled up and is emerging from a tow truck, on the bed of which sits fresh kill: a gray Audi Q3.

"I can try, *Papochka*. Remember you showed me how to hot-wire that Impreza last week?"

"Have I failed to teach you anything useful? Are you a moron? This has a different steering column," he says. "It has anti-theft built in. You need to pay attention to me when I speak!"

She doesn't mean to be critical, but . . . maybe she does! This is no way to speak to a child. A child who, now that she looks more closely, likely ought to be in school. She's not a busybody, nor is she the sort of person who feels she has the right to pass judgment on other people's child-rearing techniques, and yet why is this boy hanging around the impoundment lot at noon on a weekday?

"Shouldn't this child be in school?" she asks.

"What are you, the government?" he asks rudely. She supposes she can't blame him. She ought not be meddling.

He stares at her for a minute. "You look familiar," he says.

Sophie can't imagine she knows him, although it sometimes seems everyone knows her on account of the store.

"Wait a minute! Are you Nancy Pelosi?"

She is flattered to be mistaken for Nancy Pelosi, apart from the nearly twenty-five-year age difference, which is itself pretty insulting. She will go with the theory that Nancy looks young for her age.

"Except even Nancy Pelosi is smart enough to know there's no school in summer."

"I'm sorry, is this your version of an insult? I happen to know Nancy Pelosi; she's a friend of a friend." (Really, a friend of a friend of a friend, and she's only met her once, but this is not the point.)

"Although she probably drives a Subaru too," says the man. "Car of the American elite."

Really, she has no idea what is happening here, how or why this conversation has so rapidly devolved. Or perhaps more to the point, why she is bothering to engage.

"A Subaru? Elite? It's just a car. It's not even a fancy car."

"Look at you and your books," he says, waving toward their van, which is painted with a logo of the store and a stack of books.

Michael is suddenly out of the van, looking like he is going to level this guy with a baseball bat, or cause him to hyperextend.

"Let's all calm down and take a deep breath," Michael says.

The man looks at Michael, taking in his T-shirt and the tight, not especially flattering yoga shorts he is wearing.

"Look at this Lululemon," the man says to his son, then adds something in Russian. The boy looks deeply uncomfortable.

What is happening here, in left-leaning Maryland, no less? "Please don't speak to us like that! We would just like to figure out a way to get our car and leave in peace."

"Look, Comrade Pelosi, why don't you and Mr. No Drama Llama go home and come back when you have right key?"

"Mom, let's get out of here," Michael says. "This guy is trouble."

It's just a bad moment, she knows, but she feels responsible somehow, even ashamed. Is this what her country has become? Give me your tired, your poor, your huddled masses yearning to breathe free, your impoundment lot owners full of vitriol who think this is an acceptable level of discourse nowadays. Then again, maybe this guy is not what he seems—for all she knows he could have been a physicist or a poet back home, and now, here in this xenophobic country, he has been stripped of dignity, reduced to arresting cars.

The thing to do is leave before this escalates from regular bad to really bad.

Besides, she is worried about her car. She would like to recover it, sooner rather than later.

"I'm up for having you hot-wire it," Sophie volunteers. "I'll sign whatever waiver. I just want to get out of here."

"Please don't," says Michael.

"I have better idea: You go home, get the key, and come back tomorrow. Then I can charge you for the extra day."

END OF DAYS REPORT: Wednesday, August 16
OPENING SHIFT: Noah, Jamal, Summer
SWING SHIFT: Luke, Antonio, Vashti
CLOSING SHIFT: Carmen, Yash, Sami
EVENT: Clemi
FLOOR MANAGER COMMENTS: Nope, not a typo. It is indeed beginning to feel like the End of Days, what with the rain, the forthcoming eclipse, the calls, and all of the crazies that have crawled out of the woodwork this week. Also did I mention the rain, the rain, the rain?

- Be vigilant. Something creepy is afoot. Which is to say that someone has attacked the vacuum cleaner. It is currently resting comfortably in Mrs. Bernstein's office. She has requested that we leave it be for now. We were unable to vacuum last night, so if you see any debris, please just pick it up by hand until we get this resolved.
- Also: The police came around to take a report about Petunia, the now notorious bagel-eating Shih Tzu. They have suggested that if she returns to the store she ought to wear a muzzle, so if you see a tiny little dog that looks like Hannibal Lecter, that's the deal, and if you see her in the store without the muzzle, please let me know ASAP.
- We have a newly arrived shipment of solar eclipse sunglasses. They are on display table three near the front of the store.
- We've had several more calls asking whether we'll be scheduling an event for *Gauzy*. The answer is no, but we do have twenty copies of the book left and more on order.
- *Antifa Now!* is back on the shelf. Also, I stand corrected.

There is no such thing as *Antifada*. What I meant was *Intifada*.

- More calls about the weekend events. We've been transferring all calls over to Clemi's voice mail, which—special note to Clemi!—is *still* full.
- Also remember your *Doodles* talking points. We will have books on Saturday, and the author is coming in to sign.
- We briefly lost internet around noon—we had to use iPads to ring up sales, but it came back on after a couple of hours.
- Belinda is going to be out a few more days at least, but she is on the mend. Web orders are kind of a hot, steaming mess, so if you have time to help out, let me know.
- Oh, what's that? You want another doodle joke? Okay:

What do you call a dog that works at
an independent bookstore?
A hipsterdoodle!

You are welcome.

Autumn T

CHAPTER 8

Thursday

THE TORTOISE AND THE FRENCH FRY

Clemi would have thought that by now she'd be prepared for every event eventuality, yet the curveballs keep coming. Last night's author, a disheveled, balding, oblivious man in a trench coat who looked spectacularly unpresentable, showed up twenty minutes late, then said he needed to have a smoke and make a couple of calls while the audience, such as it was, waited another twenty minutes. He then read from *The Uncommon Quayle*, a work of speculative fiction featuring Vice President Dan Quayle, who is drafted, unwittingly, into service as an undercover narcotics agent. He spoke for forty very long minutes in a monotone voice without once looking up, then rebuffed Clemi's efforts to cut short the Q&A.

This event needed to end so they could turn off the

lights and lock up the store. Most of the remaining staff, those who were nonexempt, were by now going into overtime, which was not something Mrs. Bernstein encouraged. Also informing Clemi's sense of urgency was the fact that she had evening plans. Noah had suggested they meet up after the event, maybe grab a beer. Or maybe Clemi had suggested it, or steered or possibly manipulated the conversation in a direction that led to the idea of grabbing a beer when she said she needed to talk to him about Kurt. This was true, but also not entirely. She still found her mind drifting back to the kiss, trying to divine its meaning.

The event ran more than an hour over as the author pontificated about the reasons for choosing Dan Quayle as a protagonist for his series, rather than, say, Dick Cheney. He then moved on to a consideration of Dan's future exploits. He might send him into outer space in the next novel. Either that or to the Texas border. By then the store had closed to new customers, but the staff had to clear this anemic crowd out the door before they could lock up. When the man finally stopped speaking, he volunteered to pose for selfies with the audience, even wrapping his arms around a pair of customers who appeared to be on their way out and looked deeply uncomfortable. Jamal was still there even though he was no longer on the clock and volunteered to help Clemi straighten up, folding the chairs, putting them back in the closet, and helping to push the heavy fixtures back in place. A total of seven books changed hands—five of them to someone who claimed to have once been Dan Quayle's next-door neighbor.

It's nearly 10:00 p.m. by the time Clemi texts Noah to

tell him she is finally done with work and ready to meet up, but he doesn't respond. The rain has subsided, at least temporarily, and it's turned into a beautiful night, so she walks home slowly, periodically stopping to stare at her phone. Noah doesn't have much of a social media presence, but he posts every once in a while. She checks his Instagram to see if she might determine his whereabouts, but his last update is from about a month ago, when he went to a Nationals game with his parents when they were in town.

It's nearly 11:00 p.m. by the time she gets home—it's a long walk, made longer by her deliberately slow pace. She's been hoping he'd surface and suggest a meeting spot, which almost certainly would have sent her back in the direction from which she'd come.

It's no big deal. That Noah is a nonstarter is not exactly breaking news; her bad for thinking otherwise, if only for a few days. Starting right now, she is officially not going to waste any more time thinking about him. She is an independent career woman, happy to eat a late dinner of . . . there is really nothing in the refrigerator, and not really anything in the cupboard that she might cobble together as a meal. Even the ramen has been consumed. She finds a box of Cheerios that is only a little bit stale, and a banana that is only a little bit brown, and eats a few bites before changing into her pajamas.

She remembers, not that she ever really forgot, that she is supposed to return her mother's supposedly urgent call. But it's only 5:30 a.m. in London, where her mother lives these days after relocating a few years ago when she folded her boutique literary agency into a larger international packaging conglomerate. Clemi wonders if her move to London had anything to do with wanting to be closer to Raymond Chaucer. She could wait another half hour and call her at 6:00 a.m., a more respectable time, but she could also not.

She is twenty-three years old. Old enough to not have to call her mother back because she is a too-busy career woman who doesn't have the time. Old enough to decide to be over her mother problems, but also old enough to know that perhaps no one ever is. She is also wise enough to know that in some respects, this might be the honeymoon period in regard to her mother problems; she is an only child and her mother never remarried, which means that should anything happen to Elena, or should she need help as she ages, the responsibility will fall entirely to Clemi. Which is all the more reason to address the elephant in the room. Or rather the elephant that she is still hopeful will be at the store this weekend: the British poet with a bad reputation who is almost certainly her biological father.

Even if Clemi sets aside her mother's egregious personal behavior and her subsequent lies—a huge and impossible *if*—Elena is still a difficult, critical, unsupportive mother. Clemi's hair, her job, her bank balance, her apartment, her choice of friends, her wardrobe—there's always something Clemi could be doing a better job of, and sadly, this is mostly true.

Whatever is so urgent can wait. And besides, if it's really so urgent, her mother knows how to find her and can do so without creating drama by calling her cell phone instead of the store.

Clemi's head has only just hit the pillow when she hears the buzzer. First one staccato note, then another, then another. Then, whoever is seeking entrance to the building—a visitor, a serial killer, a neighborhood hooligan who just wants to wake people up—leans on the button, making an insidious noise that sounds like a coffee grinder gnashing stale beans.

Florence doesn't stir. Clemi isn't sure if she has taken a sleeping pill or has otherwise self-medicated, but if she's sleeping through this racket, she's unlikely to wake up anytime soon.

She fumbles around for her phone so she can check the time, and finally locates it under her pillow. It's 2:36 a.m., which means she must have conked out for about half an hour and slept soundly enough to have missed a text from Mrs. Bernstein.

> Get security please 4 poet
> Thx

This is progress, at least; her boss is apparently no longer insisting on canceling the event. Still, finding a security firm that can send guards on such short notice is going to be tricky, as well as expensive.

The noise stops for a moment, then begins again. Now this person is annoyingly composing some sort of rhythm on the buzzer, or trying to send a message in code. And now another text arrives and it's Noah:

Open the freaking door!

Noah! Good grief. Now she is fully awake. She pops out of bed and catches her reflection in the mirror; her hair looks like Cyndi Lauper's on a bad day, plus her eyes are streaked with traces of yesterday's blue eyeliner, which she had put on in anticipation of meeting up with Noah. The rest of her face looks puffy, or at least it does to her.

She catalogs the options: She could throw on jeans and a T-shirt and add a quick application of lip gloss. Or she could go with the flow and answer the door in her time-honored faded Disney princess sleepwear ensemble.

Now he is inside the building, leaning on her doorbell, one long, contentious, very loud, atonal chord. Really, he is such a jerk! She grabs her bathrobe as she heads toward the door, wishing she were in possession of more sophisticated lingerie, like, say, a silky gown that might slip alluringly off the shoulder rather than these ridiculous ratty garments she believes she got for her thirteenth birthday. She undoes the bolt on the door and finds not just Noah but also Summer and Kurt Vonnegut Jr.

How Noah has come to be in possession of the tortoise again, she's not sure; after finding Kurt Vonnegut Jr. in the events closet, she had taken him back into her office, where she planned to keep him for a while until she could come up with a better plan.

Noah doesn't even greet her—just walks right in holding the tortoise, whose legs are flailing like he wants to be set down so he can crawl to the on-ramp of the Beltway and inch toward Virginia, back to Pets! Pets! Pets! and away from these irresponsible people. Summer trails behind Noah and Kurt, wearing notably not Disney princess sleepwear but rather distressed jeans, pointy flats, and a plain white T-shirt. She looks like she just came from the all-night blow-dry bar, every hair in perfectly mussed place.

"Sure, just come on in and get comfortable," Clemi says, waving them toward the living room, such as it is with its lumpy couch and makeshift coffee table fashioned from a large, upside-down wire basket covered with a blanket. Noah either fails to detect or chooses to ignore her sarcasm. He drops onto the couch, props his feet up on the table, and puts the tortoise on the floor. Kurt Vonnegut Jr. looks around with his tiny, beady tortoise eyes, taking in his surroundings. He starts to toddle toward her, like maybe he wants to resume their conversation from a couple of days ago. Not that they really spoke—tortoises don't talk!—but just supposing that he *could* talk, she knows he'd say how happy he is to see her, to be back here with the marginally more responsible adult.

"My little sister has that bathrobe!" says Summer, still standing, looking around the room like she's afraid to sit down. Her hesitation is understandable. Clemi inherited this living room ensemble from the previous tenant and does not know the provenance of the sofa or of the plush orange armchair with a couple of cigarette burns in the seat cushion. Her general strategy involves minimizing the amount of time spent in this apartment, a goal made achievable by her work schedule.

"You didn't tell me you have a sister," says Noah. "How old?"

"My half sister. She's twelve." Summer pulls her hair back and gathers it into a ponytail with one of the many elastic bands wrapped around her wrist.

"Oh, right. That's Claire?"

"Clara, yes."

"And she lives in Denver, right?"

"Amazing. You've been listening."

"I have! Your dad's new wife is named Marissa, and she's a real estate agent and not your favorite person in the world. See? I am a master of retention!"

"Even after four beers and a cider." Summer is leaning on the doorframe facing Noah. Now she pulls the elastic out and shakes her hair loose again, a nervous tic. Or a flirtatious tic.

Clemi is having trouble wrapping her head around this scene in her living room. What, exactly, is going on? What has motivated the two of them to transport this production to her apartment, at this hour?

"Um, hi, you guys! Welcome to my living room in the middle of the night? So we have established that you have a half sister in Denver and that she is a Disney nerd. But we are less certain about the purpose of this visit."

"Oh, hey, sorry! Maybe I misunderstood—I thought you wanted to meet up after the event."

"I did, but I didn't mean at, like, 2:00 a.m."

"Hey, no judgment here," Summer says. "I like to get to sleep early too. Also, another thing in common: I've got a Disney princess thing going on too! I love Ariel. But also Belle. Obviously. She's a book nerd. But this is really tragic, you guys: I took a Buzzfeed quiz—one about which Disney princess you are—and it said that I'm *Cinderella*, not Belle, which upset me more than I ought to admit."

"That's not such a bad thing," Noah says. "I mean, that's kind of just right. You're, like, totally industrious. Plus, Cinderella's gorgeous. And she has all those sweet bird friends."

Clemi feels weirdly jealous. Not just of Noah and Summer, but even of Cinderella. She could do with some more supportive friends right now, avian or otherwise, but you take what life gives you, and right now it is giving her these two people, along with Kurt Vonnegut Jr., whose affection is definitely not imagined. He has moved toward her and his resplendent, possibly salmonella-tinged shell is grazing her foot. She places him in her lap and starts to stroke him like he's a tiny dog.

"You're reading *The Savage Detectives*?" Summer asks, picking the paperback up off the coffee table.

"No, that's been sitting here since I moved in. But I should read it. It's on my list. Have you read it?"

"I did, but when I was young. I should probably reread it. It's amazing. It's masterful. The guy is a literary guerilla. I'd get a lot more out of it now, I'm sure."

"What, did you read it when you were twelve?" Clemi asks. "I've heard he was pretty arrogant. He disparaged a whole bunch of writers including Gabriel García Márquez and I think also Octavio Paz."

"The price of genius," says Noah. "All writers hate each other."

"That's not true," says Clemi. "I'm a writer . . . I mean, I want to be a writer, and I love everyone. Mostly."

"Yeah, but just wait until you're famous," says Noah.

"Oh please. At the rate I'm going . . ."

"You're only, what, twenty-four?" says Summer. "What do you mean at the rate you're going?"

"I'm twenty-three. But still, I'm not as far along as I'd hoped to be. You know that I went to school with Raina O'Malley, who wrote *The Girl in*—"

"Yes, I've heard," Summer says.

Clemi wonders what, exactly, she's heard. It can't be good. And if Summer has heard it, whatever it is, probably everyone else has too.

"I just read somewhere that she's on *Granta*'s list of best young American writers. And I'm not even halfway through my own book. I mean, I was, but I ripped it up. I can't seem to get it off the ground."

"Um, at the risk of repeating myself, you're only twenty-three?"

"Yeah, but I think I need a couple more years to finish writing, and then by the time I give it to readers and revise and find an agent and a publisher . . . I don't know, I just don't want to be old when I publish my first novel."

"Oh, Clemi, you're brilliant," says Noah. "Nothing to worry about. You'll still be brilliant when you're twenty-six."

Clemi feels a wave of despair and anxiety. What does Noah know about her brilliance or lack thereof? False praise is worse than no praise at all. Generally she finds it's better not to talk about the writing thing. Whenever she mentions it, she feels exposed, like she's just revealed a dark secret, like she's a kleptomaniac or is addicted to prescription drugs. Which probably has to do with her mother again—the mother who is a famous literary agent. An agent to the great writers, to the literary stars.

It's late and this visit is disorienting her on several different levels; she isn't sure how much more of it she can take. "So seriously, what's going on? I'm happy to see you both and everything, but I thought we were going to meet up after the event, like at ten, not in the middle of the night. I have a crazy day tomorrow and I need sleep."

"Yeah, sorry about that! I meant to text you. I just kind of forgot. I mean, I didn't *forget*, it's just that I got around to it on the late side, and here we are! We're a little worried about Kurt," says Noah.

Clemi's ear catches on the word *we*. She looks at the tortoise and continues to stroke his shell. "What's up with him? He looks okay to me."

"He does seem a little better now."

"What do you mean?"

"We were out at the Blue Derby and . . . well, everyone was messing with him," says Summer. "Autumn L gave him a couple of French fries and Antonio poured some ketchup and he stepped in it and—"

"You saw Autumn L? How is she?"

"She's great! I mean, she doesn't like her new job, but she's making like three times as much money, so there's that, even if she's stuck in an office analyzing boring documents or whatever. I'm not really sure what she does. I'm sorry, I should have invited you. I knew you had to work so I was waiting until the event was over, and then I guess I just kind of forgot?"

"Yeah, no worries. I would have liked to have seen her

though. I miss her! I need to catch up with her. Wait . . . You took Kurt Vonnegut Jr. to a *bar*?"

"I'm really sorry. I told Noah it wasn't a good idea to take him there. We were supposed to go straight to his place, but then Autumn L called Noah and . . ."

Clemi tries to pinpoint the precise location of the wound. Is it the casual reference to the two of them having been en route to Noah's apartment? Or that everyone was out at the Blue Derby and no one thought to invite her? Or that they took Kurt Vonnegut Jr. to a bar? Or even that Summer is now talking about Autumn L like they are old friends, when in fact she has presumably never met her before tonight, whereas Clemi worked with her for months?

"He may have had a bit too much," says Noah.

"Please don't tell me you gave a tortoise alcohol."

"I mean too much of everything. Too much stimulation. He only had a little sip of beer. I'm really more worried about the French fries. He seems to have a little . . . tortoise diarrhea."

"Ew! Geez, Noah. Are you trying to kill him? What's wrong with you? Should we take him to a vet?"

"No, I really think he's going to be fine. I just think he's better off here with you. I'm not the most responsible pet owner, I guess."

"No kidding. But I can't keep him. I'm not supposed to have pets. It's in my lease."

"Mine too," says Noah.

Clemi wonders if this is true or if Noah is making it up on the spot. She looks to Summer for some sort of validation, but she is staring into the hallway, her eyes wide. Clemi hears the sound of a drill revving up.

"Oh, don't worry about that. It's just Simon. It's cool."

"What do you mean, 'it's cool'?" asks Summer. "What's he doing?"

"It's just his thing. A . . . hobby, I guess. He likes to drill. I don't really know what it's called, if it's a legitimate condition, like something with a name, or just a Simon thing."

Or if it's just another little pocket of weirdness in her already weird life: her nocturnally drilling roommate. That's how Clemi has come to think of the Simon situation, the phraseology her very own. It isn't even a *thing*, nocturnal drilling. Even the internet doesn't know what this is—only suggesting, patronizingly, that perhaps Clemi has made a typo and meant to write the words *nocturnal drooling*. This week the drilling has seemed especially bad, although it's hard to tell if the problem has become more insidious or if Clemi is just more anxious than before and now unable to sleep through it.

Typically, the noise begins each night somewhere between 2:00 and 3:00 a.m. and lasts for roughly an hour. She is aware that this has been happening for some time, but in this latest manifestation the drilling sessions seem to go on longer. Something about the entire situation grows more disturbing each night.

An intensive internet search on Simon himself has been among her poor sleep hygiene practices this week. Just last night she plunked down her almost-maxed-out credit card to do a background check on him from one of the sites that pops up on-screen when you google someone's name. She's heard of people doing this when dating on apps, and no one she knows has been hacked or had their identity stolen as a result, at least not yet, so she figures they must be at least marginally legit. In any event, there was nothing to learn. Simon is a twenty-nine-year-old male, born in New Hampshire, and he has lived in DC for seven years, in three different apartments, with as many different jobs in retail.

"This is seriously weird, Clemi. Maybe you shouldn't be living with this guy," says Noah, as though he's suddenly concerned about her. "It's just not normal . . . Speaking of normal, where's Florence?"

"She is somehow or another sleeping through this. And anyway, Simon is a friend of Antonio's ex-girlfriend's cousin, so he's sort of vouched for. Plus, he's a really nice guy and a good roommate, so let's define *normal*, okay? Is taking a tortoise to a bar and feeding him French fries normal? I mean, maybe Simon loves to drill but there's just nothing constructive to drill?"

The drilling grows louder, and Clemi has to admit that she's being absurdly defensive. This is about as abnormal as it gets.

"Does he have a job?"

"He works at Banana Republic."

They pause to listen.

"How did you find this place? It's not bad—nicer than anything I saw when I was looking."

"I took over the lease from Lulu when she left. And when Florence lost her job and we needed help on the rent, we found Simon."

Lulu is a former bookseller who quit, giving less than one

week's notice and becoming a persona non grata to Mrs. Bernstein when she announced she was going to work for a rival bookstore less than three miles away. People came and left all the time, but mostly for better-paying jobs or graduate school or random personal reasons. Rarely did they go to another bookstore in the same town. Independent bookselling is a congenial, cooperative, gentlemanly, non-competitive business. Except when it's not.

"So, I don't mean to dwell on this, but . . . I'm kind of fascinated. He drills holes in the wall and then . . . ?" Noah asks.

"Oh, no big deal. He just patches them up again. Like over here . . ." Clemi directs their attention to the wall next to the couch just under the Wilco poster. "That's one of his favorite drilling spots." It's where he'd likely be right now, goggles and earphones on, sitting on the floor, legs akimbo, were it not for the fact that Clemi is entertaining in the living room.

Noah and Summer stare at the wall, evidently not sure what they should be seeing.

"If you run your finger over the plaster you can feel where he's patched it up, but you can't really see the damage," Clemi explains.

"That's so cool," says Summer. "But also creepy. Like scar tissue."

"Exactly."

"Wow . . . it's like he's cutting."

"Yup."

"I might use that," Summer says.

"Use it how?"

163

"Just in a story I'm working on."

"You're a writer too?" Clemi feels stricken. Summer is here, in her apartment, uninvited, and now she's stealing her material, not that she had ever intended to use it. Summer probably even has an agent. She can see it already: the bidding war for her collection, the literary prizes, the massive book sales with Summer mugging on the back cover, while Clemi stays forever in place, setting up and breaking down flimsy IKEA chairs.

Fortunately the beep of her phone interrupts this bad thought spiral. She looks at the screen and sighs. "Unbelievable. It's Mrs. Bernstein again. Does she sleep?"

Get publisher to pay for security

"What does she want?" asks Noah.

"She wants me to get the publisher to pay for security for the Raymond Chaucer event."

"Will they?"

"They ought to, but it's not as easy as it sounds. Last time I asked, I was told the author had used up the entire publicity budget on first-class air travel."

"Like that's our problem?"

"Yeah. Except that it is. And I know it's been kind of a tight year at the store, budget-wise."

Another *chirp* from her phone:

Also
Have u ordered
Enough books?

Kurt Vonnegut Jr. makes a clicking noise, sticks his head up, and looks straight at Clemi.

"Look at that," says Noah. "He's so happy to be home!"

"This isn't home, Noah. Like I told you, I'm not allowed to have a pet."

"Okay, you guys, stop freaking out about this. I'm not sure what the big deal is, but *I'll* take him home," Summer says.

Clemi is now on full alert. She has known Summer for all of three days, and she's already had enough of her. No way is she going to let her take the tortoise home. But then, it's not like she has a better idea. Maybe she can talk Mrs. Bernstein into letting her keep him in her office, even though the store has a no-pets-at-work rule. She has been told that long before Clemi's time you could bring your dog to work, until someone complained about allergies, at which point a ban was introduced. A few months later someone in the finance office brought in a hypoallergenic pet lizard. It lasted a few weeks in a plastic terrarium on top of a filing cabinet until a bookseller complained that since *her* dog was hypoallergenic, too, she ought to be allowed to bring it to work. Charges of speciesism ensued, at which point a blanket no-pets-at-work rule was put in place, with the caveat that customer pets were welcome even though in reality they were the ones who caused most of the problems. Still, maybe she can find a way.

"No," says Clemi. "I'll just bring him back to my office."

"It's so depressing in there," Summer says.

"Um, thanks?"

"I just mean there's no light. It's not good for him."

"Yeah, it's not especially good for me either, but I'm okay."

"What's the big deal? How about I take him for a day or two, just 'til you figure this out?"

Clemi isn't sure what to say to this. She doesn't like the idea, but it's possibly what's best for Kurt.

"Hey, look! He got over a hundred likes on Instagram!" Noah says.

"Who did?"

"Kurt Vonnegut Jr.!"

"He has an Instagram account?"

"Don't be ridiculous. It's posted on my account," Summer says. "But you know, that's a great idea! I'll start an account for him right now!" She taps at her phone for a few seconds and then looks up, smiling.

"He's @kurtvonnegut_tortoise."

Clemi reaches for her phone and pulls up Instagram and follows Summer and @kurtvonnegut_tortoise, and there he is, there *they* are. Summer and Noah sitting at a table with a bunch of others, Autumn L and Jamal and Antonio. Zhang Li is there, too, along with one of her colleagues, whom Clemi recognizes from a meeting they once had about Blowfish events. And there's Kurt in the middle of the table, gnawing on a French fry.

"Some tortoises!" the post reads.

Some tortoises *what?* This is strangely infuriating. Clemi thinks about one of her best friends from college who is now a teacher in a Maryland elementary school. She has a hand-made poster hanging in her second-grade classroom that reads: "If you feel yourself getting angry, count to ten. If you still feel upset, sing the alphabet before responding." Each letter is a different color, cut from construction paper and glued to a poster board. It looks like a ransom note that's been accented with unicorns and glitter.

Clemi's mind frequently goes there when she is under pressure at work, but it doesn't translate well to a retail environment. She imagines herself standing at the information desk singing the alphabet before replying to a difficult customer, such as the one who came in yesterday while Clemi was covering a lunchtime shift for Autumn T. The woman, who seemed too young to be so rude (as if rudeness is the result of a lifetime of accumulating injustices, which at least has some logic to it), quipped that she could not believe Clemi had not heard of the book *Blue City*, and wondered why she was working in a bookstore if she couldn't keep up with popular fiction. With patience and determination and a few pointed questions, Clemi determined the woman was after the nonfiction book *The Devil in the White City*. She expected an apology, some sort of display of embarrassment, or possibly even praise for her keen powers of deduction, but the customer simply thanked her lukewarmly, took the book, glanced at the back cover for a few moments, then deposited it on a display table of climate change books before exiting the store.

Right now, it would take more than a few rounds of the alphabet to calm her down.

Forget about her social life. Or, rather, Kurt Vonnegut Jr.'s social life. Now she is fretting about getting Raymond Chaucer's publisher to pay for his security. And then there is the matter of finding any security guards at all on such short notice. The last time she'd needed security, when a former Afghani ambassador was scheduled to appear to discuss his memoir, she'd begun by calling the local police, the Department of Homeland Security, and the FBI, all to no avail. They each responded as if she was trying to get away with something—as if scoring security guards was her version of swag. No one had seemed especially concerned that the author had received a number of recent and credible-sounding threats. "Not in our jurisdiction," she heard repeatedly, until a kindly person at the Justice Department—the switchboard operator, perhaps—directed her to a private security firm that failed to return any of her calls.

Clemi had finally found two guards ready to serve, but once they arrived, she felt like she was in the middle of a bad sitcom. The men were right out of central casting, bumbling Keystone Kops who showed up armed. They were so unsteady around their weapons that once they reported for duty she realized she'd just invited the real threat—loaded weapons!—into the store. She asked them to disarm, to no avail, and then politely asked them to please be careful not to shoot any customers. They had, unbelievably, been named Clinton and Bill, and on top of everything else, they seemed oblivious to the uncanny juxtaposition of their names; either that or they were sick of the jokes. They began their assignment by asking Clemi to elaborate on the nature of the threat, by which they did not mean details of the alarming Twitter posts; rather, they wanted her to explain the history of Afghanistan, including the nature of the Soviet occupation and the current status of the Taliban.

Then their bill for more than $600 arrived, about which Mrs. Bernstein went mildly berserk.

She continues to stare at the picture of the tortoise and the French fry with her colleagues smiling in the background. Is she required by the rules of social media to like this post, to participate in this travesty? Not liking it, especially with Summer sitting right here, seems kind of mean-spirited. On the other hand, she actively, aggressively does not like this post. At all. Then again, she actively, aggressively dislikes most posts. She's an old soul. A generational anomaly. A young millennial who hates social media, which is kind of ironic since her job involves managing the store's social media accounts. That said, she finds it strangely fascinating and enjoys the window this gives her onto the world, where she is allowed, and even encouraged, to be a professional voyeur.

As she scrolls across Summer's grid, she is especially amused by her Instagram vaguebooking. "Sometimes it just hurts so much," she recently posted beneath a selfie looking sultry and sad, receiving 197 likes and a string of empathetic comments.

"Why are some people just the worst?" she asked the previous day, to equally popular result.

And then, on Monday, simply: "Some people . . ." Given that this was the day Summer began working at the store, Clemi can't help but wonder: Is *she* one of those people? She wishes Summer would just go back to NASA.

She scrolls back to a post from Autumn T from earlier this evening: an artful if slightly blurred shot of a bunch of booksellers hanging out at a rooftop bar. "Sometimes on a sultry August night all of your people come out and the setting sun is a gorgeous ball of fire and you don't even mind the sound of the traffic below and the world is just right."

It sounds to Clemi like a Pepsi commercial. She hates the internet, yet she can't seem to stop staring at images that make her miserable, that reinforce her own contradictions. She's a loner who doesn't like to be alone, an introvert who wishes she could turn her life into a piece of online performance art, while also a person who suffers wild anxiety when she so much as posts a picture of a cute dog she met on the street. This is yet another problem she will likely face if she ever becomes an author: she needs a bigger social media presence in order to sell the book she doesn't have time—or possibly the ability—to write.

She ought to preserve her sanity by putting her phone away, but now here's Summer again, having coffee with a friend last weekend: #bfforever #tooearly #earlybliss #messyhairdontcare #badhairday #myhairisawful #yaydonuts #booksellersrock #keds #food #coffee #amsortofbluetoday.

She's lost more time than she realizes. The drilling has stopped. Noah is asleep on the couch. Kurt has put his head inside his shell. And Summer is absorbed by whatever is transpiring on her phone.

Clearly, she is not going to get any sleep tonight, so she might as well do something productive. She goes into the bedroom to retrieve her laptop and is startled to see Florence sitting up in bed, staring at the wall.

"Flo, are you okay?"

She doesn't answer. She looks like she's in a trance again, like the day before yesterday when she sat on the window ledge soaking wet. Clemi is spooked.

"Sorry if we woke you. Noah and Summer dropped by. And Simon was doing his thing."

Now she turns toward Clemi. "Yes, I heard. I also heard you talking about Raymond Chaucer. You're having an event for him? You do know he's a misogynist prick, right?"

"I'm aware of the things people are saying about him, yes."

"People are comparing him to Ted Hughes!"

"So I've heard."

"You know how I feel about him. I wrote my thesis on—"

"Yes, I am aware," Clemi says, although in truth she had managed to forget about this. "You wrote it on Sylvia Plath and female archetypes or something?"

"No, Clemi. It was called 'The Day of the Narcissist.' It was about Ted Hughes and how he destroyed Sylvia, and then he destroyed his next lover, Assia Wevill. You know she also committed suicide, right?"

"I was an English major, too, Florence. I am familiar with the story. Why don't you go back to sleep? They're about to leave in a few minutes."

"I can't believe you're going to give him a platform."

"Look, I'm getting it from all sides. I don't need to hear it from you too."

"Mrs. Bernstein was right."

"What do you mean?"

"About the darkness descending."

"She was talking about something else entirely. You

weren't even there at the party anymore, so how do you even know?"

"You forget that I know things, Clemi. She said *dark times ahead*."

"Okay, yeah, she did say that, but she was having a bad day. I mean, the world was having a bad day. It still is. But she wasn't referring to a freaking poetry event at a bookstore."

"Interpret at your own risk."

Clemi is so not in the mood for this. She is worried about Florence, but also exhausted. She wants to help her through this bad patch, but it is becoming clearer that whatever she needs is beyond Clemi's abilities. By covering her rent and maintaining a veneer of normalcy, she is beginning to wonder if she's just enabling Florence's downward spiral. Florence needs professional, or at least parental, help, and it is probably time to reach out to them again. She suggested this to Florence a week ago, but Florence got angry and made Clemi promise not to do it.

Clemi soothes Florence back to sleep, then takes her laptop and leaves the room, gently closing the door on her way out.

Back in the living room she settles onto a pillow on the floor and logs into her work account. Seven event requests, including one from a self-published author writing about her recovery from a shoplifting addiction and one from a representative of the president of Liberia, who will be in town *next week*. And an email from Raymond's publicist in London, who says she needs to talk to Clemi urgently, and to please call her as soon as she wakes up.

Then a second email from Chaucer's publicist, checking in to be sure Clemi has ordered a sufficient number of books.

Noah begins to stir. For a moment it looks like he's going to wake. He opens his eyes and looks around the room, then he unfurls himself and stretches out on the couch. He throws an arm over Summer, who has finally gone to sleep beside him. Clemi turns away from the sight of the two of them touching.

Her computer emits another chirp. It's a third email from Raymond Chaucer's publicist:

Just a reminder—he needs fine-point Sharpie pens. Also, the *Washington Post* interview will post online today. Heads up, I've heard it's not going to be his finest moment.

END OF DAY REPORT: Thursday, August 17
OPENING SHIFT: Emma, Carmen, Jamal
SWING SHIFT: Vashti, Aaron, Summer
CLOSING SHIFT: Antonio, Yash, Sami
EVENT: Clemi
FLOOR MANAGER COMMENTS: Keisha is back! Keisha is back! (Did I tell you that Keisha is back?) No one can stay away from this place, is the moral of the story. She'll be helping out on web orders so Belinda isn't overwhelmed when she comes back, hopefully next week.

Come get free wine and pizza from our friends at Platypus tomorrow at 2:00 p.m. They will be here to present their winter catalog and will have galleys and tote bags and stuff.

- We are still a vacuum-free zone, but this will soon be resolved.
- We had several calls this morning about *Gutted!* The author appeared on *Morning Joe* today. Please take note: Confusingly, there are two new books with this title. One is about deboning freshwater fish. The other is a memoir by a journalist who has covered Iraq for a decade. We have sold out of both titles, so please take special orders and just triple-check that you have the right book.
- We are out of *The Girl in Gauzy Blue*, so take special orders. We should have it back in stock tomorrow.
- More calls about the weekend events.
- The worldwide web remained our friend today, apart from the twenty minutes when the electricity blew. We are going to get this resolved too. We are going to get everything resolved. I swear.

Okay, okay, okay. I know what you want . . .

What do you call a doodle trained by a psychoanalyst?

Drumroll, please . . .

A doodle trained by an analyst is a . . .
Freudoodle!

Autumn T

CHAPTER 9

Friday

THE BIRDS

Sophie wakes up and checks her inbox straightaway to see what potential headaches the day might bring. The first thing she sees is an email with the subject line, "Welcome to SilverBliss."

SilverBliss?

What is this *SilverBliss?* It sounds vaguely familiar, but she can't think why. Is it a racehorse? A jewelry store? A hair salon? A quick google search turns up a dating site. "Exclusive for over-fifties. It's never too late to find your bliss."

Now she remembers; she has heard of this, seen it advertised here and there, but she can't imagine what it's doing in her inbox. It's definitely not something she would ever sign up for. If she's going to meet someone, she will do so the old-fashioned way, or at least the romcom way: Someone will come into the store and ask for a book recommendation, and she will send him home with an armful of Joan Didion, including *Slouching Toward Bethlehem* or maybe *The White Album*, and he will come back a few days later to say that Didion's writing changed his way of viewing the world. And even though she knows he is just pretending—she has yet to meet a man who loves these books the way she does—she will still agree to the cup of coffee he proposes, and they will fall in love and live happily ever after. But so far nothing even remotely like this has occurred. People tend to know what they are looking for in her store, or if they do want a recommendation, it's generally within a specific genre, like, "I need a good thriller to read on a plane." People rarely ask Sophie what she herself would recommend. Plus, most of the men with whom she interacts are either half her age or have partners in tow. And that's okay because she is not actively looking for romance, she's really not, and until this week it truly hadn't even crossed her mind. But that evening with Gil, as pathetic as it was, has reminded her of the possibility of not always being alone.

Now Michael is calling on her cell. It isn't even 7:00 a.m. He doesn't usually call this early and she hopes nothing is wrong.

"Don't flip out when you check your email, Mom, but . . ."

Oh, Michael! It would not have occurred to her that Michael would do something like this, but it suddenly makes sense.

"Did you—"

"Possibly? Don't be mad! What's the harm? Besides, you get the first month free. But be sure to cancel before the end of the month because otherwise it will automatically charge your card. I put it on your Amex."

She doesn't know where to begin. Which of the presumptions and intrusions is the most egregious? Probably that he has memorized the details of her credit card.

"You seemed a little . . . not yourself when we were in the car the other day. That thing with the Canadian guy . . . and all this Anne Frank stuff. I know it's been a lot, but I think you need to start moving forward with your life."

"I am, Michael! Remember? I said explicitly that I'm trying to enjoy my carefree life while I can!"

"Yeah . . . that's kind of my point. You need to break out of this bad thought loop. Walking around quoting Anne Frank."

"Otto."

"What?"

"Otto Frank. Her father."

"To my point, Mom. Just log on and see if you can figure out how to set it up. I'll come over later and teach you how to upload a photo."

Again, she tells herself to take a deep breath. "Thanks, I do know how to upload a photo. I mean, I'm on Facebook! Or . . . I was. I haven't been on in a couple of years and now I think I'm locked out, but—"

"Okay, I didn't mean to insult you, Mom. Just let me know if you want any help."

"Thanks, Michael. That was really sweet of you. I'm not ready to date, but if I change my mind, I'll take a look."

She takes a look. Of course she takes a look. She inputs the bare minimum of information that will allow her to log in and browse. She is certainly not going to identify herself or put up a picture, but she does create a bookish handle: DCBookWoman2017. There are more "bookwomen" handles than she would have thought, so at least she is not immediately identifiable. She narrows the field to men between the ages of fifty and sixty and decides to open it up to the entire East Coast, thinking that if she were to correspond with anyone, which she would not, it would be better to meet outside the DC metropolitan area because she wants to do this as much on the down low as possible. Not that she is going to do it at all.

Oh, it is depressing, these rows and rows of men. They all look so *old*! Not that old is bad. She is no spring chicken herself, a phrase that ought to be taken out of circulation even though she is the one who just thought of it, which she has done because it is an anachronism, and she is old herself.

There is 8332Muscleman—a guy from Watchung, New Jersey, who is posing in front of a red Ferrari. Marvin123 is from Albany, a retired urologist who says he is fifty-two years old but looks more like eighty-two, and there is AnandSingh, who says he is fifty-eight and works for the Nuclear Regulatory Commission. He looks handsome, and he lists reading books among his hobbies, which also include cooking and gardening, but she is unsettled by his admission that although he is still married, he has been given permission to date.

She decides to play a game. If she *had* to date someone here—not that she would—who would it be? It's not uniformly horrible, this lineup of elderly gentlemen, but at least half of them do look fake. Maybe SilverBliss sprinkles in some bot profiles to keep people like Sophie from collapsing in utter despair.

Okay, here is someone with a sweet face. He looks . . . smart. He wears round glasses and appears to be a bookish sort. His profile lists him as a doctor from Hartford. He has been widowed for five years and has two adult children and a dog.

She scrolls down farther to see what else she can learn but accidentally clicks on something. Oh boy. What has she done? She has evidently just sent this person a message that reads, "I'm sending you a *woo* to get the conversation started. Contact me and let's get to know each other!"

This is horrifying. Completely. She goes back up to the top and tries to undo this and thinks she has succeeded, but then suddenly all of these men begin to message her. Whatever she has clicked on has sent each one of them a *woo*, whatever that means. She slams the laptop shut, then opens it again to be sure she has closed the browser. She considers sticking the thing in the tub and turning on the water, but she has already assaulted one appliance this week; taking out her frustrations on another might be the start of an expensive slippery slope.

Each morning Sophie, wrapped in her bathrobe, is reminded of Tony Soprano as she walks to the foot of her driveway and bends, or sometimes squats, to retrieve the papers. She is not a fictitious heavyset New Jersey gangster, and hopefully she looks marginally better wrapped in her robe—or at least doesn't waddle quite as comically. She nevertheless feels ridiculous, as well as slightly suspect, especially right now, because it is already close to noon and she has not yet showered or dressed, having managed to fall back to sleep after the too-early SilverBliss debacle. She also feels conspicuous because she is the only person on her block who still has the print version of the *Washington Post* delivered, but as evidenced by her SilverBliss gaffe, she is clearly better off avoiding all things digital. Still, she feels guilty contributing to the destruction of trees, admittedly an odd concern for a woman who owns a bookstore. She has never really investigated whether the newspaper, or the books in her store, are manufactured from recycled paper, even though she knows she should.

Here she is again, holding two opposing ideas, and her head has not exploded. That there is literary precedent is no excuse, but right now, it's the best she's got.

She sits at the kitchen table with a mug of coffee and begins to peruse the headlines. There's an outbreak of cholera in Yemen, NAFTA is being renegotiated, and Kim Jong-un is preparing to nuke Guam. Also there's a storm brewing in the Caribbean; they are calling it Harvey, and even though it's many days and many miles away, perhaps it will hopscotch to Washington and do them all in.

The mayor of Charlottesville is calling for an emergency meeting to discuss the removal of Confederate monuments. The president is touting the winery he owns, which is about a twenty-minute drive from where the protests occurred. A local bar is offering discounts on drinks every time a White House official is fired.

And if that's not enough, on the front page of the Style section, to which she has turned for something more life-affirming than the day's horrible news, is an enormous photograph of Raymond Chaucer. He is handsome in a disheveled sort of way, his shaggy hair a bit of a mess. He has what Sophie considers to be a distinctive and somewhat specific look that says: (a) British white male poet; (b) progeny of a formerly aristocratic family that is about to be dispossessed; and (c) just returned from an afternoon spent tromping through mud with hunting dogs, murdering geese.

The reporter, Katarina Giovanni, a well-known feature writer whose most recent profiles have been of A-list celebrities such as Oprah Winfrey, Tiger Woods, and Nicole Kidman, does not mince words regarding her time spent interviewing the not always coherent, possibly intoxicated poet who rambled on for about two hours and circled back multiple times to the unfair media treatment he has been subjected to.

The spread contains a brief introduction, a long Q&A, and a facsimile of the follow-up email Raymond sent to the reporter after the interview—in which he included the recorded transcript and proposed redacting about 90 percent of what he said.

Sophie reads, first, the softball opening: He is staying at his sister's currently vacant apartment in Navy Yard, in a sleek modern building with a spectacular view of the ball field. He arrived last weekend and hasn't stepped outside. There is the suggestion that he has been drinking a lot and eating very little. And the apartment is a mess.

Puffy background questions ensue: She asks about his unusual path to becoming a poet, and he responds by talking about his earlier career as an investment banker, explaining that he found the instruments of finance inspiring and rich with metaphor. He once wrote an entire cycle about junk bonds, he says. Another about day-trading and short-selling stock.

She homes in on a few poems from his current collection, praising them, and asks if he is comfortable discussing the inspiration. She is particularly interested in his poem "The Day of the Pushchair."

He thanks her and explains that this is a delicate poem, written about his then-toddler son on a particularly difficult day when he and Seema, his late wife, had been arguing. He had accidentally let go of his son's pushchair as they were walking along an incline on Hampstead Heath. It was an accident, he says. He was distracted and took his hands off the bar of the stroller to make a point. Nothing terrible happened; the child had only chipped a tooth and slightly broken his arm when the pushchair flipped over at the bottom of the hill, but Seema had made a huge fuss, had screamed bloody murder.

"Only chipped a tooth and only *slightly* broke his arm?" the reporter inquires.

"Yes, only slightly," he replies. "The plaster cast he wore was very small."

She asks about his childhood in Yorkshire, then points out that Ted Hughes, to whom he has been compared, both as a poet and as the husband of a woman who tragically took her own life, was also from Yorkshire.

It is around this point that Raymond Chaucer begins to lose his composure.

"It was an accident, what happened to Seema," he says. "Yes, we are, Ted and I, we're both from Yorkshire. So what? Okay, so my wife quite tragically made the extremely unfortunate decision to place her head in the oven—but what no one understands is that it was leaking, and she was simply investigating the leak!—and yes, I am a poet, and yes, I was possibly not the easiest or most faithful of husbands, but this is where the similarities to the Hughes-and-Plath narrative end."

The reporter then asks him to elaborate, pointing out that several outlets have reported Seema's death as a suicide.

"Has anyone noted that suicide runs in her family? Did you know that her grandmother's sister committed suicide?"

"Wait, so you are suggesting that it was, in fact, suicide?"

"I am not. I'm just saying it's complicated. But it was decidedly an accident."

"Yet this accident occurred after she learned about your child outside of the marriage. The one she didn't know about."

"This is a private matter about which I have no comment."

"Okay, let's move on for now. Your recent collection, *Kaboom!*, does have a crow on the cover, an homage, presumably, to one of Ted Hughes's most celebrated works."

"This is true, Katarina. What I mean to do with this collection is change the narrative. I am trying to own the situation that has been created. I am showing the world why my story is different from the story people believe. I am in no way like Ted Hughes. Apart from the bits about him that are good, like being an accomplished poet, or liking children and animals, that is."

"But there are similarities. So can you elaborate on what you mean by 'changing the narrative'?"

Sophie is beginning to feel unwell. Whatever happened with his wife is tragic. Suicide, gas leak, it doesn't particularly matter. This man is a complete narcissist. No wonder so many women are protesting his events, attempting to marginalize him, even blow him up—not that she advocates for the latter, and certainly not in her bookstore.

She wonders if Clemi has read this. Perhaps she would change her mind if she did. Is it too late to cancel? The event is tomorrow afternoon. She knows she has been wishy-washy, issuing conflicting edicts. Her thinking is all a muddle these days, full of contradictions about pretty much everything. If it was up to her, she never would have scheduled him in the first place, but that's not a helpful observation. What's done is done. Or maybe not. Maybe it's not too late to go back to where she began and tell Clemi to cancel. But she wants to give Clemi some autonomy. She feels a headache coming on from too much thinking. Really all she wants to do is crawl inside her nook.

She forces herself to read on.

"Please allow me to emphasize the following points by way of demonstrating the many differences between my story and the Ted Hughes story. Seema was a wannabe poet; Sylvia Plath, published and accomplished. Seema was born in India; Sylvia in America. Sylvia had two young children. Seema and I have three children, two boys and a girl, two in their late teens, one already a young adult. Seema's death

is truly an unfortunate thing, but what I'd like to emphasize, to have a chance to explain, is that the similarity to the
Plath-and-Hughes story is purely coincidental, having more
to do with the fight we had had about replacing the oven,
which was itself already problematic and which the technician had come to repair. It was an old-model contraption, a
classic that had conveyed with the house, an ancient thing we
had initially meant to replace. But then, with the passage of
time, it began to seem charming and quaint, a talking point,
even, with guests. Mind you, it was nothing fancy . . . I don't
remember the brand name, although it could have been from
John Lewis. By which I mean the department store, not the
congressman. Have you been to London? You must come
sometime. I can give you some restaurant tips. Happy to show
you around. (I'm not hitting on you, by the way. I would just
like to be clear about this since I'm under strict orders, and
besides, just for the record, you are not my type.)

"It was not a great oven, but then, we were not especially
great cooks. But I digress: When the emergency repairman
came, he mentioned damage to some of the coils in the back,
possibly the work of gnawing rodents—and while he had the
situation contained, it would behoove us to begin thinking
about a new oven. He'd hate to see the place explode, he
said, and while I do think he had our best interests at heart,
I also did hear him mutter under his breath something to
the effect of how cheap we must be to keep an old oven
like that around, what with the fancy cars in our driveway."

The reporter asks him if the oven was an AGA. She
explains she has heard that, for whatever reason, this has
become a point of contention.

"It was not an AGA, Katarina. But thank you for asking because I would like to set the record straight on this point. I am so tired of this AGA conversation. Bone tired. Emotionally and physically drained. I'm close to snapping, really. I wish we could just talk about my new collection. He can't say why, exactly, this detail sets him off, other than that he and Seema had been arguing about the price of ovens, on top of which he is simply not the sort of man who would have an AGA in his house."

The reporter points out that he has drifted into the third person.

He apologizes and says this happens sometimes.

She points out that about a dozen different news outlets have reported that the oven was an AGA, then asks him again why this seemingly ridiculous, minor detail is so upsetting. The manufacturer of the oven ought to be beside the point in this tragic story.

"It was not an AGA, but you know what? If you want to write your own narrative, go ahead.

"The real point is that Seema spent days looking at new ovens. She kept pressing them on me, oven after oven after oven, and as you can imagine, I'm a busy man and—let's be honest, I couldn't really care less. Plus, who wants to spend that much money on a stove? But it does matter now that you have me going down this rabbit hole, because it was, in fact, an AGA that she wanted, but in the end, we had not yet replaced the old oven, and it leaked, and she very tragically died. This is the point that no one seems to understand . . ."

Never has Sophie been so happy to have her reading interrupted by a ringing phone.

Autumn T is on the line, calling to say that Mohammed is in the store and that he's looking for her.

"Mohammed? Who is Mohammed?"

"Hang on," Autumn T says. Now Sophie hears only muffled swirling sounds for a couple of long minutes while the information is procured. It's a losing battle, getting any of her employees to put a caller on hold rather than cover the receiver with their hand. Teaching them to use an old-school phone system that involves transferring calls and juggling customers on multiple lines is harder, she suspects, than teaching a nonagenarian—okay, to be fair, even teaching someone her own age—how to download an app.

"Mohammed says his uncle sent him? Ibrahim Ahmad? The architect?"

Good grief! She thought she'd communicated to Ibrahim that this was a delicate situation, and that ideally he would come alone, before or after business hours. Instead he's sent this stranger—okay, his *nephew*, but a stranger to *her*—who has popped in without notice, as if she's the sort of independent bookstore owner who is available on demand, who doesn't have a calendar chock-full of important meetings and lunch dates with other small business owners and civic leaders around town. Or who might be very busy sitting at the kitchen table in her bathrobe, catching up on the news.

"He says there's an electrical socket somewhere that isn't working. Something about a private nook? Honestly I have no idea what he's talking about."

"I'm on my way in," she tells Autumn. "Just get Mohammed a coffee and show him into my office, then give him a book or something to keep him occupied since it's going to take me about thirty minutes. It's better if I show him the job myself."

"Okay, will do. Also there's some guy named Ed here looking for you."

"Ed?"

"He has something to do with something. Maybe the parking lot?"

"Oh, *that* Ed. Boy, do I have a thing or two to say to that horrible man right now! It's better for everyone involved if you can just get him to go away. Tell him I won't be in today and that I'll give him a call."

"Will do."

"But just to be clear, I will be in. For Mohammed. Just not for Ed. I'm going to pop in briefly to get something and then I have an errand to run, but then I'll be back again."

"Whatever!" says Autumn. "Just take your time. It's all good!"

It is not all good, really. But she will get herself dressed and persevere.

Sophie had been planning to call the car dealer to order another expensive key. She has already scoured the house for the spare, but she will take one more look before leaving for the store. She rifles through the junk drawer—again. Then the other junk drawer—again. There's Scotch tape; bottle openers; some matches; many, many pens (one of them gooey with leaking black ink); an old flip phone; Solomon's business cards; a bunch of loose AAA batteries.

For the second time today, she sorts through all of the old keys; she seems to have a spare to every car she's ever owned. Forget about the memoir in vacuum cleaners—she ought to write a memoir in keys! She finds one to the old Corolla hanging from Michael's Washington Wizards keychain. He had failed to appreciate the trusty old blue stick-shift wagon, and she'd endured much grumbling about how no one drives manual cars anymore and how his best friend had gotten a brand-new red Mercedes SL convertible for *his* sixteenth birthday.

Sophie had been spectacularly unmoved. She had privately rebelled against the affluence around them while at the same time understanding and enjoying the benefits of privilege, albeit in her possibly smug, less showy way. She and Solomon were comfortable, but his rainmaker days were over and his workflow had begun to slow. And running a bookstore was a labor of love: some months the store turned a profit, but even then just barely, and in many other months they were in the red. Still, they were never hungry, and the mortgage and utilities got paid. The final semesters of Michael's tuition had presented a challenge, and they had taken out a home equity loan, but such was the price of admission to a private liberal arts school.

Despite these sorts of luxuries, she was luxury averse. Solomon had once surprised her with a diamond necklace for their anniversary—a single stone hanging on a silver chain. It was lovely, but nevertheless, she had refused to wear it at first. She wanted to know its provenance, to be sure it wasn't a blood diamond. This led to one of their rare fights. Solomon had told her to lighten up. "It's a gift, Sophie! Just enjoy it. You sound like a Bolshevik!" That had stung. She wasn't entirely sure what sounding like a Bolshevik implied when it came to jewelry, but his remark made her self-conscious about her personal presentation, and after that she began to pay closer attention to her wardrobe.

She had never been one for fancy cars, designer clothing, or high-end kitchen appliances. She just wanted a cozy neighborhood in which to raise her son, reliable cars to drive, schools with committed teachers, a strong sense of community, friendly neighbors, and a little plot of land on which to garden—not that she had ever grown a vegetable in her life, or likely ever would. But she liked the idea. A community also needed a bookstore, and she was proud to have helped plug that hole.

There, on a purple lanyard, is the key to an earlier model Corolla, the one she drove around the time Michael was born. The black hatchback had seemed so sporty in its day and was still going strong with more than 120,000 miles when it was finally, somewhat mercifully, stolen right off a busy street while she'd been at the movies. Had it not been stolen, Sophie might still be driving it today because a car is a car is a car, and who needs a new one when the old one is still running okay?

Some of Solomon's old car keys are in the drawer as well. Also a bunch of keys to places she does not immediately recognize, plus tiny keys to tiny padlocks and gates and storage lockers long gone. But it seems that nowhere in this house is a spare key to her current Subaru Outback, which is currently being held hostage, expensively, in an impoundment lot.

She has heard about visualization exercises, where one meditates on something and thereby wills it into existence—or something like this, which sounds like hocus-pocus to her. And yet, at this point, it's worth a try. She tries to picture the key and is reminded that it is not an actual key but one of those keyless contraptions needed to start the ignition but that does not need to be inserted into anything. She thinks about this for a minute. This means the car will still start even if the key is in her pocket. Or in her purse. *Or in her vacuum cleaner.*

Why has this not occurred to her earlier? This ordeal has cost her another day of impoundment lot fees, and another night of sleep. At least now she has a plan. She will go into the store and speak with Mohammed. Then she will get the vacuum cleaner, hail a taxi, and head back to the impoundment lot.

The thing is, it's raining again, pouring, and she doesn't have her car. And she doesn't have the Uber app. And she is too proud to call someone for a ride. She stares at the umbrella in her hallway and thinks about her rainboots for a moment, but they are upstairs, and she is feeling lazy, so she puts on another pair of recycled flats.

The rain is of the insidious slashing sideways sort, and Sophie is getting wet despite her anorak and umbrella. She might as well enjoy the weather in all of its various forms, however, because when she goes into hiding—*if* she goes into hiding—she'll miss all this: the rain, the snow, the sunshine, the fresh and not-so-fresh air, the chirping birds, the man leaning out the car window and screaming at the driver who just ran a yellow light and nearly hit a kid on a tricycle.

Besides, the walk helps her *decompress*—a word she has admittedly mocked, but can now see some possible use for at this particularly fraught juncture when she is especially tightly wound. She used to walk around here all the time right after Michael was born, which was shortly after they bought the house. It was another time in her life when she'd been full of conflict—possibly the last time, come to think of it, that she'd felt this torn. She'd been on maternity leave from her editing job at the National Institute of Standards and Technology, and when it was time to go back to work, she found herself nearly paralyzed; she didn't want to leave Michael. She extended her leave, using up all of her vacation time. One day, while pushing the baby carriage past the neighborhood bank, she noticed it had closed and the property was for sale. It wasn't completely out of the blue, this idea to open a bookstore; it was a fantasy that had been germinating for a while. For a lifetime really, as she'd been a book omnivore since she'd learned to read. What about buying the bank? Or maybe half the bank, since it was enormous, and opening a bookstore?

It wasn't quite as simple as that, but it turned out to be easier than expected. There had been loans and lawyers and a steep learning curve as she'd absorbed the intricacies of the trade, which turned out to be much more complex than she'd ever imagined, but she'd thrown herself into it, visiting other bookstores and learning about inventory and point-of-sale systems, and getting to know publishers, sorting out the imprints in an ever-changing and conglomerating business, facing down the threat posed by the internet and other big-box, deep-discounting stores—and that was not the half of it! It had not previously occurred to her, as obvious as it should have been, that she would spend as much time managing her staff as she would selling books—the combination of which led to fourteen-hour days with Michael camped out in a portable crib as she got her business off the ground.

The bookstore seemed blessed from the start. She was able to muddle through largely on her own the first year with part-time help, but as the business grew, she needed a manager. Jamal had been among the first to respond to the ad, and she'd hired him on the spot. He'd been young—only in his late twenties—but he had previous experience at a local chain called Olsson's, and he knew far more than she did about how the business worked. The margins in books are punishingly tight, but she has managed, against all odds, to keep the lights turned on.

As she approaches the store, the rain lightens and she folds up her umbrella. Her feet are soaked and she can feel the water sloshing around inside her shoes. She's two blocks away and can see, in the near distance, a crowd of wet people, a few in costume, holding signs. What is happening here? It appears to be some sort of protest. Is this about the Chaucer event? But why the costumes? They are dressed like birds. Has she done something wrong? Is the Humane Society, or ASPCA, or PETA, or all three, having some event at the store? Or maybe it has nothing to do with her. Perhaps Verb is in trouble this time.

As she moves closer she can see that some of these people are wearing what look like *cat* costumes. Some have whiskers drawn on their faces; others are wearing hats with pointy ears. One man has a long, striped tail. They are standing in a separate cluster from the birds, some more elaborate than others. While a few look like their getups have been provided by Broadway costume designers, others are more homespun. One guy has glued a few feathers to his jacket, and they are soggy and falling off. A few others are wearing strap-on beaks.

"Cats are murderers," reads one banner, held, unsurprisingly, by a bird.

"Cats kill more than four billion birds and twenty-two billion small mammals nationwide," reads a piece of literature that someone has just stuck in Sophie's hand.

What is happening here and who are these people and what exactly is the problem?

The cat people are holding signs that say "Protect our cats!" and "We come in peace!" One woman is holding a sign that says "The musical has no plot!" Sophie isn't sure if this last one is a joke, or if this person has shown up at the wrong rally. She vaguely remembers protests when the Kennedy Center planned to bring *Cats* to Washington; people had complained about the terrible music and the humiliating costumes.

She loves birds. And she also loves cats. But why are they here, at the bookstore?

She picks up on some sort of conflict between these two

camps, the bird and the cat advocates. The watered-down version, as she understands it, is that bird people want house cats to wear bells or be kept indoors, whereas the cat people want to protect feline rights and bring attention to the fact that there has even been a spate of local cat poisoning. She doesn't know what to think about any of this, apart from her feeling that you can't control everything in this world. Sometimes, tragic as it may be, a cat may kill a bird. And a bird may kill a worm. And a worm . . . She doesn't know enough about worms to continue with this line of thought. She has enough on her plate; she can't worry about every little thing, can't engage in this particular hissing match, even if she should.

More cats with signs approach from across the street: "Leash laws kill cats." "Free the cats." "Homeless cats at special risk." In the middle of the crowd, and quite possibly lost or seriously confused, a guy dressed as a clown is staring right at her, giving her such a chill that for a moment she considers abandoning her car, her nook, her store; running away on her wet aching feet; and finding a bus headed to Canada.

What is it with these people? she wonders. She is an animal lover—she really is! But how can they get so worked up about birds and cats when our civil liberties are being eroded and our neighbors are being deported and North Korea has the bomb and is making plans to use it?

Whatever is going on here, she can see the potential for this to escalate, to turn into a maelstrom of soggy feathers and claws.

Now she's one block away and so distracted that she

forgets to check for traffic before crossing the street. She lets out an involuntary yelp as a bus rushes past with only about a foot to spare between her and the speeding projectile, a brush so close that her rain jacket billows in the near disaster's wake. She stops, shaken. In what had been a grim running joke with Solomon, being hit by a bus was how they presumed they were both meant to go: not via nuclear war, or global warming, or cancer, or strokes, or heart attacks, or even Nazis. They used to part each day with the tongue-in-cheek admonition to have a good day and not get hit by a bus.

One catastrophe, one possible sign from God, averted, she dashes in front of the protesters and keeps walking, approaching the strip of sidewalk that fronts the orthodontist's office, the bookstore, and Verb, where she sees a person in green body paint with a gigantic papier-mâché head who looks like a Quaker parrot. Sophie is jolted by this sight, overcome by such a wave of nostalgia that she can barely look at the fake bird. When Michael was growing up, they'd had three Quaker parrots, one after the other. The first one flew away, the second one injured his foot and died a premature death, and the third one lived for nearly twelve years. She had become fiercely attached to each one. They used to sit on Sophie's shoulder and give her a peck on the cheek and say, "I love you, Mrs. Bernstein!" Then she'd say, "I love you too!" and also, "Please call me Sophie!"

How she'd adored them! She hadn't wanted a parrot at the outset, but a friend had asked Sophie to watch her bird while she traveled to a funeral, and Sophie had fallen in love. In her mind's eye, she can still see the cage in the corner of the kitchen staring out onto a mini forest of trees back before the land was parceled and more development ensued. There'd been a backlash about that, although nothing like what is going on right here and now. Things were more civilized then, or at least she likes to imagine they were. In all likelihood people were just as divided about every little thing.

"Hey, Mrs. Bernstein, we're right over here!"

She hears the voice calling to her, but she's still back in that kitchen with her birds. She can see Solomon sitting at the table, reading the Sports section, and she doesn't want to leave. She used to bring him coffee and scramble his eggs—was that so wrong? It's not as though she'd been a docile housewife with no opinions! Lord have mercy on Solomon when she didn't agree with him on something. She was a small business owner—she still is!—so why does she think she needs to be defensive about the fact that she also took very good care of her husband, who if left to his own devices probably would have just sat in that chair and starved?

"Mrs. Bernstein, are you okay?"

Yes, she is fine, she is perfectly okay. But she is not quite ready to face the moment, to leave behind this memory of Solomon, even with its imperfections. She can see Michael under the kitchen table, playing with his Legos. Scattered around him on the floor are the colorful pebbly seeds that the birds used to eat. Sloppy eaters, they used to peck at their food, sending bits flying from the cage, which is why the old Electrolux vacuum was kept upstairs, even though they had a new, better vacuum that did the heavy lifting, which they kept in the basement. Now she can see that she will need to add another chapter to the memoir and is wondering whether it's better to write a memoir in vacuum cleaners, birds, keys, or junk drawers, and now someone is shouting at her.

"Mrs. Bernstein! Are you okay?"

The Summer person is running toward her, dodging the mob of soggy birds.

"Why are some days just so crazy?!" she asks.

"I don't know," Sophie says. "Do you know who these people are?"

"I only know one of them. I see my mom's friend, but I'm trying to avoid her if you know what I mean. It's just so awkward, right?"

"It is awkward. Very awkward. Where did they come from?"

"The internet, probably."

"And why are they in costume?"

"Again, an internet thing, we think. There's a minor-league baseball game in Bowie with some bird-themed teams and cat-themed teams, and it was dress-up day."

"But why are they here? At the store?"

"Oh, the newspaper got it wrong."

Sophie feels as if she is in a foreign country with a bad translator.

"What newspaper got what wrong?"

"I'm not entirely sure. Maybe they got the dates for tomorrow's event wrong so people think it's today? Or who knows, maybe Clemi gave them the wrong date? Maybe *we* got the date wrong? Or maybe the author got the date wrong? And they were supposed to dress up for the baseball game, but not for this event. But someone tweeted something and someone got something wrong. Whatever the reason, they are here but the author is not."

"Do you mean the poet?"

"No! I mean the *Kuddly Killers* author."

"Seriously? How did I not know this was happening?" Sophie realizes she has asked the wrong question. Obviously this was happening. She just hadn't been paying attention.

"I thought people were upset about the Chaucer event."

"They are!" says Summer. "And the amazing thing is that there's some overlap. Some of the people in favor of controlling the cat situation are also haters of Raymond Chaucer. And ditto for some of the pro-cat, anti-bird people. It's a crazy coincidence! From what I can tell on Twitter, a lot of these people are planning to camp out here until tomorrow."

Sophie is speechless. Why hasn't Clemi alerted her to this possibility? She wonders again if Clemi has seen the *Washington Post* interview with the poet and plans to find her ASAP to see if they can cancel his event.

She takes a few deep breaths and tries to calm herself down. This is not the worst thing that has ever happened at the store, is it? Isn't this part of what attracted her to the business to begin with? That even in an age of purportedly short attention spans and the many proclamations about the end of reading and the end of books, people can rally around words and ideas, even if they are about cats and birds?

Sophie takes another look and sees that several of the cat people have on those pink pussy hats worn for the Women's March on the Mall a few months earlier. At least they are repurposing. She has a pink pussy hat too—not that she ever wore it. Emma, one of the booksellers, knit it herself and handed them out to all the female employees at the store. She had tried to coax Sophie out to the Women's March, and while she fully supported the cause, it was all she could do not to ask Emma if she was out of her mind. Sophie's marching days are over. Is that not obvious? She is afraid of crowds, terrified of hordes, obsessed with descending darkness.

They have found her regardless; the hordes have come *to her*, disguised as cats and birds who have emerged from the internet on the wrong day and are determined to stay.

She has had enough of this nuttiness. She needs to go inside and find Ibrahim. No, not Ibrahim. His nephew, Mohammed. Because what she really needs to do—and now it is crystal clear!—is plug a teakettle into a functioning electrical socket, close the door, and spend the rest of her life in a quiet cubby, reading books.

So many people are flanking—or rather flocking—to the door that it's hard to move. She's unsure if she will even be able to make her way to her office once she squeezes inside the store. Fortunately, Yash and Jamal and the Darkness guy from the receiving room—whose 9:30 Club invitation she still needs to respond to—are somewhat successfully corralling people into two neat lines that snake around the block in both directions. Jamal opens the door and helps clear a path. Summer is still attached to her, which is completely unnecessary—she's hardly infirm!— yet she supposes it's possible that she's the one clinging tight to the young woman's arm.

Sophie starts down the Biography and Memoir aisle, which reminds her of Fatima, a bookseller from the late 1990s whom she had especially liked despite her insistence they separate out these two sections, resulting in many a vociferous debate. Although not as vociferous as the debate about whether to add a children's department, which they still do not have. Sophie can't say why, exactly, she is opposed, other than that they are out of space as it is and already struggling to keep a healthy supply of backlist *and* frontlist titles in stock. Also, if they were going to expand to have a children's section, she would want to do it well, and that would involve hiring booksellers with the right expertise.

For the record, Sophie had been pro consolidation of the Memoir and Biography sections. She remembers the meeting during which she had gone on a mild rant, if that's an acceptable oxymoron, about how once you go down the slippery slope of separating out sections, the possibilities become endless: instead of just Health you might have Women's Health, she'd said. Instead of Religion you might have Judaism, Christianity, and even Witches. It was humiliating to have one of the booksellers explain that they already *did* have separate sections on Women's Health, Judaism, Christianity, and Witches.

For the record, Sophie let Fatima have her way: they had separated out these two sections because, in fact, she was that kind of a boss, the sort who listened to her employees, respected their opinions, and often gave in even when she disagreed. She was definitely not a control freak, or at least she hadn't been back in the day—although maybe she had been just a little bit.

At the end of the aisle, she spots Clemi. She's about to pull her aside to ask her about canceling Raymond Chaucer again, as well as give her a piece of her mind about the chaos. What was she thinking, booking not one but two controversial events in one weekend, summoning the internet hordes? But then she sees Mohammed through the glass pane that fronts her office in the very back of the store. He sees her, too, and is now out of the chair and moving toward her.

He's disarmingly handsome, dressed too well to be about to muck around in her dusty nook. He appears to be in his early thirties. He holds a book in one hand, and with the other he reaches toward her to introduce himself.

"What are you reading?" she asks after shaking his hand. The question is her standard opening line, her icebreaker, her version of "How are you?" although conveniently in this case he does happen to be holding a book.

"Oh, good question. Someone handed this to me and told me to wait in your office. It's called . . ." He pauses to look at the title. "*Kaboom!* It's really beautiful poetry, but it's by that guy who killed his wife."

"Technically he didn't kill her," Sophie says. "In the interview that he gave this morning in the *Post*, he says the whole thing was an unfortunate accident. But still, whatever happened, it wasn't good. He's doing a reading here tomorrow."

"The poet is coming here? Are you kidding? I heard there was a bomb threat at a reading in London. And from what I can see, you've already got a bit of a situation," he says, waving vaguely toward the front of the store. "What's going on?"

"Yes, you know, democracy in action. It's a good thing! I'm not concerned," she bluffs. "We've hired security."

Now Summer is at the door.

"I'm in a meeting," Sophie barks.

"Sorry, Mrs. Bernstein, but this is kind of time-sensitive."

Summer steps inside, unbidden, and just stands there staring at Mohammed for a moment.

"Yes?" Sophie asks. "What's so time-sensitive?"

"Two things. First, I'm just wondering if you had a chance to take a look at that envelope from Zhang?"

She has not. But she is not sure what about this is time-sensitive.

Summer goes over to Sophie's desk and rifles through the pile of mail. "Here it is," she says, handing it to her again. Sophie flinches. She doesn't want to touch it. What if it's a subpoena or a summons or some other sort of legal threat? She can't handle this right now, whatever it is. She just stands there, frozen.

"Also, along those same lines, this just arrived. It looks important."

Summer hands her, or tries to hand her, a second envelope. The return address indicates that it's from the formidable law firm of Weiner, Weiner, Weiner & Ong. Sophie doesn't want to touch this one either.

"Here, I'm just going to set these on your desk, okay?" Summer says, stepping cautiously toward the back of the room and setting both envelopes on top of a pile of *Kaboom!*, which at this point is being stacked on every available surface, including the floor.

"Who do you know at Weiner?" Mohammed asks. "My cousin is a partner there!"

"Really? One of the Weiners?" Sophie doesn't know why

she asks this. It's not like she knows one of these particular Weiners from another.

"No, Mortimer Ong. He is married to my second cousin."

Perhaps this connection will be helpful. Or disqualifying. Not that she has any idea what dreadful possibility this envelope might contain. Now curious, she rips it open.

Weiner, Weiner, Weiner & Ong LLP
ATTORNEYS AT LAW
1600 L Street NW
5th Floor
Washington, DC 20036

Dear Mrs. Sophie Bernstein:

On behalf of my client, Ellen Matthews, I am writing about the incident that occurred in your bookstore on Tuesday, August 15, at approximately 5:37 p.m. when my client's minor child sustained an assault and battery by Petunia, a ten-pound brindle Shih Tzu. As is clear from the facts described below, the bookstore has breached its duty of care under the laws of the District of Columbia. Accordingly, it is civilly liable for the personal and economic injuries sustained by my client and her minor child (hereinafter referred to as "John Doe") as a factual and proximate cause of the Shih Tzu's reckless behavior.

On the day in question, my client had stopped in the bookstore with her minor child on the way to a birthday party to pick up a copy of a children's book. (To no avail, as your bookstore does not, apparently, cater to children.) As my client proceeded to leave the premises,

John Doe was sitting quietly in his stroller eating a bagel when a brown-and-white ten-pound Shih Tzu suddenly and menacingly approached the stroller and proceeded to take the bagel out of his hand with its bare teeth. In addition to rendering the $7.99 bagel inedible, this traumatic incident caused John to immediately burst into uncontrollable sobs and inflicted distress that has resulted in the emotional, pecuniary, and physical damages described in further detail below.

To address the negligent infliction of emotional distress John Doe sustained from the incident, he had an initial consultation with a therapist who believes he will need weekly sessions until the age of eighteen to work through his trauma and overcome his newfound phobia of dogs of all sizes. Because these sessions are not covered by my client's insurance, they will cost her an estimated $150,000 ($150 per session per week until John Doe reaches the age of majority at eighteen).

In addition, because the minor child is now afraid of dogs, he is unable to go to his grandparents' house for twice-a-week babysitting. Hence we are calculating an additional $156,000 in childcare. There is also the cost of the replacement bagel, the parking ticket my client received while returning to the store to replace the bagel in an effort to console the inconsolable John Doe, and the cleaning cost of the rug she threw up on when she (my client) got home because of her distress. These amount to additional damages totaling $3,243.14.

As you can see from the foregoing—as well as from the attached police report—my client has a strong claim.

If you are unwilling to compensate, we will be bringing an action in DC Superior Court, at which point we will also be seeking punitive damages in the amount of $1 million to ensure no one else suffers from the bookstore's wanton and reckless disregard for its duty of care to its customers.

Please advise at your earliest convenience.

Sincerely,

Mitzy Weiner, Esq.

P.S. My colleague has just written a comic novel called *Pro Se*. It's hilarious! Can you tell me who to contact at the store so she can schedule a reading? Thx!

"Mrs. Bernstein, are you okay?" Mohammed asks.

"It's not from your cousin," is all she can think to say.

"I'm not surprised. I think they are in Hawaii right now."

Summer is still standing at the door.

"Is there anything else?" Sophie asks.

"Yes. Just one more thing. Noah asked me to tell you that one of the bird people just slashed open a pillow— don't ask me why . . . I think they were trying to make a point about a bird holocaust or something—and there are tiny feathers all over the place, so basically we were just wondering if you ever got the vacuum fixed."

Sophie's eyes drift over to the spot where Querk III stands, his wounds still raw. But she's not thinking about the battered vacuum; she's thinking about . . . She has so much to think about that she's completely overwhelmed, but for some reason her brain sticks on the absurd question *How can a bagel cost $7.99?*

"Sorry, I've been distracted, but I'll take care of it today, right after this meeting. I'm going to take it in to be repaired, but in the meantime I'll bring in my vacuum from home. It's not as industrial as this one, but it ought to help."

"It's okay. I mean, you don't need to deal with it. Noah says he'll take it to the shop. Probably it's done for, but he can try, and if they can't fix it he can pick up another. So basically . . . a related question: He asked me to see if you have the keys to the store van. Also, where *is* the store van?"

Oh boy, where *is* the store van? When Michael dropped her off at home on Wednesday, he said he'd return the van to the store. She will have to give him a call to see where he parked it and what he did with the key.

"I'm not sure. But I'll deal with it in a bit. As for the feathers, I don't know what to suggest about them . . . Maybe just sweep them into the corner or pick them up?"

"Do you want me to look at the vacuum?" offers Mohammed. "I mean, vacuums aren't my specialty, but I'm pretty good with electrical devices generally."

"Could you?" Summer asks.

This is not the worst idea, but she doesn't want to have to explain to anyone how her keys came to be inside Querk III. She is aware that she is making too much of this situation, that people do stupid things all the time, that accidentally vacuuming up her keys is not a sign that she is completely losing her grip, except that right now, perhaps she really is.

"I have an idea . . . I need to take the vacuum somewhere in a few minutes, but when I return, maybe you can look at it then, Mohammed? Or Noah can then take it to the shop?"

She knows this makes no sense. Where in the world

would she possibly need to take a broken vacuum cleaner? Out to lunch? Best to change the subject.

"Right now we have more important things to do," she tells Mohammed. Which is true. She feels a genuine urgency now that she is about to be sued. She looks at her desk and realizes she hasn't opened the *other* envelope yet. Is this a bad reality show? What sort of nightmare might that second one contain?

"Let me show you where the outlet is," she says to Mohammed. "But I should warn you, it's in an awkward spot." She's still trying to figure out how to get him into the nook without drawing attention to the fact of its existence. She also remembers that she needs to ask him to look at the electric switch for the door, the one on the inside of the nook. The good news is that the store is in the midst of such complete and utter chaos that maybe no one will notice them removing the row of Graham Greenes and sliding open the shelf just long enough to squeeze inside.

"No worries. I've been in many awkward spots. You should see some of the bizarre ways people wire their houses. It's as though they think they will never need to access their breakers again. I've had to cut through drywall on a number of occasions. Hopefully this won't be quite so bad.

"Before we go, though, I want to pick your brain about something," Mohammed says. "I hope this isn't completely inappropriate, but I'm writing a book and I have some questions about publishing."

"You're a *writer*?" asks Summer.

Another writer? Seriously? Sophie can't take much more

of this. She's not sure which is worse: Summer's fawning over this handsome young man, or the fact that he, too, is writing a book. Never mind this Mitzy Weiner person's completely tone-deaf ask.

Sophie learned this morning that even the organizer of the rally in Charlottesville has written a novel—about a homeless dwarf. Next thing she knows, he will be asking for an event too.

"What's it about?" Summer asks.

"It's a novel, and I confess it's somewhat autobiographical. It's based on my family's story. You know, my uncle, my father's brother, is a tunnel builder in Gaza, and his son—my cousin—is still in an Israeli prison, and it's a generational saga about the cycles of history, about each generation being unable to break free of the past. It's a story of how the personal and the political are inextricably intertwined, with the tunnel as a metaphor and . . ."

Oh boy. His cousin is in an Israeli prison. This is terrible. Sophie would like to pause to explain that even though her last name is Bernstein, she hasn't liked an Israeli leader since Yitzhak Rabin and that the entire Middle East situation is a catastrophe and feeds directly into one of the many reasons she needs Mohammed to electrify her nook.

Instead she says, "I'm sorry to hear about your cousin, Mohammed. But the book sounds amazing. Full of potential. We'll be happy to carry the book once you write it, but for now let me show you the work that needs to be done. We need to be discreet, though . . ."

"Happy to, Mrs. Bernstein. Maybe after you read it, you can give me some guidance."

"Absolutely. I'm not an editor, but happy to try to help."

"I've got it from here," Sophie says to Summer. "It looks like Autumn needs some help back at the information desk." She does not want Summer to follow them to the nook.

They push through the crowds, and as they make their way into the Fiction room, one of the birds approaches Sophie from behind and startles her with a peck on the cheek.

"Sophie! My goodness, it's been so long! How are you? How is Michael? I saw Juliana last week, can you believe it? She said Violet finished medical school already and is a resident at Hopkins doing a cardiology rotation. And Howard is married with three kids."

Sophie stares at this woman who, to be honest, does not look even remotely familiar—although that may have something to do with her bright red plumage—and she doesn't have a clue what to say, so she blurts out a question about whether she is a cardinal.

"No! I'm a summer tanager."

"Oh!" Sophie says. She has absolutely no idea what to say next. She doesn't know who this woman is, who Juliana or Violet or Howard are, and she has never heard of a summer tanager. And frankly, right now, she lacks the capacity to care. She knows this is terrible, because part of what attracted her to owning a bookstore in the first place was fostering a sense of community. Getting to know her customers. Seeing old friends and acquaintances browsing the stacks and stopping to chat.

"Also, you won't believe who I saw at the protest last week . . ."

Sophie knows this is a cue of some sort. She's supposed to ask, "Who?" Or she's supposed to say, "Which protest?" but she feels besieged. Mohammed stands beside her patiently, presumably on some very expensive electrician clock.

After an awkward silence, the summer tanager answers her own question. "Marjorie! I mean, it's not like I don't see Marjorie all the time—we're in a book group together—it was just a surprise.

"You know, Sophie, you should come to our book group! You'd be more than welcome. It's at my house in two weeks. You'd be so great. You could recommend books, maybe you could even give us a discount . . ."

Sophie's head begins to throb. She knows this is terrible, that something is wrong with her, that she's on a steep downward slope, but she truly can't stand listening to this woman prattle on so cheerfully.

What has happened to her, to Sophie Bernstein? She used to have *friends*. Has she lost her humanity? Has she traded in her friends for a life in books?

That may not be the worst thing in the world. She sometimes thinks the world divides into two types of people, those who think books are for reading when there's nothing else to do, and those who avoid other things to do in order to read books—and unsurprisingly she's in the latter camp, but really, is that so awful? And yet this chatty, friendly, name-dropping woman is not the enemy; she's merely inviting Sophie to join her book group! She ought to at least inquire about the nature of their meetings and about their reading habits. Do they look for lightweight escapist novels, or are they looking for books with some intellectual thrust? Do they attempt to excavate previously unseen relevance in time-honored dystopias? Or do they read serious nonfiction about the world coming to an end? Maybe they just want to redecorate, destress, or declutter.

"What are you currently reading?" Sophie asks.

"Our next book is about a girl wearing blue . . . or something like that. By Raina-something-Irish. I just tried to buy it but you are sold out. Is she coming to speak at the store? We read a big profile about her in the *New Yorker*. They're saying she's like Lauren Groff meets Haruki Murakami meets Judi Picoults."

"Picoult."

"Pardon?"

"Judi. Picoult. Singular."

"It's Jodi," says Mohammed.

"That's what I said," Sophie says, taking Mohammed by the arm and pulling him toward the shelf with the Graham Greenes. She's got to get out of here. Truly she has had enough of this business, of these people, of this store.

Sophie stands on the corner, one hand waving frantically in the air, attempting to hail a cab, the other hand gripping the neck of the overpriced, underperforming, oversize, godforsaken, key-swallowing monstrosity of a vacuum cleaner. She feels a trickle of rain, looks up, and sees storm clouds gathering, then hears a rumble of thunder in the distance. She hasn't even finished drying off from this morning's downpour. How much more rain could this one sky possibly contain?

She's been standing at this busy intersection through six cycles of the light and has yet to see a single taxi. She considered calling Michael to ask for another ride in the store van—the van she presumes he still has—but she doesn't want to listen to him complain about the drive, nor does she wish to revisit the subject of what a dingbat she's become. On the other hand, she might possibly use the time to try to begin a more productive conversation. About what, she's not entirely sure, but she knows what it would *not* be about: jobs, yoga, money, online dating sites, or anything to do with the bookstore.

Truly she needs to download one of those ride-hail apps. She tried recently but had trouble recovering her Apple ID. The problem is that she believes her account is linked to Solomon's and he's—well, he's dead. She knows there's a way around this and that Michael could probably help figure it out, but she'd rather walk the twenty-five miles to the impoundment lot in her soggy shoes than ask this particular favor of him.

A man holding an umbrella and sporting a gray beard walks toward and then past her. He looks preoccupied. She entertains the fleeting and embarrassingly retro thought that some preoccupied-seeming gray-bearded man will come along one day and save her. Save her from what? She's a semicompetent woman in her midfifties and the owner of a successful small business, not some damsel in distress. She amends the thought to make it more progressive. Instead he will just be there for her, will have her back in moments like these, will smash the vacuum to smithereens, give her a ride to the impoundment lot, and then simply be her friend.

Now that she thinks about it, the preoccupied man is vaguely familiar. He must recognize her, too, because he doubles back and stares at her. Who is he and how does she know him? She thinks hard on this for a minute, running through a mental list of the preoccupied gray-bearded men she knows, and then decides it must be a customer. That's the problem with owning a bookstore in a relatively small community. Pretty much everyone you run into is a customer, and the customer is never wrong, which means that you are never right, and also that you'd better be careful. No giving the finger to drivers who cut you off or fail to give you the right of way, and no speaking your mind when someone unloads a cart with fifty-seven items onto the conveyor belt in the supermarket express lane.

Oh! Wait! She realizes it's Bradley Graham, owner of Politics and Prose, another beloved local independent bookstore.

"Sophie?"

"Brad?"

"Ed."

"Ed?"

"Ed Altman," he says, extending his hand for a shake.

Ed Altman? She knows this name but is having a mental block.

"I've been trying to get in touch. I bought the parking lot behind your store last year."

"Oh, Ed! Sure!" Ed Altman, the evil czar of the parking

lot. She is shaking his hand but really wants to strangle this Ed Altman now that she has physical proximity. She'd probably get a light sentence—any reasonable jury of her peers who has ever had a car towed would understand her rage. Were it not for Ed Altman, she would not be standing on this corner, trying in vain to hail a cab. "What are you doing here? I thought you lived in Pittsburgh."

"I do, but I wanted to check in on my empire."

"Your empire?"

"That's a joke, Sophie. I'm thinking of repaving the lot, so I'm just down here talking to some contractors. Also my nephew lives here. My nephew's girlfriend works at your store. Small world. A shtetl, really! But it's serendipitous running into you because, as you probably know, I really have been trying to reach you. I don't know if you got any of my messages. I have something I want to talk to you about. Maybe we could sit down over coffee. Are you free right now? Or maybe later today?"

She does not want to talk to this horrible man, this man who is regrettably not her gray-bearded savior but rather a greedy parking lot magnate who, now that she thinks about it, is probably in cahoots with that other horrible man at the impoundment lot.

"I'm not."

"You're not free at all today?"

"No."

"Okay. No problem. When might you be free? Tonight? Tomorrow? I'll be here for a couple more days, and I'm pretty flexible."

"No, sorry. I'm just busy."

"Okay, well, here's what I wanted to say: I'd like to talk to you about buying the store."

"My *store*?" She's not sure why she asks this, or why she is feigning such shock. She already suspects as much.

"Yes. I mean, I already have the parking lot, right? So why not buy the store as well?"

She stares at him, incredulous. Has this been his actual strategy all along? Something they teach you in MBA programs, perhaps: Buy the parking lot, erode the value of the business by aggressively towing customers, and then snap it up cheap? Okay, she is getting carried away here, making ridiculous assumptions. She's just angry that she's been towed.

"I'm joking, Sophie. I bought the lot because it was for sale. That's what I do. But I do, sincerely, want to discuss possibly buying the store."

Sophie hears a clap of thunder. The rain begins to fall and a car horn honks and a dog barks and a baby cries and maybe this is the universe speaking to her, telling her that maybe this man *is* her gray-bearded savior. He's going to solve her problems by taking this headache of a store off her hands, because maybe that really *is* what she wants. Or thinks she wants. Or wanted a few minutes ago. Maybe she can even work out an arrangement to have herself convey with the property, and she can live unobtrusively inside the nook.

"I've had my lawyer draw up an offer, and I'd like to sit down with you to go over the details, but I need to get back to the cheesecake folks by next week."

"The cheesecake folks?"

"Yes, well, it's not for certain, but we've got the Cheese-cake Factory interested in the spot. In addition to a couple other national chains."

"You are going to turn my bookstore into a Cheesecake Factory?"

"As I was saying, there are some other interested par-ties. Chipotle and sweetgreen among them, but that might mean subdividing the property, leasing to someone else upstairs . . . We've had some preliminary conversations with a group of psychotherapists too."

"I see a cab!" Sophie says. And she does. It's red and has a light on top that indicates it is available. She waves both hands manically, like her life depends on getting away from this man. The vehicle glides to a stop and she opens the door.

"Let me help you with that," Ed says, picking up the vacuum cleaner. "Do you want me to put this in the trunk?"

"No!" Sophie shrieks. "Put it next to me on the seat. Right here."

"Sure. If you insist. The thing is kind of stinky, but whatever."

She takes another long look at this man, puzzled on too many different levels to count. "Has anyone ever told you that you look just like—"

"Richard Dreyfuss? Yes, I get that all the time."

"Oh . . . that isn't what I was thinking, but I see what you mean."

Whomever this is, Richard Dreyfuss, Bradley Graham, Ed the parking lot czar . . . she wants to get away from him right now. She hears a snippet of something on the radio, waves goodbye, closes the taxi door, tells the driver where she is going, and then asks him to please turn up the volume.

And now for a quick news update:

At least four people have been arrested in connection with yesterday's terror attacks in Barcelona. The latest toll: thirteen dead, more than one hundred injured. The Islamic State is claiming responsibility. Early this morning in Cambrils, a town about seventy-five miles south of Barcelona, another vehicle attack killed one pedestrian. Police shot all five suspects. These attacks are believed to be related, as is an explosion yesterday in a house in Alcanar, another coastal town about three hours' drive south of Barcelona.

Belle and Sebastian, the popular Scottish indie rock band, reboarded their tour bus after a pit stop at Walmart in North Dakota, accidentally leaving behind their drummer, Richard Colburn. Wearing only his pajamas, with no phone or passport, Colburn eventually managed to get on a plane to Minnesota in time for their concert that evening. The band says they had become "blasé" about their protocol for getting on and off the tour bus and will now put more stringent measures in place.

Unusually mild weather today in our nation's capital, where we can expect a high of 91 degrees. It will be sunny for a while, and then it will be overcast for a while, and then it will rain. Then the sun will come out again. Then it will rain some more and the roof of an independent bookstore in DC will spring another leak and the birthday cards on the spinner rack near the back left window will become a costly, soggy mess.

Also, fun pro tip re: the total solar eclipse on Monday. (That's when the moon will completely cover the sun and you will be able

to see something called the corona *if you are in the path of totality,*
which will extend from Lincoln Beach, Oregon, to Charleston,
South Carolina. Those outside the path will still be able to see a
partial solar eclipse and you can do weird stuff like take a cheese
grater or a spaghetti colander and project the eclipse onto the
ground or a piece of paper.) Don't forget: do not look directly into
the sun! Bad things can happen, like your pupils will get large
and all the light will go in there and your retina will get burned
or something like that. We don't really know because we are a
poorly funded public radio station and we had to let our science
reporter go, but the thing to know is that you should buy solar
eclipse glasses, which you can receive free with a donation of only
$100 to WAMU, so just dial our toll-free number or visit us at
yourlocalpublicradiostation.com.

And now, everyone's favorite radio host, Boris Lewinsky.
Today's guest is award-winning poet Raymond Chaucer, here to
discuss his latest collection, Kaboom!

"Can you turn it up even louder?" Sophie asks, her body
tensing.

Boris Lewinsky: *Welcome, Raymond Chaucer! We are happy*
to have you here, and I've always wanted to ask you . . .
sorry, what's that? Ah . . . yes, apologies. That's KaBOOM!
Bold emphasis on the second syllable, exclamation point.
Mr. Chaucer, sir, we have limited time and much ground to
cover, so I'm going to launch right in. You had an unusual
apprenticeship as a poet, one might say. Your award-winning
first collection, Black Monday, *was inspired by your position*
at the time as a vice president at the investment firm—

Raymond Chaucer: *Sorry to interrupt, Boris, but I just wanted to go over the ground rules again. I need to confirm that we aren't going to be talking about the AGA. In the last interview I gave, the reporter ignored this, and it ended badly. So if you only want to talk about the AGA, I'm already done.*

BL: *The what?*

RC: *The AGA.*

BL: *I'm afraid I don't know what that is.*

RC: *The oven.*

BL: *The oven?*

RC: *You know, the one that Seema—*

BL: *Oh, right. Well, since you've broached the subject, let's just get that out of the way. Because of your wife's regrettable suicide, you are being compared to former British poet laureate Ted Hughes, which one might assume is both an honor and a curse. Ted Hughes is generally considered to be one of the twentieth century's greatest writers, but his brilliance is often overshadowed by the suicide of his wife, Sylvia Plath.*

RC: *Do you have anything to drink?*

BL: *We have water. Diet Coke. Regular Coke. Coffee.*

RC: *Surely there's something else here.*

BL: *Oh, sure, I think we have some LaCroix. A few flavors. Razz-cranberry is my personal favorite, but it's not always stocked. Have you ever sampled it?*

RC: *I'm thinking more like bourbon. Maybe someone has some in a drawer?*

BL: *Um, bourbon . . . Marylou? Can you see what you can find?*

RC: *I don't need anything fancy. Drawer-grade will do. Just put it on the rocks.*

This is horrific. Sophie wonders if she should ask the taxi driver to turn the volume down instead.

BL: *Got it. Meantime, let's get back to this AGA situation. Can you tell us more about this? I confess I've not heard of an AGA before.*

RC: *I've been assured we are not going to talk about the AGA.*

BL: *I'm not sure I understand. You brought it up. I don't even know what an AGA is.*

RC: *Also, it wasn't an AGA, Boris. So just forget it. And, heading off potential lines of questioning, I have no idea what Sylvia Plath used to set forth on a journey to a happier place, not that it matters much, does it? They had an apartment, I am reasonably sure—and what kind of nitwit would want to confront the challenge of installing an AGA in an apartment? I am told their weight is pegged to that of an adult African elephant. Male elephant. A bull, they might call them.*

BL: *Okay. Marylou is making hand signals . . . not sure what she is trying to say . . . Oh, I see, she is suggesting we switch right over to take some calls. What a great idea! On line one we have Leonard from Woodbridge, Virginia.*

Leonard from Woodbridge, Virginia: *Hi there, Boris. I'm a big fan of your show. I don't think I've missed a single one in the last seven years, since I retired from the fire department out in Des Moines and moved here to be with my late wife's sister. I have a question for Mr. Chaucer. What's an AGA?*

BL: *Thanks, Leonard. Glad to hear you enjoy the show! And that's an excellent question. Raymond, can you enlighten us?*

RC: *Thanks, sweetheart. Just a bit more ice. Do you have a straw?*

BL: *Raymond, can you respond to Leonard from Woodbridge, Virginia, please?*

RC: *I wish I could, but as we've established, I'm not going to talk about the AGA.*

BL: *Okay, moving right along, on line two we have Sally from Chevy Chase, Maryland. Hi, Sally, what's your question?*

Sally from Chevy Chase, Maryland: *Hi, Boris! I'm a big fan too. I don't have a question, but I was just looking it up online, on Wikipedia. The AGA was invented in 1922 by Nobel Prize–winning Swedish physicist Gustaf Dalén, who, interestingly, lost his sight in an explosion while developing his earlier invention, a porous substrate for storing gasses.*

BL: *Thank you, Sally. That's very enlightening.*

Sally from Chevy Chase, Maryland: *I'm not done.*

BL: *Thanks, Sally. We've got lots of callers on the line and we are apparently not going to talk about AGAs, so if there's time we'll get back to you. Now we have Paul from Cleveland Park, Washington DC.*

Paul from Cleveland Park, Washington DC: *Is it possible to get an AGA in the United States? Also, assuming the answer is yes, is it true, as that poet was just suggesting, that it can't go on the second floor? Is it too heavy for a 1970s townhouse?*

BL: *Hi, Paul, as I told our last caller—*

Paul from Cleveland Park, Washington DC: *I'm just wondering if—assuming I can get one in Washington—do I have to move the kitchen to the English basement? I mean, I can, I suppose. It's something I've been considering for a while, but it can be awkward when you're entertaining and have to keep going up and down the stairs. I guess the problem could be overcome by installing a minifridge in the living room, or even installing a dumbwaiter, but I don't want to take away from the aesthetic by—*

BL: *I'm afraid we are going to have to leave it right there, Paul, but thanks for the call. I am confident that your unwavering attention to detail will guide you out of this pickle. Excuse me a moment . . . Raymond? Are you okay?* [Muffled noises in the background.] *Um, let's go straight to Maurice from Vienna, Virginia.*

Maurice from Vienna, Virginia: *Hi, Boris! How are you today?*

BL: *I'm just great.* [Crashing sound. Many muffled voices speaking at once.] *Just really, really, really great.*

Maurice from Vienna, Virginia: *So, I wanted to tell you that after I met my wife, Estelle, right after the Battle of the Bulge, we were living in North London and had one of those AGAs you are talking about. It was an amazing contraption. You could dry your gloves on it.*

BL: *Thank you, Maurice. Does anyone out there have a question about poetry? Or want to discuss the latest collection,* Kaboom!, *by Raymond Chaucer, who is here with us live in our—*

Paul from Cleveland Park, Washington DC: *I have a question for Maurice. Well, two questions. First, since it was always on, did it keep the house warm? I guess what I'm really asking is whether you saved on the heating bill? Second question: Did you have any trouble getting it through the door? I guess I have three questions, now that I think of it. I just went to their website, and I liked AGA in their version of red, which they call "claret," but which looks more like burgundy to me, but never mind that last point—is it a shade that will clash with my fire-engine red Le Creuset pots, pans, and Dutch ovens in which I am so heavily invested? So . . . would it be safer for me to just get a simple classic Wolf stove with red knobs? Because those knobs are somehow both bright and muted at the same time, if you know what I mean—and a stainless-steel body on a stove is always in good taste. So maybe an AGA is just not in the cards for me. My grandmother used to call this "nisht bashert" in Yiddish. You know the expression, Boris?*

BL: *I'm not unfamiliar . . . Marylou? Please . . . How are these calls coming through? We seem to be having some sort of systems failure.* [The sound of something like a head hitting a table.]

Marylou: *You'd better call a medic or something.*

BL: *We are running out of time.* [Sound of sirens.] *We are now going to switch over to our lovely producer, Liz, who is going to tell you how you can get yourself a pair of free solar eclipse glasses.*

Unknown caller: *Hi! My name is Florence, and I live in Columbia Heights. I want to talk about the solar eclipse on Monday and remind everyone that this will be a time of total cosmic disarray. You might feel like you've been picked up without warning and dropped somewhere you don't recognize. But you should be patient and—*

BL: *Hi, Florence, I don't know how your call got through the switchboard, but thanks for those sage words of warning. We are here to talk about poetry today, and one more thing: it seems you don't actually have a question. But not to worry as we are going off air for a while.*

Florence from Columbia Heights, Washington DC: *Oh boy, do I have a question! My question is:* How is this okay?! *Why does a publicly funded radio station give a platform to an overrated, misogynist, wife-killing, so-called poet? This is even worse than the fact that he's appearing this weekend at*

a beloved local independent bookstore. Have you considered
all of the women writers you could be giving a platform to?
Women with no voices who—

BL: *Thank you, Florence. I'm going to have to cut you off here, but*
we appreciate your insight.

Florence: *Oh, perfect, Boris. Perfect. Cut me off just when I'm*
talking about women with no voices!

BL: *Marylou? Is there a plug here we can pull? What about this*
one here?

Florence: *I'm just saying, Raymond, I want you to hear my words*
directly: I'm coming for you. If you won't talk to me here,
Raymond, fine. I will see you at the bookstore, Raymond!

BL: *Wait, did you try pulling that cord over there? No . . . oh no, oh*
no . . . whoops . . . no, that was my computer. How about this
one here? It's connected to the—

END OF DAY REPORT: Friday, August 18
OPENING SHIFT: Vashti, Carmen, Jamal
SWING SHIFT: Summer, Yash, Noah
CLOSING SHIFT: Antonio, Luke, Sami
EVENT: Clemi
FLOOR MANAGER COMMENTS: Unfortunately, Keisha has realized that she needs to spend more time with family, so if anyone can pitch in fulfilling web orders, please let me know. We are still hopeful that Belinda will be back next week. Also thanks to everyone who has been working extra shifts without acknowledgment—it's been kind of bananas around here. Props to Jamal especially!

- As you already know, Clemi got the dates all wrong on the Bird and Cat event, so the throngs of the irate and aggrieved animal lovers showed up early. Whether this means they will return tomorrow is a known unknown. There are, alas, feathers all over the store, and the vacuum status is also unknown. Hopefully we'll get this resolved soon. Stay tuned.
- We have more Gauzy books on hand. Round of applause. You're welcome.
- Just a reminder that the new Bob Woodward book is embargoed. That means you can't sell it even though we have it downstairs. This is for real, people. We can get in trouble.
- We will have security on hand for the Chaucer event.
- A reminder that the *Doodles* guy will be here on Sunday.
- Does anyone know what happened to the store van?

And now, doodle joke of the day:

What do you call a doodle in the
midst of an existential crisis?
A Camusdoodle!

Not to be confused with a doodle that drinks out of toilets, a commodedoodle, which is different from a doodle that pulls hard to the left, known as a Commiedoodle, or his ideological cousin, the pinkodoodle.

Your friend in bad doodle jokes,

Autumn T

CHAPTER 10

Saturday

I'M LOOKING
FOR A BOOK

*C*lemi is in her office, trying to make a dent in her email.
She should be downstairs in the store, setting up for the
events, but she's stalling; if she can get through just a dozen or
so messages, she might be able to at least whittle the number
in her cache to 4,132 and still have forty-five minutes or so
to pull the Nisses and the Gundes out of the closet and set
them into neatish rows.

She begins at the top, although she could also begin at
the bottom; it doesn't matter hugely since all of these emails
have arrived in just the past five days.

The first one opens with "Dear sir" and is from the
author of a self-published book from 2009 called *Ivy on the
Inside*. The author of this thin volume would like to hold a

reading at the store to call attention to the plight of white Ivy League–educated men in federal prison, he explains.

Clearly this is a no-brainer, a triple *no*. The book was published more than ten years ago, they hold very few readings for self-published books, and the guy, who has called her "sir," sounds like a jerk. She doesn't need to explain any of this to him—all he needs is a polite *no*—yet after a childhood of plucking manuscripts from trash cans, she believes everyone deserves a personal response, even though this is both impossible and absurd. Which is part of why her inbox is always full.

The next message is from a guy who would like to present his book on a post-divorce, soul-searching solo climb in the Cascades gone wrong, which he describes as the next *Into Thin Air*. He has also, unbelievably, addressed his letter "Dear sir."

If it really is another *Into Thin Air*, she suspects she would have heard of it or read about it in one of the industry trades. But you never know. Give everyone the benefit of the doubt, except, perhaps, those who presume to call you "sir." When she attempts to look him up she realizes he has failed to provide the title of his book, and no fewer than 149,000 people share the author's name.

The next email is from someone who says she's a regular customer, suggesting that Clemi invite the guy who wrote the book about the Bernamacrocrocodoodle to come speak. She heard people talking about it at the dog park this morning and it sounds amazing!

And the email after that is from an author she hosted last week for her book of gluten-free dessert recipes, thanking

Clemi for "all the good work that she does." Clemi knows this is a nice gesture for which she should be grateful, but it's also the sort of vaguely patronizing sentiment—such as being told that her job is "cute"—that she hears a lot from authors and customers alike. It tends to rub her the wrong way.

Next up, she is being invited to a party. A party in New York! A party at a fancy restaurant in honor of Raina O'Malley to celebrate the publication of her book, *The Girl in Gauzy Blue*, featuring four varieties of craft cocktails, each one named for a character in the novel.

Unfortunately, or fortunately, Clemi's ringing phone forces her to abandon this exercise. At least now her inbox is down to 4,127 unread, except the computer has just dinged, announcing the arrival of twelve more.

It's Summer on the phone, calling from the information desk with a number of things to report. "OMG it's so totally bonkers over here," she says. "You're probably going to want to set up extra chairs."

"Sure, I'll be there in a second, but—"

"You totally won't believe how many people are out there. The ones from yesterday plus a bunch more. Some of them are really wet."

"Okay, I'll be there in a second, but—"

"Also, there are about forty people from PETA back here again."

"Oh boy. Okay, I'll be there in a second, but is there anyone around who can lend me a hand?"

"I'll ask, but you know, Belinda is still out and Yash is helping with web orders and we're kind of—"

"Short-staffed. Yeah, I know. If there's anything you can do, even just a little help . . ."

"Also . . . oh crap . . . hang on . . ." Clemi hears commotion in the background. She thinks she even hears Mrs. Bernstein, which is definitely not good. It's going to be a rough afternoon as it is, and she had been hoping to get through it without the added stress of trying to manage her increasingly mercurial boss.

"Summer? Hey, are you still there?"

There's no answer. She continues to wait and then finally Summer comes back on the line. "Sorry, talk about chaos. It's not just the cats and birds but also . . . you ought to know . . . Florence was just in here looking for you, and she seemed . . . not okay? Also, there are some Chaucer haters here already, even though that's not until tonight. I think since you got the date wrong for the bird thing everyone is just generally confused."

"I didn't get the date wrong! I don't know who did, but I think it might have been the author who tweeted it out incorrectly."

"Sure. Whatever. My point is that there is some cross-over in this Venn diagram of wet, angry people, so I'm guessing some of the pink pussy hats are also here for him? That's a thing, right?"

"What's a thing?"

"That women hate the poet."

"Some do, yeah."

"Well, they are saying something about . . . oh no, hang on a sec. I told Florence to leave but she just walked back in and seems pretty weird . . ."

"Okay, I'll be right over. I need to check on the number of presolds and see if they've all been put in the events closet, anyway." Clemi takes a deep breath and begins to log off her computer but then sees another email drop in. It's from Shelf Awareness, the bookstore blog that she subscribes to, and the lead item reads: "Raymond Chaucer's NPR Debacle Goes Viral as *Kaboom!* Heads into Third Print Run."

Okay, so Summer wasn't kidding. It's a busy store generally—sometimes when the opening shift arrives customers are already lined up outside—and a big-name author can draw big crowds. But in all her time working here, Clemi has never seen anything quite like this. She has only just set foot on the book floor when Jamal asks if she can pop behind the information desk and help a customer who has been waiting for a very long time.

"What the heck is going on here?" asks an elderly man in a rumpled suit who is either familiar or just has the look of someone familiar. Maybe he was once a congressman or, who knows, even a vice president back when Clemi was in diapers.

"Just a lot going on today." She scans the store for Florence while trying to help the customer. "What can I do for you?"

"I'm looking for a book," he says.

"Great! Anything in particular?"

"Do you have anything about wellness?"

"Sure, we have an entire section. Any particular aspect of wellness?"

"Yes, my granddaughter is into freezing herself or something, and her birthday is coming up. Is it called cryogenics? But I thought you do that when you are dead, and she's only seventeen."

"Cryotherapy, I think it's called. I'm not sure if we have a book about that precisely, but I can show you the Wellness section."

"Do you think that's safe? Isn't it better to be warm than cold? Whatever happened to steam baths and saunas?"

"Those are great questions. Let me show you the Wellness section." As she leads him toward the back right quadrant of the store, she keeps an eye out for Florence, who is nowhere in sight.

"Why are those people wearing hats? Is there another Women's March today?"

"No, it's just that—"

The customer's phone begins to ring so loudly that people turn and stare.

"Hang on, I've got to take this," he says. "I'll be right back."

Clemi heads back toward the information desk when another customer calls to her.

"Excuse me, can you help me?" It's a young woman with a baby strapped to her chest.

"Sure. Are you looking for a book?"

"No, I'm looking for the bathroom."

"Oh, it's right over there," she says, pointing toward the front of the store. "Just turn left when you get to the Fiction room."

"Clemi, can you answer the phone?" Summer yells to her.

"I can't find Florence," she yells back.

"I think she's gone now," Summer says. "I saw her go out the back door."

At least that's one less body in this nearly suffocating room, Clemi thinks. She has seen the store packed with crowds so large that they have had to shut the doors and turn people away. She has dealt with controversial events that have required the presence of police, but this is definitely the most extreme. The bird camp is assembled over by the World War II section, and they are rehearsing a protest squawk. On the opposite side, milling in front of the area where the event will take place, are the cats. And it's now pouring again and everyone is squeezing inside. Three phone lines ring. She answers line one and—what are the odds of this?—it's a call for her! It's a publicist asking if she wants to schedule an event for the host of a popular HGTV show called *Flip-o-rama* who has just written a book.

"Um . . . yes! No! Maybe! Send me an email," Clemi says. "It's not a good time to talk."

She picks up the ringing line two. "Hi! I'm looking for a book!"

Clemi sees Autumn T and hands her the receiver just as line one begins to ring again. She decides this would be a good time to slip away and check on the current number of presold books.

She has almost made it to the events closet when she is accosted by an elegant woman who explains she is in town from Brazil and is looking for a present for her eleven-year-old grandson.

"So sorry, we don't carry children's books," she says.

"Oh no, no, he's very advanced. He's already read the first volume of My Struggle. I'm wondering if you have the others?"

"Um, yes," Clemi says, pointing her toward the *K* books in the Fiction room. Normally she would get it herself, but in this case, she wonders if she ought to instead call social services and request that someone put a Harry Potter book in the poor child's hand.

They are good people, these customers! She loves them all, even the difficult ones! Have mercy on these poor souls who have wandered in to browse, who merely hope to quietly peruse their local independent bookstore and pick up a novel to read on this clammy August day, who are standing in line with their arms full of Gauzy books and *Kaboom!* and *Kuddly Killers*, prepared to pay full retail price.

As Clemi continues what is beginning to feel like an epic journey toward the events closet, she pauses to check the thermostat. It is hot and getting hotter. The air conditioner is set at full blast, but there are simply too many people in here for the system to keep the place cool.

Clemi is no bloodhound, but she smells him before she sees him. Several unpleasant odors are competing in the store right now: damp carpet, the wet customers, the clash of deodorants and perfumes, and even an overripe protester or two. But she's pretty sure that among all of this is also a note of tortoise. His time with Summer sure did not last very long.

She unlocks the events closet and there he is again, precisely where he is not supposed to be—on the shelf in the very back, nestled between the presold books for *Kaboom!* And oh boy, between these and the hundred-plus books in Mrs. Bernstein's office, there sure are a lot of presold books for *Kaboom!* People may hate Raymond Chaucer. It's plausible, even, that some of the especially angry women out there may actually want to kill him, but it appears that close to three hundred people have called the bookstore or placed orders online, hoping to get a copy signed by the famous poet. For Clemi, this means a couple of different things: One, she needs to get these books out of the closet and into the office with the others so that Raymond Chaucer can sign all of these tonight with his fine-point Sharpie pens, a box of which she pulls from a bin. Two, it means that despite all of the messages and warnings about being sure she has ordered enough books, and her confidence that she has done so, it is quite possible and even likely that they are going to run out of *Kaboom!*

She approaches the terrarium by squeezing through the narrow aisle between the tightly packed Nisses and Gundes. Kurt looks up at her and . . . does he seem to be imploring her to pick him up?

Pick me up!

He doesn't really say this because he is a tortoise and he can't talk.

Nor does he say:

Thank goodness I'm back here with you! That girl, Summer, is a total ding-dong, and I don't know what Noah is doing hanging around with her when he could be spending time with you. (By the way, girlfriend, you could do a lot better than that clueless, privileged dude.)

He doesn't say any of these things because, again, he is a tortoise. A poor, sad, smelly tortoise, and tortoises do not speak. But they do stare. And he is staring at her through the terrarium with what seems to be a longing of sorts, just like he did that first night at the pet store. She wants to do right by him, to give him some TLC, maybe detox him for a few days, put him on a juice cleanse, get him some exercise and fresh air.

Yes, he seems to be saying. *Please.*

She puts her head right up against the terrarium, and he stares at her with a spooky intensity.

They are in the midst of this moment of tender, anthropomorphized communion when she hears a snippet of a conversation coming from the other side of the wall.

"No, no, please, let me have that back." It's the voice of a man, and he sounds somewhat alarmed.

"I've got it!" says the unmistakable voice of her boss.

"Mrs. Bernstein, please, I don't think you want to do that. It's not going to serve any purpose. In fact, I think you are more likely to blow out the electrical system again."

"Call me Sophie, please!"

The events closet begins to vibrate, and Clemi braces herself. Is this the early rumbling of an earthquake? Kurt Vonnegut Jr. feels it too. He sticks his long, leathery neck up high and looks around with mournful eyes. She then hears a high-pitched electronic whine that she knows is a drill, but she's probably just imagining this, experiencing some sort of posttraumatic drill syndrome from too many nights spent listening to her weird roommate putting holes in the walls.

Then she hears another, different noise. It's Kurt. He is chirping, hacking, wheezing. It sounds like he has kennel cough. Maybe he's run down from all the partying. For all she knows, Noah and Summer might have given him something to smoke. He makes another throaty hacking noise, and his eyes bore into her.

Help! he seems to silently plead.

Again she hears the whir of a power tool, and now some energetic banging, and then Mrs. Bernstein lets out a scream just before there's a loud *thud*.

"Geez, this thing is powerful," she says. "I had no idea!"

"Mrs. Bernstein. Sophie, I mean. Really, I think it's better if you just let me do my job. This isn't the right spot. It's going to be a little complicated. I need to drill through to the electrical box and do some rewiring and—please don't take this the wrong way, but it will be easier if you leave me to it. It will take a couple of hours. Then I'll be out of here."

Where is here? Clemi wonders. She has never stopped to think about what is on the other side of this wall. Suddenly there is a *whack* sufficiently hard to cause books to fall from the shelf. Flakes of plaster float in the air, and she sees light streaming in from a couple of pin-size holes in the back wall, through which she sees Mrs. Bernstein looking right at her. Her boss quickly looks away, as if this is not really happening.

"Okay, okay, okay!" she hears Mrs. Bernstein say.

Clemi feels like she's in the middle of a bad game of Pin the Tail on the Donkey, like she's been blindfolded, spun in circles, and presented with so many things that require urgent attention that all she can do is stumble around in a daze. Now another *whack* to the wall is so powerful that it knocks the terrarium off the shelf.

Summer is at the door, knocking.

Clemi opens it just a crack and listens to Summer's status update, as if everything is business as usual in a lunatic kind of way.

"Just a few more things, Clemi. The security guys are here, and they're asking for you. And there's a reporter here from News Channel 4. He's doing some live shots from outside the store but also wondered if he could have a moment with you."

"Um, great . . . just give me a second," Clemi says. "The security guards aren't supposed to be here until tonight, but whatever. I'll be out in just a minute."

Clemi closes the door and makes her way to the back of the closet again, squeezing through the narrow aisle between the Nisses and the Gundes. The terrarium has landed on its side, the top has come off, and the contents have spilled out and Kurt Vonnegut Jr. is nowhere in sight. She gets down on the floor and looks around, but there's not enough light in this back corner. She needs to get her phone or find a flashlight so she can see into the crevices and find poor Kurt, even though she is entirely sympathetic to his escape.

Just then, more banging, and another bunch of books falls from the shelf, a couple whacking her on the head, and she lets out an inadvertent yelp.

"Is everything okay in there?" Summer asks.

"No! I mean yes! Totally," Clemi says. "Totally and completely and 100 percent under control." It's so totally and completely not under control that she might burst into tears.

She recognizes them, for better or worse, these unlikely purveyors of security. The one named Clinton is so round around the middle that he looks misshapen, which perhaps he is. His head is too small and his legs are so twiggy that they look like they might snap. The wispy mustache does little to improve the overall effect.

Bill is of more normal proportions, but sickly in his own way, his skin tone suggestive of a diet of quarter pounders with cheese.

Clemi is about to explain that they are several hours too early, and to tell them to leave and come back, but just then Mrs. Bernstein appears. She looks stricken. She has what look like bits of plaster in her hair, and next to her stands a handsome young man who is holding a toolbox in one hand and a power tool in the other, its long cord dangling. He, too, has plaster on his clothing and in his hair and looks exasperated. Mrs. Bernstein is about to speak when Bill pre-empts: "We'll be right back; we're just going to strap on our guns in a secure area."

"Guns?" Mohammed asks, looking at Mrs. Bernstein. "Why do these men have guns? I thought this was a bookstore."

"That's a very good question," Mrs. Bernstein replies. "Clemi?"

"These are the security guards, Mrs. Bernstein. Remember, you told me to get security? For tonight? They're just early. Talk about a mess. This was the best I could do. I asked for unarmed guards, but this firm, they only do armed."

"I thought I told you to cancel! On top of which, you know how I feel about guns!"

"You told me to cancel, but then you told me to get security," Clemi says, both confused and exhausted. Has she missed something along the way? "And truly, I asked for unarmed guards. This is just what showed up." She looks at Clinton and Bill, worried that she has offended, but their expressions are inscrutable.

"Why do you need security guards?" Mohammed inquires.

Mrs. Bernstein seems to be on the verge of formulating a response, but before she can speak, Summer appears. "Sorry to interrupt, but one of the bird people just spilled a bag of seed—yeah, don't ask—over in the Political Theory section and I can't seem to find the vacuum. Has anyone seen it?"

"Just leave the vacuum—I'm taking care of it," Mrs. Bernstein snaps. "I've got my Roomba. It's in my car. I'll get it in a minute."

"I'll get it, Mrs. Bernstein!" Summer volunteers.

"No! I'll get him! Don't go near my car!"

Summer looks like she's about to cry or go running back to NASA.

"I'm sorry, I didn't mean to snap," Mrs. Bernstein says. "It's just been a day and like all of you, I'm a little overwhelmed. Just give me a minute and I'll get him."

242

"Him?" Mohammed asks.

"Roomba. Sorry. I've sort of anthropomorphized my vacuum, I guess? He's become something of a friend?"

Mrs. Bernstein seems to be making a joke, but Clemi, Mohammed, and Summer just stare.

Clemi is getting a bit woozy watching Roomba swirl around the store, spinning in circles, his sweeping brushes alert and fluttering. She doesn't know where Kurt Vonnegut Jr. is, and she hopes he and Roomba don't bump into one another. Relative to the store's regular vacuum, Roomba is a tiny thing, but he's nevertheless at least double Kurt's size. She's not sure what would happen should they accidentally collide.

Roomba is clearly trying his best, but he can only ingest so much birdseed before making a sound suggestive of gastric indigestion and coming to a halt, indicating the need to be emptied. Noah is back on vacuum duty, but he is only giving this partial attention and at the moment is nowhere to be found. Clemi has picked Roomba up and cleared out his gut more than a few times already.

She follows Roomba into the Fiction room. She is beginning to understand Mrs. Bernstein's attachment to this endearing appliance. After only a couple of hours, she already feels she is getting to know his rhythms and can sense that he is moments from needing to recharge. She is right; a few seconds later he comes to a full stop at the feet of a woman clad in all white. Clemi bends to pick him up, and as she rises she sees several women are wearing identical white trousers and billowing white tops. They are congregated in front of the *P*-authored books, which brings to mind Tom Perrotta's book *The Leftovers*. She has no idea who these women are, or what they want, or which event they are here to attend, if any, but they make her think of the cultlike group Perrotta depicts in his dystopian novel about a large chunk of the population that suddenly and inexplicably disappears—the self-proclaimed, chain-smoking living reminders of the missing called the Guilty Remnant.

If characters are beginning to emerge from the pages of novels, if the tortoise is speaking to her, if she is feeling affection for a robotic vacuuming device, if her mother has just texted to say she has moments ago landed at Dulles and is in a car, en route to the store . . . She's not sure what conditional probability she is attempting to formulate. She just knows that the outcome is bad.

But right now she needs to set that thought aside and stay the course, because a surprisingly tiny, soft-spoken woman in a leopard-print dress is sitting in Mrs. Bernstein's office. Her name is Lili Chandrasekaran, and she is the author of *Kuddly Killers*. Clemi has already walked her through the details of the event, and now it's 3:00 p.m.—time to begin.

"Ready?" Clemi asks.

"Thanks for asking. But no. Not really."

"Okay, no problem if you need a few minutes. Do you want me to get you a cup of coffee or something?"

"No, I think caffeine would just make it worse. I'm already shaking. See?" Lili holds out a small bony hand,

and it is indeed trembling, causing the many heavy bangles adorning her wrist to jangle and clank.

"Wow, just relax. It will be fine. How about some herbal tea? I think I have something called 'Calm' in my office. I could run over and grab a tea bag."

"No, I think I would probably just throw it up. I have issues with reflux."

"Oh, okay," Clemi says, taking a step back. "We definitely don't want that to happen. Listen, I'm just going to check on the microphones and be sure everything is okay out there. We'll begin the event in about five minutes."

"I'd rather not use a microphone. It makes me sound so loud!"

"Well, yes, I guess it does. But that's helpful. The store is really busy today and we want people to hear you."

"I'd rather they didn't."

"You don't want them to hear you?"

"Not really. I'd rather they just buy the book. I hate public speaking, but my publisher told me I have to do this."

"Sure, I get it. I really do. It's kind of ridiculous to think that the personality traits that make someone want to sit in a room and write a book for months, years, whatever, is the same sort of person who wants to stand up in front of an audience and speak! There's just so much pressure to perform! Why can't writers just write?"

"Also, if you don't mind, can you ask them to be quiet out there?"

"What do you mean?"

"All those people, they are making a lot of noise. Squawking. Meowing. Talking. I'm very sensitive to noise."

"Honestly, I'm not sure there's much I can do. It just kind of is what it is. But you are going to be okay. Just go out there and take a lot of deep breaths. Smile. Do some of those visualization things, you know—like, picture yourself in some place that makes you happy and calm. Like the beach or whatever."

"I'm—I'm having trouble breathing. I feel like I'm about to have an asthma attack. Is this one of those bookstores that has a cat? I'm allergic to cats."

"No, no cats. Not real ones anyway. There are various dogs wandering through. And a tortoise. But he doesn't have fur, so probably it's not him." Clemi feels a fresh wave of dread and guilt and panic having mentioned the tortoise, and now she wishes she could get back out there and try to find Kurt. But for now she has to deal with this fragile, unstable potential catastrophe of an author who is starting to cough.

"Do you have an inhaler?" Lili asks.

"You mean, like, for asthma? No."

Choking and hacking ensue. She sounds like a cat trying to cough up a hairball.

"Should I call an ambulance?"

"No! For the love of God, do not call an ambulance. I don't have health insurance. Well, I did, but I just lost it in the divorce."

"Okay, wait, I have an idea. I think Sami might have asthma. Maybe she has an inhaler. I'll go check and will be right back!"

Clemi elbows her way through the crowded book floor until she reaches the information desk.

"Do you know where Sami is?" she asks Autumn T.

Autumn puts up a finger, meaning, *Wait, I'm busy talking to a customer.*

A small boy looks up at Clemi and says, "We are looking for a book about how to make a vegetable garden." He is holding the hand of a woman in a hijab who says something to him, and he translates. "We want to grow tomatoes."

"Oh, nice!" Clemi says. She points him toward the side wall and tells him that's where the books on gardening live. She would like to lead him over there herself and learn more about this boy and the aspirations for his vegetable garden, but there is no time for pleasantries. The store is a three-ring circus right now, and more urgently she has an author who can't breathe.

"Has anyone seen Sami?" she asks again.

Autumn T points toward the staircase, which could mean she's upstairs, or it could mean she's downstairs. Clemi decides the more likely possibility is that she's downstairs, in the receiving room, maybe taking over from Yash on web orders. As Clemi heads toward the stairs, she sees that a bus from a local retirement home has pulled up in front of the store and is unloading its passengers. Some twenty elderly residents begin to make their way through the door. A man who looks to be about 102 years old accidentally pushes his walker into the #BlackLivesMatter display table, sending about a dozen copies of *Between the World and Me* flying and skidding across the floor.

Clemi's hunch is right. She finds Sami sitting at the web order desk, her thick brown hair in two long braids, her wire-frame glasses propped on top of her head, an empty can of buffalo ranch–flavored Pringles beside her. She is surrounded by stacks of books that are piled dangerously high. It looks worse down here than it typically does during the holiday crush.

"It's hopeless," Sami says to Clemi. "I give up. It's like that Mickey Mouse book where the water just keeps pouring in faster than he can mop it up."

"Do you mean *The Sorcerer's Apprentice?*"

"Yes. I think so. I used to read it as a kid. But you know, I've always been confused about whether that's the same thing as *Fantasia?*"

"I think so. But I'm not certain."

"Hey, do you want to come over sometime and we can watch the movie? I haven't seen it since I was a kid."

"Yeah, that would be really nice!" Clemi says, excited by this idea. She has always wanted to get to know Sami better and could use a light, normal, watching-stupid-movies-with-a-girlfriend sort of evening given all of the recent stress of her friendship with Florence. "I actually came to see if you have an inhaler. Our author upstairs is having an asthma attack, I think. Do you have one?"

"I do! Which is really amazing because I rarely have it on me. I usually leave my bag upstairs, my lunch, too, but since they sent me down to web orders I brought it with me because I want to leave at 5:07 exactly to catch the bus because I have dinner plans tonight, and before I go out I want to go to a spin class, so I have my gym bag too."

"Great," Clemi says, not sure she has absorbed all of the nuance here, but it doesn't hugely matter because the answer is yes to the asthma inhaler. She takes it from Sami, promising to bring it right back.

She runs up the stairs and pushes her way through the crowd, makes her way back to Mrs. Bernstein's office, and finds Lili Chandrasekaran talking on her cell phone. She turns to Clemi. "Can I have some privacy, please?"

"I'm here with the inhaler," Clemi says.

"Oh, no worries. I found one in my bag. But thanks."

Clemi is determined to stay strong here, to not give this woman a piece of her mind. Nothing good will come of that. She will stay focused and keep the trains—and the Roomba!—running, albeit at this rate, not on time.

"Great! Such good news! Let's get the event started then, shall we? We're already late—it's ten minutes past the start time."

"If you could just give me a minute. I'm talking to my therapist, and she's told me it's okay if I change my mind. That I don't need to give in to all this societal pressure to constantly perform. So I'm going to just kind of slip out of here, if that's okay. I might try to go for a swim or something to calm myself down."

This is just too much. Clemi has deferred to every author's every wish for as long as she's been in this job. She once procured Absolut Elyx for a very famous author and poured it into a water glass so no one would know it was vodka she was sipping at the podium. Another time she did a last-minute run to Ben's Chili Bowl to get an author a half smoke, but this—just abandoning ship—this is not okay!

"It's not okay!" she says, surprising herself. "These people are all here to listen to you. We have ordered your books. We have given you an events slot. Maybe you don't like to speak. I get it. But it's just part of our . . . of *your* . . .

profession. It's an honor to publish a book! So please just pull yourself together and get out there and do your job."

Lili looks a little stunned, but remarkably, she obeys. She pulls a small mirror from her bag and takes a moment to preen—fussing with her hair, applying a coat of lipstick, and smoothing out her dress, her bangles jangling with her every move (like a cat with a bell on her collar, Clemi can't help but observe). She then follows Clemi out onto the book floor and clears her throat. But before Clemi even has a chance to introduce the author, the customer they refer to as Chatty Cathy is at the microphone.

"I have a question!" she says.

"Not yet!" Clemi says.

"I would like to talk about owls, and where you stand on the spotted owl versus barn owl controversy. I heard a story about it once on NPR, and I wonder if you think it's okay to shoot the owls—I forget if they are shooting the barn owls or the spotted owls because one of them was there first, right? Like one of them was an East Coast bird that somehow wound up on the West Coast and then reproduced out of control and—"

"It's not time for the Q&A yet, so if you wouldn't mind sitting down, please—"

"It reminds me of an argument that we had . . . okay, maybe *argument* isn't exactly the right word, but a contentious meeting of my neighborhood association to do with how to keep the deer population under control because, while you might not think so in an urban area like Washington DC, we have a lot of deer, even in my yard, and honestly I don't know how they get in there because we have a very high fence, but that's beside the point. My point is . . . What was my point?"

There is the sound of retching from somewhere in the back rows, followed by a very bad smell, and she can see Antonio rush over with carpet cleaner and paper towels and air freshener. Lili Chandrasekaran makes a soft moaning sound and then crumples, in slow motion, into a heap on the floor.

"Someone call 911!" Clemi yells. "Someone bring me a cold towel!" Lili's lack of health insurance is not going to stop Clemi from seeking medical help. She doesn't want to have a dead author on her hands.

She squats down and slaps Lili gently on the face. The woman appears to come to for a moment, looks around, and then her eyes roll back in her head again. As Clemi cradles her, she sees something out of the corner of her eye skitter by. Is that Kurt Vonnegut Jr.? She gently sets the author's head back onto the carpet and crawls over to the spinner rack of calendars to see if there is a tortoise underneath. Something is indeed moving under there and she is very excited until she realizes that it's just a mouse. A mouse!

"There's a mouse!" she accidentally screams.

"We just had a call that Doodle Guy is on his way in," Summer says, appearing beside her.

"There's a mouse!" she repeats.

"Get one of the cats on it, ha-ha!" Summer says. "Anyway, you need to deal with Doodle Guy."

"Who?"

"You know, the self-published author guy? Bernie and the Doodles or whatever?"

"Oh, yeah. Him. That's not my problem. It's not an event. He's just signing some books. I thought he was coming tomorrow."

"I don't know. I'm just reporting the news."

"Can you deal with him? I have an author in distress, lying on the floor behind us, and I need to call an ambulance. This is probably the worst day ever!"

"Yeah, well, take a number. I'm having a bad day too. We're short-staffed. Someone's got to help."

"Maybe ask Noah?"

"He wasn't feeling well, so he went home. He said he's sick but I think he's really just hungover, which is kind of annoying of him if you think about it. Last night was so wild. You should have come!"

Clemi is debating whether to take the bait, to find out where it was she was not invited this time, probably accidentally on purpose by Summer, who clearly has designs on Noah—but she hasn't gotten very far in the pro and con process when she hears a too-familiar voice.

It's her mother, who has already arrived and is standing beside her. "Darling," she says to Clemi, "it looks like you've put on a little weight!"

CHAPTER 11

RAYMOND WASHES UP
AT THE BALLPARK

The ballpark is the last place Raymond would have expected to find Seema, her silky hair hovering above him, tickling his chin, smelling of that lovely, expensive Moroccan oil she used to caress into her locks after shampooing. Only the best for Seema. Don't even get him started on her face cream. La Mer de Something, more than $2,000 for a sixteen-ounce tub. Made of algae and eucalyptus and zinc and the tears of some extinct animal like tyrannosaurus rex. Not that he cared as much as his pained expressions might have suggested on the occasions she returned from her shopping trips.

He has been longing for this moment, to apologize and explain: I didn't mean to let go of the pushchair! If you want an AGA, you can have an AGA! You are beautiful and smart! I never meant to imply that your poetry wasn't any good. If you want me to go with you to marriage counseling—well, count me in! And while you're at it, spend whatever you want.

"I'm sorry! Truly!"

"It's okay, but you are not supposed to be here. I don't know how you got in. Are you here to apply for a job?"

Is he dreaming? He is dreaming! Obviously he is dreaming!

Also, he already has a job, a fact he is eager to convey: "I already have a job!"

"Sir?"

"I am employed! I'm a poet. And before you laugh—why people think the occupation of poet is funny eludes me—please know that I'm the real deal. I've won awards! *Kaboom!* has just gone into a third printing!"

"Sir?"

"You can call me Ray."

"Um, Ray? The line for the job applicants is on the other side of the concourse."

Raymond opens his eyes and sees a woman in uniform sporting a badge. A couple of lanyards dangle around her neck. She is leaning over him, her long, Seema-like hair dark and tickling his forehead.

He pauses before answering. He is feeling confused, suspended between catastrophic interviews, between countries and time zones. He's hovering over third base, like a plane. He's not sure how he got into the ballpark, but it's good to be back. He's missed baseball, and he wonders if forfeiting this simple pleasure might be part of what's doing him in. Is it possible that reengaging with the game is one component of landing his plane? That said, he's not really a plane—he's a drone. But he's not really a drone—he's a poet. A poet drone. An autonomous poet drone. An APD.

"Excuse me, sir, can I help you?" she says, this time more loudly, as if he is deaf. She is aggressive now. More aggressive, even, than Seema, who persists with aggressive questions inside his head.

One of the various labeling devices she wears identifies her as Martina, and he is quite touched by the offer because he is, in fact, in need.

"Can you tell me what time this place opens?" he asks, pointing toward the concourse with all of the shuttered concession stands. Before collapsing into this seat, he had seen one with an especially alluring name: Distilleries of the DMV.

"The stadium isn't open today, sir," she says. "Can you tell me how you got inside?"

He honestly doesn't know. Presumably he walked in through an open gate. All he knows is that he's here. She is reaching for something as she continues staring at him. He hopes it's not a gun. He is, after all, in the US now, the land of the Colt 45 and the .357 Smith & Wesson Magnum, go-ahead-make-my-day. But her hand settles on some sort of communication device that appears to be strapped to her hip.

"Sir, can I ask what you are doing here?"

"I'm . . ."

"Are you . . . applying for a job?"

"A job? You mean here? Are there jobs?"

"Yes, there are interviews today for seasonal ushers."

"Ushers? I am not certain I see how I would be helpful with that. As I have already explained, I'm a poet."

"A poet?"

Now she has the talking device pressed to her ear and is reaching for some other contraption affixed to her other side. He is, for a moment, terrified.

Raymond feels a drop of rain. Then another. Then hears a crack of thunder.

"Let's take shelter," Martina says.

"Great idea," says Raymond as the skies open up. "Also, if you could help me get a cab, that would be great. I have to be at the bookstore pretty soon. How long do you think it will take to get there?"

"Which bookstore?" asks Martina. "DC is a big place, you know. We have more than one bookstore."

"Ha! Very funny. It's not a one-bookstore town."

Martina does not appear to be amused.

"You know, like a one-horse town?"

"You don't need to explain your bad joke to me."

He won't take offense. He is a poet. An uncontrolled, unmanned drone poet, if you will. He's never claimed to be a humorist.

"Now that you ask, I realize I don't know the name. Let me just find the address on my phone . . ."

Before his hand reaches his pocket, Martina has him slammed up against the concourse wall. She yanks his hands behind his back and slaps some handcuffs on his wrists, and even though this is intriguing in its own way, he is aware that under these circumstances this is not a particularly good thing. She rummages through his pockets, evidently looking for the offending weapon she has presumed to be inside, but produces only some spare change—a few pence—a loose button, and his phone, which she confiscates.

Martina leads him a quarter way around the concourse, past Base Line Brews, Dos Locas Nachos, Senators Sausage, Grand Slam Grill. These come-hither names make him practically salivate. He really needs a drink. He is located liminally between the last tug of bourbon consumed after breakfast and whatever he can find next. (Americans medicalize everything. Mood, learning, sex—even drink. But let the record show he has no drinking problem. He just needs a drink.)

Then they turn right and descend down a long corridor and into a small room somewhere in the bowels of the stadium. He can hear the rain pounding on the roof and he's stuffed in a chair and his phone is placed, faceup, on the desk. He can see the text messages appear and is comforted by the fact that Fiona, his publicist, is still there, inside his phone, telling him what to do—but he is, alas, unable to reach over to reply.

> NPR may have been an eff-ing disaster, Ray, but go figure
> If there's a bright side to any of this, there seems to be even
>   more of a run on your books
> The bookstore girl just emailed again to be sure you will
>   come early
> Ray please reply
> Ray are you there . . .
> ???
> When you see this let me know
> Okay well now she wants you there at 5:15

And yes. I reminded her about the pens.
Fine point Sharpies.

"*Ultra*-fine point!" Raymond screams in frustration.

"And those look like fountain pens!"

Martina is now back in the room with two men.

"Ultra-fine point what?" asks the older-looking one, the one brushing water from his too-tight suit, the one who has a big belly and no hair and a speaking device in his ear. The other man is in a police uniform with an impressive number of things going on—badges, stripes, holsters, electronic contraptions that periodically beep—he is so well fortified that he looks more cyborg than human, like one of those Transformer toys one of his boys once asked him to help assemble. He can't remember which one.

"Sharpies," Raymond says, then realizing that potentially sounds like a weapon, he quickly adds, "I mean, Sharpie pens. See, there's fine point, which is typically what the bookstores supply, but that's too thick. I like to put a more elegant touch to my name, and I find the so-called fine point bleeds, especially into the curvature of the *R*—"

"Are you going to watch the eclipse on Monday?" asks tight-suit.

"The eclipse?" Raymond asks, puzzled. Ah, apparently he is not the intended recipient of this question.

"You betcha," the policeman replies. "In fact, I'm taking the weekend off, driving down to Charleston with the kids."

"Charleston? I wouldn't go anywhere near there after last weekend!"

"You mean Charlottesville?"

"Oh, right. I knew that. I'm just kind of dyslexic with all the *chuh* sounds, if you know what I mean. Also there's Charles Town, the place with the racetrack in West Virginia. I get them all mixed up. So yeah, South Carolina. Why?"

"My daughter lives down there. She's also a cop, if you can believe anyone in my family would go into this profession after growing up with me! But the other reason we're going is because Charleston's in the path of totality."

"Groovy. That sounds like the title of a Pink Floyd song," the suit remarks.

"Or it sounds like the best place to watch an eclipse. Anyway, my wife is a science nerd. She's really into it and it's kind of a once-in-a-lifetime thing. And my daughter, it's her twenty-third birthday, so we're just going to do it up big."

"Raymond has a child who must be about twenty-three. One he didn't even know about, one he's never met," Raymond says.

"Hey, Martina, can we get this guy some coffee? Sober him up?"

"You're asking *me* to make coffee? What, is this 1950?"

"Thanks, gentlemen, Martina, but what I really need is a drink."

Martina opens a minifridge and for a moment Raymond is hopeful, but she produces a bottle of water.

"There's another eclipse in February," she says, setting

the bottle on the table in front of Raymond. The water is right there next to his phone, and it's a lovely sight except that his hands are cuffed behind him.

"Yeah, but that's just a partial eclipse."

What if, God forbid, the pushchair had failed to come to a stop at the bottom of the incline? Raymond sees, in his mind's eye, the baby spilling out, rolling down the hill. He can hear Seema's screams.

"True. I think there's supposed to be a big one in something like 2050."

"In 2050? I should be turning ninety-two years old in 2050, God willing," says Raymond.

"Martina, who is this guy?" the cyborg asks.

"He says he's a poet."

"I *am* a poet. You may have heard me on NPR yesterday. I can't say that I fully understand what the fuss is about, but they say I caused what they so quaintly call 'a tweet storm,' which sounds pretty awful to me, but Fiona, my publicist, says it's a good thing and there has evidently been a rush on my books—even more of a rush since there was already one on account of some of the things my wife's, my late wife's, friends said to the press."

"Like what?"

"Oh, like I was having an affair with my agent. Like I have a child out of wedlock. Like I was unsupportive of her as a writer. Like I was a negligent father of our own children."

They are all looking at him, slack-jawed.

"But, moving on, I need to get to the bookstore early to sign all of the stock and so, therefore, please, a moment, if you will!"

"I did hear about this! You were on Boris Lewinsky! You're the AGA guy, right? Geez. That was really a crazy interview."

"This guy was on NPR?" Martina asks, seeming to reevaluate him, like maybe he's a little more interesting than your run-of-the-mill hallucinating drunk in a ballpark.

"Yeah, here, I've got the app on my phone. Do you want to hear?"

Raymond does not want to hear. It was an unpleasant experience and he's been trying to convince himself that it was perhaps not as bad as it seemed.

"Bring it on," says Martina.

Raymond wonders whether this qualifies as some sort of cruel and unusual punishment, being forced to sit in a room, cuffed to a chair, and listen to himself make an ass of himself on National Public Radio. He braces as he is asked a series of questions having to do with that AGA. *Not* the powerful imagery of the boy in his pushchair, or what the poet might be working on next, or what inspired some of his more celebrated poems, such as the one about the child in snow boots.

Just the AGA, the AGA, the AGA.

"I've always wanted to see an AGA for real," says Martina. "I was reading a novel once and the AGA came up so many times I had to stop reading to figure out what it was. At first I thought it was a family member, or like an ayah, which is what they call a nanny in India. Which was obviously wrong. Then I thought maybe it was a kind of dog or something, the way everyone was always huddling around it."

"Did you read him his rights?" the suit asks Martina.

"She's not a real cop," the cop explains.

"Thanks for the vote of confidence," Martina says. "Plus, even if I was a cop, I wasn't arresting him. I was just getting him back here so I could call you."

"Am I under arrest?" Raymond asks. "I can explain. But also can you hand me my phone?"

Again all three pairs of eyes turn to him and stare.

"Seriously, I'm supposed to be at the bookstore. But now my publicist is telling me to get there at 5:15 because . . . well, you heard it. Whatever I said yesterday is ginning up sales."

He doesn't remember much after that, apart from tight-suit giving him a summons to appear—something to do with public intoxication, disorderly conduct, trespassing, etc. But somehow, hard as it is to fathom, Raymond winds up stuffed inside a taxi and then deposited on a bench outside the bookstore next to a homeless man who looks at him for a moment before exclaiming, "You're the AGA guy!"

"Technically I'm a poet."

"Yes, I'm aware. I'm a fan of your work. I was flipping through *Kaboom!* this morning and I think 'Change the Narrative' is the strongest in the collection."

"Oh, interesting. I hadn't planned on reading that tonight, but maybe I should?"

"Please do! It's really disarming. Kind of devastating really. Also I appreciate your avoidance of the usual poetic tropes, you know, like the way you almost go there in that line about the falcon but then you dial it back just as the boy looks skyward and sees the F-16."

"Funny you should say that, because I'm struggling right now with a new cycle that seems to be devolving into pure trope."

"Well, yeah, I mean, you have a lot on your plate right now. Sorry about your wife, man. That must be rough."

"Um, yeah. Thanks. No one ever says that, so I really appreciate it. It *is* rough. And that's not the least of it. I'm kind of afraid to go inside that store. I've been on a weeklong bender but it doesn't seem to be helping."

"I've tried that. Take it from me, it never helps. But yeah, you *should* be afraid. There are some women in there who are waiting for you. They want blood."

"I'm used to that. But this situation is worse than you know."

"What do you mean?"

"Can I tell you a secret?"

"Everyone confides in me these days. They see a guy on a bench, you know, and I guess they think I've got no one to talk to. I'm as good as a bartender or a priest."

"Well, if you were a bartender, you'd at least be able to give me a drink. But anyway, who are you? What's your story?"

"No story. I'm a poet too, although that's not really how I identify. I was an assistant professor at American University, and then at GW, but I never got tenured. After a while I took some time off so I could focus on my writing, but I couldn't get hired again, so I went to work in a bookstore. But that bottomed out too, so I'm just hanging out here. It's a pretty good place. They bring me donuts sometimes. The kids are okay. Especially that girl with the red hair."

"She's the one."

"What do you mean?"

"It's complicated."

"Yes. I see. She seems to have your chin."

"What do you mean?"

"I see the resemblance!"

"I haven't even told you."

"You said it's complicated. Plus that chin. That's really all I need to know. And speaking of the devil, here she is!"

Raymond sees the girl, the girl with his chin, open the door just as an ambulance arrives. She flags the medical technicians and directs them inside the store. A few minutes later they reemerge with a tiny woman in a leopard-print dress strapped to a stretcher, and they load her into the back of the vehicle.

He stares at her like he's just seen . . . what? Something astonishing. Even as a poet he doesn't have the language to describe what it is like to see your daughter, the one you have pretended away for more than twenty years.

She is a beautiful child—ethereal, somehow not of this world. And yet there she is, giving orders to everyone, running the show here at the bookstore. If you think about it, given her DNA, it's not at all surprising that she has wound up here, hiding amongst these books.

CHAPTER 12

SOPHIE GETS A GUN

It worked. She would just like to say that it worked, her plan to engage the keyless ignition by placing the vacuum cleaner inside the car. Querk III rode home shotgun, his articulating floor brush and various other suction parts on the floor, his torso buckled into the passenger seat. Sure, there was probably an easier, more elegant, less awkward solution, but it worked, and she would like this to be duly noted.

Another small victory: she did not have to deal with the flaming moron who owns the impoundment lot this time. He had not been inside the booth, nor had his son. Instead there was a pretty young woman with intriguingly bold balayage with whom she was able to engage in a more straightforward transaction. Sophie wondered if she could pull this look off at her age. She considered inquiring about how balayage is different from highlights, one of the many things in this world she does not understand, but the woman seemed to have no interest in anything other than Sophie's credit card, which she swiped and then waved vaguely in the direction of the impounded car.

As she'd made her way back onto I-270, hail the size of golf balls began to pelt the Subaru, one slamming so hard that it made a small dent in the hood. Suddenly the wind picked up and the trees started swaying. The word *pestilence* had come to Sophie's mind as traffic ground to a halt. *The darkness will soon descend.*

She had then gone home, changed into dry clothes, picked up Roomba, and returned to the store, where she'd tried for quite some time to help Mohammed—notwithstanding the fact that he kept urging her to go.

Now she's home, hoping to rest for a couple of hours, fantasizing about squeezing in a quick nap—but here is the store, haranguing her by phone.

"Hey, Mrs. B. It's Summer here! How are you?" She doesn't wait for a reply before continuing. "I feel like I keep calling and bugging you and I'm really sorry."

"It's no problem. You're just doing your job," Sophie says, although now that she thinks about it, this young woman, who only just started working at the store a few days ago, certainly does seem to be omnipresent.

"Yeah, although now that I think about it, maybe I shouldn't call you at home about something that can wait."

"No problem. You have me now, so what's happening?"

"Super! Listen, do you have any thoughts about the thing from Zhang?"

Oh boy, not this again. "I'm sorry, I've been swamped. I haven't had a chance to look."

"Okay, what should I tell her?"

"Tell her I'll do it soon."

"Do what soon?"

"Look soon. Give this my full attention."

"Um, okay," Summer says. "I'll tell her. Not that she cares, by the way. She doesn't even know that I gave you the envelope."

"Okay, now I'm confused," Sophie says. "What's in the envelope?"

"Hang on a minute," Summer says.

Sophie hangs for more than a minute. The phone has once again been set down on the counter rather than being put on hold, and she can hear snippets of various conversations, including a customer asking for a copy of *The Girl in Gauzy Blue*, and another asking for directions to the nearest supermarket. Five minutes tick by. Then she is up to ten. She is just about to hang up when someone picks up the receiver on the other end and puts it back in the cradle, hanging up on her.

Now her phone pings. She assumes it's Summer again, but it's that stupid SilverBliss, sending her a notification. She has no memory of providing her phone number, but then realizes that Michael must have set her up for alerts. Someone has sent her a private message. She remembers the accidental woos, or whatever they are called, and feels ill. She could choose to ignore this. Or she could take a look.

She takes a look.

Dear DCBookWoman2017,

I saw your profile and can't wait to meet you! I think we are a perfect match! I love books too! I just finished reading a book called *The Ultimate Dad Joke Book*. My daughter gave it to me for Father's Day, and it was great! (Watch out: I've got some good jokes for you!)

A little bit about me: I am divorced going on eight years and it's a long, sad story, but in short my wife is now married to our son's orthodontist and they have moved to Baltimore, even though that is in violation of our custody arrangement but I'm out of funds to contest it right now having lost my job last month. That's another long, sad story, but I have a bunch of job applications in right now and I'm living with my mom for the time being, which is great because she isn't charging me rent. Anyway I can tell you more when we meet. Are you free tomorrow?

SadDadDC

Sophie deletes the message, then harnesses her latent tech abilities and manages to unsubscribe.

She is not opposed to online dating, but she will do it when she's ready, and on her own terms.

It is pouring again, a ridiculous, epic rain that makes it tricky to drive, but she is so keyed up about the event with the poet that she needs to get back to the store. So much for napping; she has the rest of her life to rest.

Even with the wipers swishing at full speed there is little visibility, and Sophie drives over a pothole that feels big enough to swallow her Subaru whole. It takes twice as long as it should to get to the store, but she will not complain. She's just happy to have her car again, with her errant suctioning device still securely buckled into the passenger seat.

As she pulls into the parking lot behind the store, she sees a few stray soggy cats and birds leaning against the wall smoking cigarettes, united, at least, in their nicotine addiction. They should be gone, these people from the afternoon event—or rather, the nonevent, as she learned from Clemi, who had called to report that the author was recovering from what had been diagnosed as anxiety and dehydration. Clemi also mentioned the inadvertent, unexpected crossover among the pro-free-range-cat, anti-free-range-cat, death to Raymond Chaucer, and minor-league bird- and cat-themed baseball camps and warned Sophie that many of these people are planning to remain at the bookstore for a two-for-one day of events.

One small problem that she hadn't foreseen—or rather, one of many—is that she can't lock the car. Not only that, but unless she takes Querk III back inside, anyone can climb into the passenger seat and drive away. This seems highly unlikely—she hasn't heard of any cars being stolen from this lot—and besides, if there is a car thief in this crowd, her Subaru seems a less likely target than either the Mercedes parked in the spot beside her or the BMW in the next row. Nevertheless, given her luck these last few days, she'd rather not take the risk.

She is walking around to the passenger door to unstrap Querk III when a figure emerges from the back door of the store. It's what's his name, the Darkness enthusiast. She wants to call to him, but she can't remember his name, so instead she just waves like she's one of the bird people, flapping her arms until he notices her.

"Hey, Mrs. Bernstein," he says, approaching. He's carrying a large box and smiling adorably. Really, he is so sweet, so menschy, she can't imagine what compels him to drape himself in chains.

"Did you ever get my email?"

Had she failed to reply? She is embarrassed to have been so rude. "I did! Thank you so much!"

"Do you want to join us?"

"Let me check my calendar. Can you remind me of the date?" Why is she saying this? She absolutely does not want to go to the 9:30 Club, stay up late, and listen to loud death metal music.

"Sure. I don't remember offhand and my phone is back at my workstation, but how about I email you the info again?"

"That's perfect. Meantime I have a quick question: Do you happen to have any tools on you?"

"I have a couple of knives," he says, setting down the box, which Sophie can see is full of books. He carries knives and is absconding with books?

"Where are you taking those books?" she asks in what she hopes is not an accusatory tone.

"Oh, these are just old galleys. No one wants them. Believe me, we've tried to find them homes. They sat in front of the store all day with a sign that said 'Free Books.' I think that diminished the pile by maybe three?"

"So what are you going to do with them?" she asks.

"I'm going to recycle them. Unless you want them."

"Someone spent years writing these books and you are tossing them into the recycling bin? That seems pretty sad."

"Yeah, that's what Clemi says, too, but that doesn't mean she wants to take them home. Although last year she made a Christmas tree out of them. It was pretty cool. A galley tree! Anyway, they're just advance copies. They aren't real books."

Sophie knows this is the case—it's not like any aspect of this business is new to her—and yet it is also a reminder of how disengaged she's become, as well as the fact that there are, counterintuitively and unbelievably, even more books being published, and unloved and unread, than in the past.

"Still, there must be something we can do with them."

"Sure, do you want them? I could put them in your car," he says, gesturing toward the Subaru.

She considers the box full of galleys, takes in all of their beautiful covers, contemplates the painstakingly written acknowledgments thanking editors and agents and baby-sitters and beloved high school English teachers and children and husbands and wives and friends and partners and thera-pists and cats and dogs.

"No, not really, I guess. I've got too many books as it is. But what were we talking about?"

"You asked me if I have any tools. I have a knife," he says. "Well, a couple of sharp box cutters. I don't know if that qualifies as a tool."

"Why in the world do you carry box cutters?" She wishes she could stop being so negative, so suspicious of this boy.

She hates herself for profiling him just because he wears chains, but she can't help it. Box cutters make her think of the 9/11 hijackers.

"I carry box cutters because I have a job that requires cutting open boxes," he says. "I work in the receiving room. Where we receive the books. That come in boxes."

He is such a nice boy! He manages to say this without any hint of annoyance.

"Of course, of course. I'm sorry to have asked! I'm not sure that will do the trick though. I need something really heavy-duty. Like a machete."

"I don't have a machete, but . . . well, depending on what you are trying to do—and I'm just guessing here—an ax might be better. But I don't have an ax either. Is there something else I can do to help?"

"Sure. Can I ask you a favor? And can I ask you to keep it a secret?"

"Um, sure, I think. I mean, I work for you, so you can ask me to do anything you want. Within reason, that is . . . If you asked me to do something illegal, like kill someone or something, or help you put a body in the trunk, I'd probably rather not, if that's okay. But I'll pick up an extra shift or help tonight with the event or whatever you need."

"No, no, I just need you to be discreet."

"This is making me kind of nervous. I'm technically just on my break, so I don't have a lot of time."

"Oh good grief, just go get me some kind of sizable tool, okay?" she says.

"A sizable tool? Can I just ask what it's for? Like, say, for unscrewing something, or for smashing something?"

"Smashing something! Definitely! Find me something that can smash something."

The boy just looks at her. He blinks a few times, like he doesn't know how to respond.

"Again, discretion, okay? It's for this," she says, pointing to Querk III.

"Sure. Why the big secret though? And why not just let Noah take care of it? I thought he was dealing with the vacuum."

There's no good reason, really. She's just embarrassed. At this point she wishes the vacuum cleaner would quietly go away. After she retrieves her keys, that is.

"I need to get this plastic piece off, but I've tried everything, so at this point I want to smash it open. Whatever it takes. I swear I've tried everything."

"Let me take a look." He produces his box cutter as well as a Swiss Army knife and fidgets with the plastic case for a few minutes, trying to pop it open from the side. He then tries to stab it through the middle, but the plastic won't so much as crack. He then kicks it a couple of times with his heavy boots and admits defeat.

"You're right. It won't budge," he says. "It's like it's bulletproof."

"Oh, that's a good thought! But do you really think so?"

"Do I think what?"

"That it's really bulletproof?"

"I don't know, it's just a figure of speech."

"No, it's a good idea. I mean, I hate guns. I think they ought to be banned, at least in a city like DC, and I'm furious, actually, that there are armed guards in my bookstore right now and I plan to talk to Clemi about this later, but for now, could you just go find me one of those security guards?"

"I think I know where you're going with this, Mrs. Bernstein, and I don't think this is a good idea. Why don't you hang on while I go look inside? Maybe I can find a hammer."

"No, I'll take care of this. If you don't mind, just stay here with Querk III while I go find a security guard."

CHAPTER 13

MOTHER

A lso, sweetheart, you'd look so much taller if you'd just stand up straight . . . There! Yes, that's much better!"

Next to Clemi's mother is a handsome, soggy poet in an expensive, wrinkled suit, and he's staring at her like he's just seen a ghost.

"The man on the bench says she has my chin," he says.

"Sober up, dear . . . Darling, can you get him a coffee?" she asks Clemi. "Over at that Noun place?"

"Verb."

"Right. He takes his coffee black. Maybe a croissant or something too. Let's get some food into his system. This is Raymond Chaucer, by the way. He's a poet and an old, dear friend."

Seriously? *This* is how her mother is going to play it? Just pretend this explosive situation away? Including this rather undeniable resemblance of the chins, which is even more striking now that she sees him in real life.

"I'm not really in the mood for coffee. Some sort of whiskey drink would be better."

"No, darling. Coffee."

"I can't go on without a drink. Truly, Elena. Just one."

"You're in a bookstore, darling. You need to sober up."

"Do I? After all those stories you've told me about your various clients . . . Didn't Hannah Arendt once send you out for Cognac?"

"What, do you think I'm 150 years old?"

"Who am I confusing her with?"

"Maybe Remi Colbert?" Clemi suggests. She's not entirely sure why she has offered this information because she would rather not participate in this theater of the absurd that is her mother and the poet.

"No, it wasn't her," Raymond says.

"Was it Bianca Allende?" her mother says.

"Yes!" says the poet. "That's it!" And now he is staring at Clemi again. "Also my eyes."

"Darling," says her mother. "Coffee. Verb. Now."

"I met her once," Raymond says. "She was wearing a bandana."

"Who was?" Clemi asks.

"Bianca Allende."

"Is anyone listening to me? We need coffee, pronto, now. We need to sober him up," Elena says.

"I'm sober as a judge. Give me a case and watch me adjudicate. In fact, let's adjudicate this right now. Bring it on! Find my gavel! Why didn't you tell me?"

"I did tell you."

"I would have remembered, Elena. I had to learn it from Seema, who learned it from a friend."

Clemi is taking this all in, trying to remain forensic and not let emotions get in the way.

"I was just trying to spare everyone pain."

"But obviously it wasn't much of a secret."

"What can I say?" Elena offers, shrugging as though this was an insignificant oversight, like putting mustard on a sandwich instead of mayo. "I told maybe one, two, maybe three friends? It's a small world. And not all friends stay friends. Remember Linda Tripp? It was that sort of situation."

"No one thought to tell *me* either," Clemi says boldly. "I had to read it in the *Guardian*!"

"What does everyone want from me?" asks Elena.

"Honesty? Truth? Transparency?" Clemi says. She, too, is sober as a judge, and ready to adjudicate this right now, right here, herself. And to find some sort of emotional resolution. This is why she has invited him here, why she has pressed so hard not to cancel this event, even though she had her own doubts. She may be a poorly paid, overworked events manager earning just over the minimum wage, but she has the power to direct this play, to summon all of these people to the bookstore stage. Still, she wants to hear her mother say it, to confess that she has been telling Clemi a lie for all of her twenty-three years, to apologize.

"I don't know what you're going on about," Elena says, changing the subject. "You look different, darling. You look less . . . tentative."

Now a bespectacled man appears. He has thick gray hair

277

that stands straight up. He looks startled, or maybe electrified. Beside him is what looks like a stuffed animal that is jumping up and down like a yo-yo, barking and chewing on his own leash.

"Cute dog!" says her mother.

"We had a dog named Sadie," the poet says. "When the children were young. We used to walk her on Hampstead Heath."

"I'm Bernard McAndrews," the bespectacled man says, extending his hand to Clemi. "Author of *The Doodles*. I'm here to sign books."

"Oh!" Clemi says. "Great! Everyone follow me to the office—you too," she says to the poet. "You have a bunch of books to sign."

The poet continues to stare at her as she ushers this unlikely trio into the office, where stacks of *Kaboom!* cover every available surface.

"I'm just going to grab more books from the closet," she says.

When she returns she sets a tower of *Kaboom!* in front of him—there are so many books that have been presold that it's going to take him at least an hour to sign—but he is distracted by the dog, who is chewing on the leg of his trouser.

"Bernie, sit!" Bernard says.

Bernie has no interest in sitting. Instead he jumps onto Raymond's lap and lifts his leg and begins to pee.

"Oh, he's such a little monster!"

"You terrible little dog!" Elena says. "Clemi, get us some paper towels. And don't forget the coffee. Also some water to blot this up. And some pens."

"You have ultra-fine-point Sharpie pens, right?" Raymond asks.

Clemi has no memory of the particulars of this particular detail. She has entertained many peculiar requests from authors, some to do with pens. She understands and appreciates that some writers prefer ballpoints to Sharpies, and that some prefer certain colors. She once watched an author, who brought her own stash of art supplies, decorate each title page with gold and silver markers and stick-on stars—unsurprisingly, the signing line moved very slowly that night. But she has never had an author specify the need for ultra, instead of normal, fine-point pens.

"I have fine point. I'm not sure there's really such a big difference between fine point and ultra-fine point," she bluffs. "This is what most of the authors use." She hands him a fistful of pens, hoping perhaps they can glide past this issue.

They will not.

"There's a *huge* difference. I can't get the loop in the *R* right without the ultra-fine point. It takes a light touch to turn that corner."

"Well, I . . . I can . . ." Clemi can't finish the sentence because she has no idea what she can do, right now, at this moment in time. She can offer to run to CVS, but it's not likely they will have this particular pen, and even if she drove to the nearest art supply store, by the time she arrived it would likely be closed.

Raymond takes the box of pens and flings them against the wall. The flimsy cardboard receptacle splits open and the pens go flying. The dog goes chasing after them like they're tennis balls, and then he's out of the office and out on the book floor where hundreds of people are milling about. Bernard calls his name, chasing him through the store, and Bernie begins to bark, but he's a tiny dog—they don't call them Micro Bernedoodles for nothing—and he slips under the chairs and into the crowd.

"Bernie Bernie Bernie Bernie Bernie!" Bernard shouts. A few heads turn, but no dog emerges. He begins his chant again.

Clemi gets down on her hands and knees, searching not only for Bernie but also for Kurt, who is still MIA. She doesn't see either one of them, but she does see Roomba, stuck in the corner by the World War II section. He keeps backing up and then ramming back into the wall like an SOS; he can't take much more of this.

Now someone is standing behind her, trying to get her attention. "You're Clemi, right?"

It's the handsome man who was poking around doing who knows what with Mrs. Bernstein earlier today. Mohammed, she thinks, is his name.

"I have a quick question for you," he says.

"Sure. But I'm having a bit of a moment. Can it wait just a minute or two?"

"Sure. But I'm having a moment here too. There's something Mrs. Bernstein wants me to do, and she wants it completed today, but my drill stopped working. Actually, Mrs. Bernstein tried to do a little DIY, and I don't know what she did, exactly, but I think she hit a stud with the tip of the drill and now it's not turning on and I'm wondering if the store has a drill."

"Not that I know of, but there's a hardware store a few blocks from here."

"I already tried that. It just closed."

"Oh! I know! I have one at home," Clemi offers. "Or, rather, my roommate does." She immediately regrets saying this. Why is she always so eager to please? It's not that she doesn't want to help him—she does! But she doesn't have time to deal with this right now, and besides, it's not even her drill! She has no idea if Simon would be willing to loan out his power tool, to which he seems to be so creepily attached.

"Fantastic. Do you think I could borrow it? Do you live nearby?"

"Well . . . it's only a couple of miles away, but I don't have a car."

"Clemi, I hate to keep asking, but can we get some coffee for Raymond?" her mother asks, approaching from behind. "It's kind of critical. Also, while you're at it, I wouldn't mind one myself. Some nondairy creamer for me. Almond is best. But not vanilla almond. Maybe a little something to eat as well? Just a snack—we're having dinner later."

"Really, Mom?"

"What?"

"I don't know, you've barely said hello and already you're sending me to fetch coffee?"

"Darling, you are so sensitive!" Elena laughs and grabs her by both shoulders, kissing her on the cheek. "Hello. Hello. Hello! Okay? Happy?"

"Raymond? Do you mean Raymond Chaucer, the *Kaboom!* guy?" asks Mohammed. "Is he *here*?"

"Yes," Elena replies. "He's in the greenroom."

"She means Mrs. Bernstein's office," Clemi explains.

"I'd love to meet him! Do you think he'd be willing to give me some advice? I'm working on a novel."

"I'm sure he'd be happy to. We just need to . . . sober him up."

"What is that?" Raymond asks, sticking his head out of the office. "That's the most terrifying thing I've ever seen!"

Clemi turns to see Petunia, her tiny teeth bared behind her little muzzle, charging toward them. She has broken free of the leash that Chatty Cathy was holding and is now on the loose. Somehow in the ruckus Cathy fell backward, and one of her green Hunter boots flew off and smacked Antonio on the head. Or something like that. Clemi isn't sure but Cathy is mumbling something to this effect. Probably Petunia smells the Micro Bernedoodle. Or the tortoise. Or the Roomba. Or the mouse.

"I'd be honored to help," says Mohammed, talking right over the dog chaos. "How about I run next door and get some coffee, and Clemi, maybe you can look into getting me that drill?"

She hears Bernie yapping from somewhere across the book floor, and then Petunia bolts from the office and races around the room with him, dodging the crowds, zooming in circles. They are yapping and yapping and yapping. Running and running and running. It reminds Clemi of a scene from *Go, Dog. Go!* If she waits another minute, perhaps they will all appear in party hats.

But they do not. Instead the two dogs suddenly turn their attention to the Standardized Tests section, where they stick their snouts beneath the shelf, their chests on the floor, and their tails in the air like they are doing their best downward dogs. Now they bark and they bark and they bark like they've just seen a ghost.

"Seriously, I'd like to help, but I've kind of got a situation right now."

"Clemi, just help this lovely man out, okay? Go get him his drill. Or send someone for the drill. Whatever. Just figure it out. And, Mohammed, coffee would be great. Then come on back and I'll introduce you to Ray. He's my client."

"Your client?"

"I'm his literary agent."

"Seriously? What serendipity! I'm looking for an agent! Do you have a few minutes for me to tell you about the novel I'm working on?"

Maybe Clemi's mother should work at the bookstore. Her presence is unwelcome, but she seems to know what to do, and right now Clemi is happy to let her take charge. She has enough to deal with already, such as corralling animals and procuring power tools.

Half an hour later, Clemi ushers Simon into the bookstore carrying his Black+Decker 20-Volt MAX Lithium-Ion drill. Most of Clemi's interactions with him have occurred either late at night, when he is in the midst of a destructive drilling fugue, or in passing, when he is coming from or going to work. She has never seen him quite like this: posture straight, hair gelled, shirt pressed, looking cheerful. It occurs to Clemi that he has perhaps been waiting for this moment all his life, where he is needed and has something constructive to drill.

They enter the office and find Bernard the Doodle Guy and Raymond and Mohammed engrossed in a conversation about something called a Whoodle, which is a cross between a Wheaten Terrier and a poodle.

"My neighbor has what she says is a Double Doodle," says Mohammed, "which I don't really understand."

"That's easy," says Bernard. "It's just a mix between a Goldendoodle and a Labradoodle."

"Oh. So then what's a Schnoodle?"

"Just use your common sense. Obviously it's a mix between a schnauzer and a poodle."

"I hate to break this up," Clemi says, "but you need to start signing all of these books. It's getting late. And, Mohammed, this is Simon. He has the drill."

"The books are all signed," says Elena. "I found a couple of ultra-fine-point Sharpies in my bag."

"Of course you did," Clemi is tempted to say but does not.

Mohammed and Simon head toward the back of the store, and Clemi watches them walk until they seem to disappear. Where they have gone? She has no idea—although she sort of does. Clearly there is something—a space of sorts—behind the events closet, but how is that possible? Clemi has never been especially good at spatial relationships, and the geography of this is hard to fathom. She thinks of *The Lion, the Witch and the Wardrobe* and wonders if there is a situation here involving magic, akin to the way the children in that novel simply slipped behind a wardrobe wall and into an entire other world. One with delicious taffy. Magic would be a welcome explanation. That way her mother would not really be here with the drunken poet who seems to be her father, and the AWOL talking tortoise would not be an indication that she is in over her head.

Speaking of which, out on the book floor, Bernie has abandoned his attempt to ferret out whatever was under the Standardized Tests shelf and has resumed barking and running around in circles, periodically pausing to sniff under the shelves, and Petunia has mercifully been put back on her leash.

Mrs. Bernstein rushes by, looking distracted. Alas, not distracted enough.

"Clemi, good grief, what is going on here? And where did that security guard go?"

"Which one? Clinton? Or Bill?"

"Whichever. Either. Both."

"This is no big deal, Mrs. Bernstein. Everything is under control. Clinton is . . . somewhere. I'm not sure where exactly. Maybe he just took a quick break. And Bill is . . ." She has no idea. Where are the security guards?

"Just find one and bring him to me out back," Mrs. Bernstein snaps. "Either one will do."

Now it is nearly 7:00 p.m. and time to begin the event. Clemi takes a deep breath, drawing the smell of all of these fresh, new, unread books deep into her lungs. While she is quite certain there are empirical explanations for everything weird that is happening right now, she nonetheless invokes a bit of magical thinking herself.

I am Super Book Girl! I can make it through this day!

She reminds the audience to silence their cell phones and then begins to give the poet an introduction:

"I'm pleased to welcome you here today for the US launch of Raymond Chaucer's new collection, *Kaboom!*

"Chaucer is an award-winning poet. He's also a former financier who held senior positions at several international investment banks. His new collection is getting great reviews and is drawing comparisons to Ted Hughes . . ."

She means this in a good way, upon which she is going to elaborate with comparisons to *Crow*, but she has already inadvertently set people off, and the audience begins to jeer.

"Wife killer!" someone shouts.

"Misogynist!"

"Bird killer!"

"Pedophile!"

Okay, he is not known to be a bird killer or pedophile. Maybe he's a huge jerk. A relentless philanderer. A man on a bender. A person with a chin not entirely unlike her own. Maybe she is starting to suspect that he had something to do with the reasons that her father—by which she means the man who raised her—got behind the wheel drunk, but she doesn't really know this any more than anyone really knows what happened to Raymond's wife. This sort of speculation is not helpful; there is no need for her to embellish a story that is already dramatic enough.

She continues to speak into the microphone and can hear, in the store's ancient sound system, the echo of her own voice, and it sounds unfamiliar. Confident and bold. She sets aside her notes and looks up into the audience and tells them not to prejudge Raymond Chaucer. To listen to his affecting poetry. She recites the *New York Times* review that called him "an insider trader of language."

As she speaks, Bernie the Micro Bernedoodle begins another yappy barking jag. She sees him zeroing in on a different bookshelf, over near Sports. The telephone rings and she can see Mrs. Bernstein standing at the information desk, looking extremely distressed. More jeering. People booing. She hears her mother scolding the people who are booing. Bernie ratchets up his volume in response.

Clemi can't fully explain it, but this beautiful bookish landscape, this crazy bookish chorus, fills her with a bookish joy. It's a bookstore opera. A bookstore ballet. A bookstore sitcom. A bookstore comedy, and right now, a bit of a dark one at that. But it's a privilege to be here—and she hopes to not be here for the rest of her life.

"Please quiet down!" she says, as if she is a woman in control. She looks out into the audience and sees her mother looking back at her, listening for a change.

"A bookstore is a place of language and ideas. A forum for civil discourse and the committing of art. This man is a poet, an *acclaimed* poet. Let's suspend our personal judgment for the time being and listen to his words."

There is the sound of approximately one set of applause, and her mother nods her approval for the first time in years.

Raymond steps up to the microphone and begins to speak.

"I would like to read to you a poem about one of my darkest hours," he says. The room quiets. "Of which, alas, regrettably, there have been many," he continues. "And I am grateful to you, Clemi, and to everyone in this room, for the opportunity to read from my new collection. This first poem is called 'The Day of the Pushchair.'"

Raymond begins to read a poem about a baby. A baby in a pushchair. A baby on the Heath. A baby in a blue jacket. A baby with chubby little hands held high. A baby with a red balloon. A bloody baby in a pushchair with chubby hands and a blue jacket and a red balloon. On and on it goes about the baby, circling back to the pushchair over and over.

Clemi can't tell if this is terrible or brilliant or just an exercise in exorcising whatever it is that happened to this poor child. She is no poetry critic—this seems more likely to be awful than good—but it is said to be one of the stand-outs of *Kaboom!* Maybe people just like this insight into the psyche of the train wreck that is Raymond Chaucer.

Her mother, too, looks pained. It's not clear if anyone else in the store is listening until she sees that Cathy, despite her earlier mishap, is back on her feet and already at the microphone. "I've been wondering—"

"Please," Clemi interrupts, "it's not time for questions yet."

"Just a quick one! Was that poem inspired by the

1925 Soviet film *Battleship Potemkin*, directed by Sergei Eisenstein?"

"Please!" Clemi tries again, to no avail.

"You may remember the heartbreaking scene in act four where the baby carriage goes bouncing down the Odessa steps, while Cossacks fire on unarmed civilians."

Raymond appears to think about this for a minute before replying. "Yes, precisely! Any resemblance to the events in this poem and in my personal narrative is purely coincidental. The imagery in the poem is drawn straight from this magnificent film about the baby carriage in Odessa!"

"It's not really about the baby carriage—that's just a single, haunting scene. The film is about the 1905 mutiny when the crew of the *Potemkin* rebelled against its officers. The British Film Institute named it the eleventh greatest film of all time."

"Okay, thank you, let's get back to our poetry reading now," Clemi says, this time more insistently and with surprising success.

Raymond resumes reading. Now he is going on about changing the narrative. For something like ten stanzas he goes on and on. Change the narrative, change the narrative, change the narrative . . . He is emoting. Punctuating each word theatrically, his hands in the air like he is conducting a philharmonic.

The Micro Bernedoodle is still barking near the Sports section. Clemi knows that something else is transpiring. She can sense unrest, a change in the equilibrium of the room. Scanning the crowd, she locates the source. There's Florence, at the information desk, talking to Summer. They are arguing, and their voices carry from across the store.

Clemi is terrified. What is Florence doing here? What

is she wearing? It looks like a unitard, like maybe she's an acrobat about to do a few cartwheels across the book floor. Wait! It appears to be the outfit Florence wore that day in college, when she did a flame dance through the quad. Florence couldn't possibly be thinking about setting herself on fire, could she? Not in a bookstore, which would ignite like a tinderbox. Not even Florence would do something like that.

Now Florence is in motion. She comes hurtling in the direction of the podium, and Clemi runs toward her and knocks her to the ground, grabbing the matches from her hand.

Raymond appears oblivious. He is still talking about changing the narrative, except that he has stopped reading from his poem and is now talking about the *Guardian* story.

"This AGA situation, you see, it's not about the AGA itself, so much, as that I've lost control of the narrative," he says. "The AGA is just a tiny piece of it, but it haunts me because of the way the press has created a portrait of me that bears no resemblance to the man that I really am. I'm going to change the narrative while I can!" He has just spoken those words when Clemi and Florence crash into him, knocking him to the ground.

He appears unfazed as the two women continue wrestling for the matches. He continues to read his poetry, horizontally. He is now back to the baby and the pushchair and how it was only a broken arm and a chipped tooth and he is trying to join this moment up to the 1905 mutiny on the battleship, to a film it is doubtful he has ever seen.

Clemi composes herself and tries to help him stand.

Florence has moved to the corner and is curled up in the fetal position, sobbing.

There is suddenly a very loud noise that sounds like *kaboom!* The bookstore is thrown into darkness but for the early evening light that seeps through the windows.

From the other side of the wall, Clemi is pretty sure she can hear Simon say, "Whoops!" and Mohammed say, "Oh no!" and before she can give any further thought to what in the world might have motivated her to invite her enigmatic roommate and his electric drill into what was already a chaotic scene, she hears the terrifying, unmistakable sound of gunfire from the store parking lot, followed by a scream and a plaintive wail of pain.

As she rushes downstairs to see what has happened out back, Clemi finds the Micro Bernedoodle face-to-face with Roomba, barking fiercely. Roomba is making a whirring sound but doesn't move. Something looks off. This is the least of Clemi's concerns right now, but she nevertheless takes a second, closer look. There is Kurt Vonnegut Jr., head inside his shell, hitching a ride on Roomba's back.

For a brief moment there is absolute silence in the store. Raymond has stopped reading, the audience has stopped jeering, and she doesn't hear any noises coming from out back.

Then there is a voice at the information desk that says, "Hello? Can anyone here help me? I'm looking for a book!"

END OF DAY REPORT: Saturday, August 19

Hey, y'all, there is no electricity at the store so obviously no internet. Pepco is on it. A transformer blew, and it will be another day or so before they can repair it.

I'll send a proper Report out tomorrow, but for now, just know

1. We ran out of books at the event.
2. We are closed until further notice.
3. Mr. Zielinski called to say he lost his cell phone. I found it near Travel Health and put it on the shelf beneath register three.
4. What do you call a doodle that has nothing to live for? (An AGAdoodle)

Sent from my iPhone

CHAPTER 14

Monday

SHADOWS

Geez, Mom, be careful," Michael says as he helps Sophie navigate the floating metal stairs that lead to the rooftop of Autumn T's apartment building. "I think it's better if you hand me the crutches and just kind of hang on to the railing and pull yourself up."

"Ouch! Wait! I think I might be stuck," Sophie says, pausing on the penultimate step. "The crutch is stuck between the slats. Maybe this wasn't such a good idea."

"You're okay, Mom. I've got you," he says. "Just give it a yank. You're almost there. Only one more step to go."

He does have her; she can feel his hand on the small of her back, and she knows he's not going to let her fall.

She is glad Michael agreed to come with her, although *agree* is perhaps not the right word. Giving her a ride to the party was the outcome of a negotiation, a bargain they'd struck when he admitted, sheepishly, that yes, he still had the store van. Or rather, he sort of had it. He had it but it had been towed when he'd parked outside his apartment building and failed to notice the sign about street sweeping on Thursday between 9:30 and 11:30 a.m. First they had towed it just a block away, but then it was Friday and time to sweep this other street, so it was towed again, this time to a lot, but at least it is only a few miles away. Sophie agreed to help him retrieve the van and get it back to the store in exchange for spotting her up these stairs, which Autumn T has warned her about in advance. The elevator in her building goes to the seventeenth floor, she explained, but it's still necessary to climb to the roof, where they are all gathering to watch the solar eclipse.

They reach the rooftop and stare into the distance, awe-struck. It's a startling, stunning, panoramic view. She can see everything from up here: There's the Capitol and the Lincoln Memorial and just below are people picnicking at Malcolm X Park. And over there—there's a plane across the Potomac, coming in for a landing, and she can even read the letters on the tail that spell out *Southwest*. Off in the other direction is the National Cathedral. She could stay here all day, identifying landmarks from this unexpected perch, breathing in her city.

"Mrs. Bernstein," says Autumn T, "I'm so glad you made it! How's the foot?" Even Autumn T looks different up here. But at the same time, exactly the same. She's wearing a bright orange summer dress with large yellow flowers, and although it's a dress Sophie has seen before, it looks different in this non-bookstore setting.

"Oh, the foot. *Sigh*. It's not so bad," she says. "It could be worse."

Her answer makes her think of Solomon again. He was a Yiddish dial-a-joke, with one for every occasion.

TWO JEWS MEET IN THE STREET AND ONE SAYS TO THE OTHER:

How's by you?
Not so good, my store lost electricity yesterday!
Could be vorse!
Could it? We had to close for the day! We are losing
  business!
Could be vorse!
But we ran out of books!
Could be vorse!
I'm on crutches for a month.
Could be vorse!
My husband is dead, and I'm lonely and I miss him every
  day.
Could be vorse!
I'm being sued on account of a bagel and a tiny little dog,
  so I'm really sorry, but how could it be worse?
It could have happened to *me*!

Sophie is in some real pain, but she's not going to complain. She knows she's lucky, and a lot worse could have happened when she shot herself in the foot. Well, not directly—she had shot the bullet into Querk III, liberating a cyclone of dust, three pens, thirty-two cents in change, a pearl earring, and a set of keys, so it was a partial, if dangerous and harebrained, success. But then the bullet kept going, lodging in the dumpster, sending a piece of metal ricocheting back in her direction and grazing her left foot. Her big toe is broken, she has a deep gash that required eleven stitches, and she's been told not to put any pressure on her foot. What had she been thinking? It had been a moment of pure madness on her part. A wake-up call of sorts.

On a more positive note, however, she can still drive, and she now has her keys back.

"Would you like a drink?" Autumn T asks, presenting her with a glass of amber liquid in a red plastic Solo cup.

"What is it?"

"I'm calling it Penumbra Punch. It's got rum—like three different kinds—and pineapple juice and grenadine and—"

"It's not just any rum. It's from a private reserve," says the man who looks like Bradley Graham or Richard Dreyfuss. She gets that he is not either of these, that he is the parking lot magnate who would like to purchase her store, but what is he doing here? Is she being stalked?

"I was recently in Bermuda," he says, "and brought back as much as I could get through duty-free. Nice to see you, Sophie! Sorry to hear about your . . . er . . . accident."

"What were you doing in Bermuda? Buying parking lots?"

"What do you mean? Oh . . . I see. It's a joke. No. Funny though. I own a hotel there."

"Sure you do," Sophie says. *Of course he owns a hotel. He's a capitalist*, she thinks, as if she has just discovered

some dark, dirty secret about him. As if she is not, by definition, a capitalist herself. But she's a *good* capitalist. She's
a bookstore capitalist!

"What are you doing here?" she asks.

"I think I mentioned I was in town visiting family."

"Yes, but what are you doing *here*?"

"At this party, you mean? This is my apartment. I used to
live here, and I might move back, but right now I'm renting
it to my nephew, who lives with one of your employees,
which is what I'm doing here. They told me to come."

"That's me," Autumn T explains. "You've met Zach, my
boyfriend? Zach is Ed's nephew."

"What a small world!" says Sophie. It's a shtetl indeed.
She hopes Ed isn't going to start talking to her about the
Cheesecake Factory / Chipotle situation here in front of
her employees. But then she thinks about it for a minute,
realizing that selling the store to Ed would possibly solve all
of her problems. Well, some of them.

"Hypothetically speaking," she says, "if a man bought a
bookstore from a woman who is hypothetically about to be
sued, would the legal threat possibly convey?"

"Why would anyone sue you?"

"Because Washington."

"Seriously?"

"Seriously. Because a ten-pound dog took a bagel
out of a kid's hand last week and because, as I say, this is
Washington."

"That's absurd. Let me help you with that."

"What can you do about it?"

"I'm a lawyer. I can make it go away."

Before she has a chance to say anything more, Antonio appears and hands everyone a pair of solar eclipse glasses.

"Come on, you guys. It's almost time. Five minutes until it begins."

Sophie dons the glasses and looks skyward, but she's not really sure what she's supposed to be looking for. She's been so self-absorbed this week that she hasn't been paying much attention to whatever is about to happen here, celestially.

"What are we supposed to be looking for?" asks Zhang.

Zhang? Sophie's heart begins to race. She hasn't even opened the envelope from, or rather to do with, Zhang.

"Hi, Mrs. Bernstein," she says nonchalantly. "Sorry about your foot!"

Sophie is so embarrassed about the entire situation that she is having trouble formulating a reply, but she does manage to thank Zhang for her concern and says she's going to be fine.

"Summer said she gave you the cleaning bill. I'm sorry—I didn't really want to give it to you, but Summer insisted. I know it's kind of a lot—nineteen dollars since they had to do something extra to remove the stain—but Summer said you wouldn't mind covering it since you offered. She really insisted! But really, if it's too much, don't worry about it!"

Sophie is astonished. "Oh my goodness, you absolutely should have given it to me, and my apologies for the delay—I'll take care of it right away!" That's all that is in the envelope? An invoice for nineteen dollars? She is deeply embarrassed on too many different levels to parse on the spot.

"Also don't forget to let me know if you need any more

copies of *Gauzy*! We just learned that it's going to enter the *New York Times* bestseller list at number two!"

"Oh, fantastic. Congrats to all of you! Let's be sure to talk to Antonio about this after the party and see what he thinks. He'll know how many we have in stock."

"You guys!" says Summer. "The earth, the moon, and the sun are about to be in perfect alignment, which basically means the moon will cover up the sun, which means it will go dark. Although not completely dark here in DC because we aren't in the path of totality. We'll have what is called a partial phase eclipse."

"Why is this such a big deal though? Isn't there a solar eclipse, like, every couple of years?" Emma asks.

"There is," says Antonio, "but this is the first time a solar eclipse has passed over the entire country. From Oregon to South Carolina."

"It's not the first time!" says Summer. "It happened ninety-nine years ago."

"I think it was like fifty years ago," says Antonio.

"No, it was ninety-nine years ago. I worked at NASA, you guys. I think I know what I'm talking about."

Sophie shifts her weight. She should probably sit down and take the pressure off her foot, even though she has managed to forget about it for a few moments. She doesn't know if it's the extra-strength Advil or just being up here on this spectacular roof, but she's not feeling any pain.

She sees Michael holding a glass of punch and talking to Jamal and Clemi. He throws back his head and laughs at something funny, then dons his glasses and looks up at the sky.

A new group appears at the top of the stairs, including Kevin and a person who is wrapped in what looks like shrink wrap. Is Sophie hallucinating, or is this person dressed up as . . . a giant penis? Circumcised.

"Hey, you guys! Sorry to be late!" the penis says.

"Noah?"

"Not Noah. I'm Protection Man."

"What the . . . ?"

"What part don't you get?"

"That you are in costume?" says Clemi. "The superhero party is tomorrow. This is the solar eclipse party."

"Damn!" says the penis. "I had a feeling something was wrong."

Sophie laughs. At first just a little laugh, but then she laughs a little louder, and longer, and then she nearly loses her balance, she is laughing so hard.

"Go easy on the punch," says Michael.

Sophie hasn't even had a sip. "I'm fine, I'd just better sit down," she says.

Clemi takes her arm and helps her settle into a chair a few feet away.

"I wanted to talk to you anyway," says Clemi. "I want to apologize for yesterday."

"For what?"

"For everything. But for Florence especially. I just want you to know that she's going home for a while. I called her parents this morning, and her dad is coming to pick her up. I'm just really sorry and embarrassed. I don't know what's going on with her. Well, I sort of do. Her family is having problems, but it's more than that. I thought I could help her, I really did. I should have gotten her medical help or something sooner."

"Oh sweetheart, it's not your fault," Sophie says. Did Sophie just use the word *sweetheart*? She has never been one for endearments, and she can't explain how or why this lovely word has managed to slip from her lips. "It was a complicated situation. She needs more help than a friend can provide."

"She's never been easy, but I know she's been especially difficult and scary and weird these last few weeks, and since I'm responsible for her working at the store, I just want to apologize. That thing she said about your stars—that was really messed up. Plus she totally disrupted the event."

"I'm the one who screwed it up. Mohammed warned me. He said we were going to blow out the entire electrical system, and I refused to listen. And besides, she was right."

"About what?"

"About my stars being scrambled."

"Yeah, well, mine are pretty scrambled too. I guess now I know why," says Clemi. "I mean, I already knew, but I was in denial."

"What do you mean?"

"About Raymond Chaucer and my mom. And me. What do you do with that kind of information? Am I supposed to start calling Raymond Chaucer *Dad*?"

Sophie tries to interject, but Clemi is on a roll.

"Why didn't they tell me? Every once in a while I entertained the thought. Everyone knew my mom and Raymond were 'friends.' But I figured that was just my imagination run amok until the *Guardian* interview. I confess that's why I booked the event. I wanted to actually *see* him. To see what would happen if I brought him to the store. I sort of knew without knowing that my mom would show up, and that things would sort of . . . combust. I didn't expect an actual explosion, like that you'd get shot and the lights would go out and that Florence would show up and . . . well, there you go.

"She says she wants to talk to me about all this. And so does Raymond. They want my *forgiveness*."

"I didn't get shot, for the record. But I know that's not the point. You need to do whatever feels right. And what feels right today can change tomorrow. It's up to you. The situation is yours to control. It's in your power."

"Yeah. My power, such as it is. I'm Super Book Girl!"

"You are, actually."

"It's kind of pathetic to admit, I know, but sometimes I pretend that I am. I like to stand on top of the shelving ladder and breathe in the smell of books and imagine that . . . oh, forget it. It's so dumb."

"No, I get it. Like doing that gives you powers. Like helping people not hyperextend."

"Not hyperextend?"

"It's a yoga thing."

"Ah, right. It's so cool that you do yoga, Mrs. Bernstein! I really ought to start."

"Yeah, that's another story."

"I agreed to have dinner with him tomorrow. But I said I don't want my mom to be there. I want to just talk to him, figure out who he is. I mean, I have his DNA, for better or worse. But still, to think that smarmy guy is my father . . . I don't know, it's just a lot."

"Life is complicated. Raymond may be a snake, and I'm

sure this is a hideous thing to say, but I'll say it anyway: he's a brilliant poet. Maybe you've inherited his writer genes."

"Ugh," Clemi says. "I should just give up on the whole writing thing. Florence is the one who told me I was going to succeed, and now it's obvious that she's probably just delusional."

"I'm not so sure about that. I'm sure some of what she said is real."

"Yeah, some of it, like even a coin flip is tails some of the time."

"Well, it is. And I'm here to tell you that you are going to succeed. Let me help you make that happen. What do you need?"

"Confidence. Time to write. Talent."

"I hereby hoist this glass of Penumbra juice or whatever it is and declare that you shall have confidence. Time to write. And talent."

"What? Are you the Wizard of Oz? If only it was that easy."

"Work less."

"Can I?"

"Sure. Just tell me what you need."

"Help?"

"Hire help."

"Wow! That would be amazing! Now, if only you could give me confidence and talent!"

"Clemi, you are going to succeed. I know it. Just sit down and write."

Michael appears, a Penumbra Punch in each fist, and offers one to Clemi.

"Condom guy was just telling me about the tortoise and the Roomba," he says. "That's hilarious!"

"What tortoise?" Sophie asks. "What about Roomba?"

"It's the strangest thing!" Clemi says. "It's like they bonded! Which kind of makes sense, right? They're cousins in a way—two round objects with hard shells. It's almost like they fell in love. Kurt likes to ride around on Roomba's back."

"Kurt?" Sophie asks.

"Kurt Vonnegut Jr.," says Michael.

"What the . . . ?"

"We have a tortoise and he's named Kurt Vonnegut Jr.," says Clemi. "But he has no home, so he's kind of been in and out of the events closet."

"Is that what's been going on? That smell?"

"I can't have him in my apartment, and neither can Noah, so he became like a hot potato. We kept passing him around, and somehow he kept winding up back in the closet."

Sophie's spirit of generosity evaporates with this news. "We have a strict no-pets rule! I've really had it with all these animals. You saw what just happened with Petunia—I'm afraid we're even going to have to ban the customers' dogs now."

"You guys, two minutes!" says Summer. "Stop talking and put your glasses on and look up!"

There is a sudden bustle at the top of the staircase, where Belinda has just appeared. Jamal and Autumn T rush toward her and pull her into a hug.

"Belinda! Oh my!" Clemi runs toward her too. Soon a cluster of people surrounds her.

"This is perfect!" Summer says. "Belinda, such good

timing! Here, put on these glasses. We've got, like, only a couple of minutes left!"

"Are you doing okay?" Jamal asks. "It must have been awful. I can't even imagine. I mean, I can, but . . . you right in there, in the crowd with that woman who died."

Belinda is limping slightly and has a big gash across her chin, and Sophie can see the bruises. "Hey everyone, thanks. I'm so glad to be back," she says. "But I'm not ready to talk about any of it. It was unspeakably awful. I just want to do something restorative right now, like watch this eclipse. Give me a few more days and I'll tell you everything. I might try to write about it."

"You totally should," Clemi says.

Summer continues to try to get everyone's attention, but it's a party, and Belinda has just walked in, and people are too busy talking to pay much attention to what is about to happen above them.

"Mrs. Bernstein," Autumn T says, "I know we aren't supposed to ask you this straight up, but since it's a weird day, and I've had a couple of Penununumbaras . . ."

"Penumbras."

"Yes. Whatever. There are rumors that you are selling the store."

Ed Altman has apparently overheard, and he's right there to follow up. "There are rumors that you won't so much as have a cup of coffee with someone who is offering to buy the store."

Is he possibly saying this in a flirtatious sort of way? Michael seems to think so. He is jabbing her playfully in the ribs.

Sophie's phone rings, and she takes the call. It's Sami, calling to report that the electricity at the store has been turned back on, but that they need to find an electrician because there are some larger problems with the grid.

As long as Sophie has her phone out, she takes a quick look at her email. There's a message from Raina O'Malley's publicist, mentioning that the author will be in town in a couple of weeks for a private dinner with the Obamas, and would Sophie like to have her stop by and sign some books? She is about to say something to Clemi about this, to tell Clemi to find Zhang and talk to Antonio about upping their book order, but then stops herself. They are at a party. This can wait. She's going to be more thoughtful about harassing this poor young woman night and day.

It begins to grow dark; it's been raining so relentlessly this week that Sophie's first thought is to seek shelter, but then she realizes that the darkness is the result of the eclipse.

Everyone dons their glasses and looks skyward.

"You guys, look," says Summer. "This is an even cooler way to see the eclipse." She takes a spaghetti colander and holds it over a piece of paper, where it projects hundreds of tiny shadows, hundreds of tiny crescent moons. "That's basically what the sun looks like right now, covered partially by the moon."

"Oh my God, that's so cool!"

"So the shadow is the sun?"

"Well, no. It's the moon's shadow, passing over the sun. It's the shadow that's tracking across the planet's surface right now."

Sophie may not understand the science, but the art of

it, the symbolism, is startlingly simple: Behind the darkness there is light.

She's been so stuck inside her head, so consumed by her loneliness and fears and her petty and not so petty concerns, that she's sort of forgotten there is an entire universe out there that contains amazing things. The sun, the moon, the stars, her scrambled ones included. Solomon is out there somewhere too—in what way, or what form, she can't say, but she can feel his presence, especially right now. Who knows what else is out there: the souls of her pet birds and her many broken vacuum cleaners, although she supposes the latter is less about the cosmos than the landfill.

And back here on earth there are smart young book-sellers, like this brave one, Belinda, who was in the crowd at Charlottesville and thankfully has made it back. And there are literary novels that blow the mind. And there are the book products penned by the celebrity chefs and the self-help gurus and the rock stars and the former and would-be presidents and the athletes whose devoted fans show up at the crack of dawn and stand in line for hours to get a signed book and a selfie with the author. So let the trucks haul in all the books, and let the booksellers read them and staff-pick them and hand-sell them, every last one.

This feels like the end of something in her mind, like the epiphany at the end of a book. But it's not quite over. After the sky opens up again, and the sun returns, she walks over to Jamal and gives him a long hug.

"I'm going to miss you, my friend," she says.

"I'll miss you too, Mrs. B, but I'll be back. You'll see me more than you can imagine. I'll go from being your longest-term employee to being your best customer once I'm back in DC."

"That better be true," she says. "And I know you will be an amazing lawyer."

"I'll be there to help you anytime."

"Be careful with that offer, Jamal. At the rate things are going, I may need you on retainer."

"Don't worry about any of that, Mrs. Bernstein. I think it will work itself out. Maybe this eclipse took care of it somehow, like it purified the atmosphere. For a moment at least."

"Yes, exactly. For a moment. But let's embrace that moment."

"Let's try. I guess we'd better enjoy it while we can, because I get the sense that there are some choppy waters ahead."

"No doubt. I'm sorry to say that I think you're right. But let's just enjoy this carefree life . . . okay, not this *carefree* life, but maybe just this moment, while we can."

EPILOGUE

Among the many volumes stacked high on the shelf in the nook, which has now been converted to the Children and Teen department, is one called *The Russian Tortoise Handbook*. It is not the most well-written book, and Sophie finds herself having to refrain from picking up a red pen and line-editing the thing, but grammar aside, she has learned quite a lot about Russian tortoises, including the fact that they can live as long as sixty years, and that there is a definite celestial connection here, as they were the first creatures from earth to travel to the moon.

She has learned something else as well. Kurt Vonnegut Jr. is not a boy—the gender easily identified by the length of the tail and the presence of a spur. Sophie called Clemi when she learned this news, but after a brief discussion, they have decided to have Kurt remain Kurt.

They have created an enormous terrarium for Kurt, replete with rocks and small logs and tunnels. Kurt also has a shelter to retreat to when she needs a bit of solace. A nook within a nook. Now that Sophie thinks about it, Kurt is thrice nooked, given that she can always hide inside her shell. A nook within a nook within a nook. How she envies her. Or maybe, more accurately, she once did. It's nice to know a nook is there if you need it, but like Kurt—who still comes out of her shell and joyrides on the back of a Roomba every once in a while—Sophie is moving past her isolation fantasies too.

Surrounding Kurt's new habitat are cushions and toys and children's books. There's also a small table where kids can sit and color in books. The space is not quite done: Mohammed's handyman friend is still installing the shelves and putting on a final coat of paint. While he is at it, Sophie has asked him to touch up her office so she doesn't have to look at the coffee-splattered walls and think about the Zhang Skim Cap incident every minute of every day that she's there.

They will have a grand opening of the nook next week, and children from the neighborhood elementary school will come to visit for story time. Mrs. Bernstein is going to read to them herself.

Michael, much to her surprise, asked whether he might read to them too. He's working here now, a couple of days a week, helping Belinda sort out the web order backlog. Sophie doesn't want to get carried away or jinx anything, but he seems to be enjoying himself, interacting like he's just one of the gang, going out with everyone after work.

She may have given up her hiding space, if that's what it ever really was. It was more about peace of mind, but at the same time it was representative of the opposite. Still, she doesn't know what she will do should that dark day come; it seems entirely possible that it will. At least these past few weeks have been a sweet respite. The sun has come out. And the publishing reps have been dropping by with their winter catalogs, and some of the forthcoming titles seem especially compelling. She is midway through a historical novel told from the point of view of a whippet named Astrid who lives in Sweden and who digs up a bunch of ancient bones, unraveling secrets to do with a haunted mansion once owned by Queen Christina. Or something. She's not sure what's going on in this book, but it's weirdly captivating and the author is drawing comparisons to Hilary Mantel if Hilary Mantel wrote from the point of view of a dog.

When she looks up from her spot in *The Russian Tortoise Handbook*, Ed Altman is standing there holding two coffees and a couple of donuts from Verb.

"It's a beautiful day, Sophie," he says. "I want to pick your brain about a book idea I have. Do you have a few minutes to talk?"

"Sure," she says, alarmed. He's writing a book too? She wishes someone out there was *not* writing a book. "What's it about?"

"It's a romance," he says. "It's about an evil parking lot magnate who tries to buy an independent bookstore and also help the owner with her legal problems . . . It's like *You've Got Mail* except with Shih Tzus and quinquagenarians."

"Please tell me this is a joke. And that you are not really an aspiring author. And also, quinquagenarians? Is that actually a word?"

"No, I have no desire to write a book. It's a joke. And yes, it's a word. I looked it up."

"Does he succeed?"

"In his romantic pursuit, or in buying the bookstore?"

"In making the legal problems go away."

"Ah. I see. That's all you care about then?"

"Not really. I'm not entirely disinterested in seeing how this ends."

"A double negative."

"I guess I mean where it leads."

"How about we let it lead to a bench outside. I have some coffees." He begins to walk toward the rear door.

"Let's first be clear. I am not going to sell you the store."

"Roger that. Come on, it's a nice day." He props the back door open for her.

"You really want to sit out back and stare into the parking lot, instead of in front of the store? Oh wait, I get it. You want to watch the cars being towed. How romantic!"

"Give a guy a break, okay? I mean, I even brought you a treat. Donuts and . . . let's see, I have one coffee straight up, and one cappuccino. I wasn't sure what you drink, so I just took a chance. You look like a cappuccino person to me. And I guessed skim milk, just because, I don't know, it seems like everyone wants skim milk these days."

He produces a cup that says "Skim Cap."

"I'll try not to take that too personally, but seriously, no. Please. Anything but a skim cappuccino."

"You are a complicated woman, Sophie Bernstein."

"You have no idea. Sometimes I feel like my head is going to explode."

"It's all those multitudes you contain."

"Cheers," she says, holding the cup aloft.

"Cheers."

They sit on a bench and they talk about the weather and they talk about books and they talk about their respective kids and then the UPS truck pulls up to the dock and begins to unload many boxes of books.

While they are talking Sophie sees Michael getting out of the store van, and then, out of the passenger door, she sees Clemi emerge. Together they open up the vehicle's back doors and remove a couple of boxes of books that appear to have been purchased from another store. She watches them walk toward the receiving room, and then they return to the van for another load.

She overhears a snippet of conversation as they walk past once more, this time with what appears to be the final haul. They are talking about books. Clemi is apparently worried that even with these extras they just scored from Barnes & Noble, they still won't have enough for tonight's just-scheduled event with Raina O'Malley.

"Probably you'll have too many," he says.

"It's more likely I won't have enough."

"Maybe you'll have just the right number."

"That hasn't happened yet," she says. "But there's always hope. Also I'm a little nervous. I haven't seen her since college. Did I tell you we went to school together?"

"I've heard."

They walk into the receiving room, but then Michael comes out with a long rectangular box, inside of which is clearly something other than books.

"Oh, hey, Mom, you're right here!" he says, surprised to see her on a bench on the outer edge of the parking lot. "I was just going to bring this to you. You got a package."

"A package!" Ed says. "Lucky you."

"It's no big deal," says Sophie. "It's almost certainly just our new vacuum cleaner."

"Do you need it? I saw that little Roomba thing going around just now. It seemed to be working just fine."

"Roomba is great, but it's too big a store for one little vacuum, so I'll let him just take care of the nook. I bought a brand-new cordless model. It's the next-generation Querk. I think it's called a Querk IV."

END OF DAY REPORT: Friday, September 29
OPENING SHIFT: Melissa, Rajiv, Claire
SWING SHIFT: Antonio, Aaron, Genevieve
CLOSING SHIFT: Summer, Yash, Michael
EVENT: Clemi
FLOOR MANAGER COMMENTS: Please stop by the information desk and meet Rajiv! He comes to us from the law firm of Boyne, Gilchrist, Rabinowitz, Krug & Wideman, where he was a litigation associate specializing in bankruptcy. He is taking what he calls a "literary break."

Also, meet Claire. She is a part-time student at American University and she's training on the register today; she'll be helping Clemi with events.

Also be sure to stop by the Blue Derby tonight at ten for drinks to say goodbye to Noah, who is unbelievably leaving the world of books behind for a life in finance and nepotism. Go figure. He leaves tomorrow for Boston where he will be working in his father's hedge fund.

A few notes from the day:

- We have been receiving outraged calls all morning about tomorrow night's event for a biography of Raymond Carver. The author has gotten into a Twitter fight with another of his biographers about the influence of Gordon Lish on Carver's work. Protesters are expected. Clemi is looking into security.
- And speaking of Clemi—last night it was standing room only for Polly Kim's debut, *Mr. and Mrs. Lincoln*, and we ran out of books. Send complaints to Clemi. (Also note to Clemi—your voice mail is full.)

- People are asking about E. V. Krug's new book, *Five Easy Steps to Nirvana*. She was on *The View* yesterday. We don't have it in stock but it's on order.
- Speaking of which, we have again run out of *Kaboom!* It's going into its eleventh printing and will be back in circulation soon.
- The internet went down for a couple of hours but it is now back on.
- Kevin asked me to mention that he has extra comp tickets to see the Darkness at the 9:30 Club tomorrow night. Mrs. Bernstein will be there, but she says to tell you all that it is not a requirement of the job that you show up.

IMPORTANT VACUUM CLEANER UPDATE: Something is wrong with the new vacuum—not sure exactly what's going on but it's making a weird clanging sound. Props to Rajiv, who has volunteered to take a look.

Autumn T

ACKNOWLEDGMENTS

This book was supported by a grant from the DC Commission on the Arts and Humanities, and I am grateful for their generosity. I would also like to thank the corporation of Yaddo for giving me the time and space to begin working on the project that became this book.

Thank you to booksellers everywhere, and especially to my former Politics and Prose colleagues, some of whom have now gone on to seed other corners of the book world in DC and beyond. Brad Graham, Lissa Muscatine, Liz Hottel, Hannah Oliver Depp, Abby Fennewald, Anton Bogomazov, and Sarah Baline generously agreed to read early drafts of this novel. And enormous thanks to every one of my former colleagues but especially Mark Laframboise, Angela Maria Spring, Adam Waterreus, Ron Tucker, Becky Meloan, Claudia Oliver, Lena Little, Candace Wilkenson-Davis, and so many others, too many to name, for friendship and book love and refuge during a difficult period of my life.

Everyone at Harper Muse has been a dream to work with, especially my wise and insightful editor Kimberly Carlton, who helped make this a better book. Thank you to Amanda Bostic for creating such a warm and welcoming book culture, and to Joceyln Bailey and Jodi Hughes for saving me from errors small and large. Also to the great marketing and publicity team, Nekasha Pratt, Margaret Kercher, Kerri Potts, Taylor Ward, and Savannah Summers. And thank you, Suzanne Williams, for additional publicity support.

I'm grateful to everyone at HG Literary, especially my agent, Josh Getzler, who pep talked me through the dark days of Covid and did not give up, or hang up—and to Jonathan Cobb and Rhea Lyon, as well as Hilary Zaitz Michael at WME.

Thank you to everyone at the PEN/Faulkner foundation for the community and bookish conviviality. I am fortunate to have again landed in the warm embrace of such smart, literary people. And to everyone in the lovely, supportive writing network in DC, especially at The Writers Center, where I have taught for nearly 20 years, and The Writers Room in DC where I wrote portions of this book. Friends who generously read the novel, or pieces of the novel, or listened to me kvetch about the novel include Michelle Brafman, Jean Heilprin Diehl, Dylan Landis, Julie Langsdorf, Molly McCloskey, Valerie Strauss, Paula Whyman, Marion Winik, and Lisa Zeidner.

I don't know where to begin thanking my family. I would not have completed this book without the encouragement of my husband Paul Goldberg, whose jokes I steal. Ally Coll lent her brilliant legal mind to help craft the tortious legal memo that appears in the book, and Katie Goldberg coached me on vaguebooking. Emma Bivona, Max Coll, and

Sarah Goldberg were all helpful and insightful readers. I am fortunate to have the best kids imaginable. Thank you to my mother, Marian Keselenko, with whom I like to talk about books.

And special thanks to Charlie, who tells the best stories.

DISCUSSION QUESTIONS

1. Sophie reflects that the world divides into two kinds of people: Those who think books are for reading when there is nothing better to do, and those who avoid other things in order to read. Does this resonate with you?

2. What value does comedy bring to difficult subjects, and can you think of other comedies that are set during dark times?

3. Mrs. Bernstein struggles with what to do about books that contain material that may offend some readers. This is a complicated subject that even like-minded people do not agree on. What do you think?

4. Mrs. Bernstein also struggles with the question of whether the private life of an author ought to impact the way he is received by readers. What do you think?

5. Why are vacuum cleaners inherently funny? (Or are they?) Do you have any home appliances that seem ripe for comedy?

6. What is the role of independent bookstores in your life?
7. Everybody in Sophie's world wants to write a book. What kind of problems does that create?
8. Clemi observes that bookselling is a collegial business, except when it's not. Does this seem especially true right now?
9. Clemi believes the tortoise is talking to her. Is he?
10. Have you ever heard of an AGA?

ABOUT THE AUTHOR

Photo by Sarah Pavlovna Goldberg

Susan Coll is the author of six novels, including *The Stager*—a *New York Times* and *Chicago Tribune* Editor's Choice. Her third novel, *Acceptance*, was made into a television movie starring the hilarious Joan Cusack. Susan's work has appeared in publications including the *New York Times Book Review*, the *Washington Post*, *Washingtonian* magazine, *Moment Magazine*, NPR.org, Atlantic.com, and *The Millions*. She works at an independent bookstore in Washington, DC, and is currently president of the PEN/Faulkner Foundation.

Visit Susan online at susancoll.com
Instagram: @susan_keselenko_coll
Twitter: @Susan_Coll
Pinterest: @susancollauthor